MW00490499

Murder on Devil's Pond

Murder on Devil's Pond

A HUMMINGBIRD HOLLOW B&B MYSTERY

Ayla Rose

NEW YORK

PUBLISHER'S NOTE: The recipes contained in this book are to be followed exactly as written. The publisher is not responsible for your specific health or allergy needs that may require medical supervision. The publisher is not responsible for any adverse reaction to the recipes contained in this book.

Published in the United States by Crooked Lane Books, an imprint of The Quick Brown Fox & Company LLC.

Crooked Lane Books and its logo are trademarks of The Quick Brown Fox & Company LLC.

Library of Congress Catalog-in-Publication data available upon request.

ISBN (hardcover): 978-1-63910-711-7
ISBN (ebook): 978-1-63910-712-4

Cover design by Brandon Dorman

Printed in the United States.

www.crookedlanebooks.com

Crooked Lane Books
34 West 27th St., 10th Floor
New York, NY 10001

First Edition: July 2024

10 9 8 7 6 5 4 3 2 1

In memory of Amby Pickarski,
for whom the flowers still
bloom and the birds still sing.
We miss you.

Chapter One

Ezra Grayson may have felt the presence of his late wife in the old Victorian house, but all Hannah Solace sensed there were smoke-tinged air and the lingering haze of grease from Ezra's breakfast. It's not that Hannah doubted Ezra's sincerity. The eighty-year-old had lived in this house on Main Street his entire life, forty plus of those years with his late wife, Molly. He was a fixture in Jasper, Vermont. Everyone knew the silhouette of the tall, weedy, slightly hunched-over man who ambled down Main Street at dusk for his daily walk beside his aging dog. Ezra's cantankerous disposition was as notorious as his dilapidated, cluttered home.

Hannah watched as the old man sank into the Queen Anne-style chair by the dining-room window. He looked particularly pale today, his skin tinged yellow against his plaid flannel shirt, a pallor Hannah attributed to the cigarettes he snuck when he thought she wasn't looking. He was gazing into the connected living room, and his focus darted from the soot-coated fireplace hearth to the blackened ceiling to the singed curtains. A gaping hole in the plaster veneer stared back at them both accusingly.

"What brings you here today, Hannah?" he asked quietly, as was his way. His dog, a rangy brown mastiff mix Ezra had named

Moose, lay on the floor beside him, his body angled to fit perfectly within a thick sliver of sunlight. Ezra reached down absentmindedly and patted the dog's head. Moose's tail thumped against the gouged wood flooring.

"My bellflowers aren't doing so well. I came to ask you for help. But I also brought you a snack."

Hannah placed a basket on the newspaper-littered dining-room table.

"Strawberry jam, fresh raspberries, and home-baked sourdough bread. I can pick the basket up whenever."

Ezra made a face and waved his hand. "I don't like strawberries, and I won't eat that sour bread."

"I always make you sourdough bread, Ezra, and you *do* like strawberry jam. I've been bringing it to you all summer. You're just being stubborn."

"I'm not stubborn, and I'm not hungry."

"You're a stick. You need to eat something other than fried meat and Oreos." She nudged the basket forward. "At least eat the berries. You could use some vitamin C."

Ezra scowled. "I had applesauce yesterday."

"Oh, Ezra. You're being ridiculous. Why don't you join me and Reggie for dinner tonight? Reggie's bringing food to the inn. I'm sure there will be something you like."

"Will Peach be there?"

"Of course."

"I don't like kids."

Hannah let out an exasperated sigh. "Yes you do. And you especially like Peach." She shook her head. "You're being particularly ornery today."

"Yeah, yeah. Peach is okay." Ezra flashed Hannah a mischievous half-smile, then pushed himself up from his chair with a grunt and wandered into the living room. Staring out the marred picture window that overlooked Main Street and the horse farm across the road, he touched the floral curtain gently between gnarled fingers, almost reverently. "Molly made these. She made most of the curtains in the house."

"She made this house special."

"I wanted to fix the old place up. I told Molly we represented Jasper, being on Main Street and all. Molly was practical. She loved the woods and flowers. She said we didn't need to spend our savings to please others. She said the only person one had to respect was oneself." His shoulders seemed to slump farther, and he stroked the curtain one last time before pushing it away. "She made these to appease me, I think. I would have done more, but . . ." Ezra's voice trailed off.

Hannah knew the "but" was Molly's life ending unexpectedly on the heels of their forty-second anniversary. Hannah remembered Molly as the sunnier half of the couple, always ready with a glass of lemonade or a maple biscuit to make someone feel at home. "Molly seemed happy in this house just as it was," Hannah said, feeling her words were inadequate.

He nodded. "And now the vultures are here. They want me to leave."

"I know. They've descended upon the inn."

"I'm sorry you have to endure that lot."

That lot were Ezra's two nephews and niece, the children of his two sisters and one brother. They'd come to convince their uncle to sell the ruined house and move into a retirement home in Rutland. Hannah figured they had a week, at most, before Ezra booted them out of town. Only they weren't totally wrong. This home was more than Ezra could care for, physically or financially, and the fire had rendered it barely inhabitable. It was only a matter of time before the town stepped in.

Hannah said, "Given the fire, I'm not sure you can stay in this house, Ezra. Maybe it is time to think about an alternative."

"Nonsense. I'll keep spraying everything down with vinegar. The smell will go away eventually."

"It was an electrical fire. You're lucky the house is still standing. Didn't the electrician tell you there may be more faulty wiring in the house?"

"Nonsense. She was confused. It was just a squirrel."

A squirrel that is no doubt still living in the attic, Hannah thought. Nothing in the house worked. The plumbing was unreliable, the heat was sporadic, and the one window air conditioner had pooped out years ago. And Ezra's house was quite literally tilted. From the outside it looked like the wonky, wacky house from a children's book, with sagging turrets and a skewed porch. What had once been well-tended flower gardens were now overgrown by wild roses, Canadian golden rod, morning glory, and purple loosestrife, an invasive species that Hannah had been trying unsuccessfully to weed out. It was as though Mother Nature was reclaiming Ezra's house one plant, one tree branch at a time—and Ezra was letting her do it.

Inside, the house was a maze of books and papers, with slanted, scarred, random-width pine floors and weathered, water-stained wallpaper. He'd left it exactly as it had been when Molly was alive and then filled it with *stuff*. Thankfully the room where the fire had started was kept empty of the stuff, which by some miracle had helped to contain the fire. The huge living room, lined as it was with photographs of Molly, had been Ezra's homage to his late wife; now it was a charred relic.

"Ezra," Hannah said softly, "You know I'm your friend."

Ezra's head turned sharply. "Is this where you also ask to buy my property?"

"Oh for God's sake, Ezra—"

"I'm sorry, Hannah," he said more softly. "I'm just so tired of the vultures. It seems like everyone wants a piece of this place. Now that the housing market is booming again, the jerk next door calls me every day. Like I would sell to him. Damn Henry Yarrow sent me another written offer. Why does a ski resort need my land? Don't they have enough condos? Even Cheating Chad wants it."

Hannah's eyes widened at the reference to Cheating Chad, her sister Reggie's ex-husband. It was a nickname Hannah had coined, and now the whole town had adopted it. She wanted to say something to make Ezra feel better, but she knew he was truly troubled by the interest in his property. Brian Lewis, the Connecticut owner of the big house next door, had had his eye on Ezra's house for years. Brian complained frequently to the town's selectboard that the house was an eyesore, but Jasper had no zoning laws, and anyway, no one wanted to turn Ezra out of his childhood home.

Henry Yarrow, a longtime Vermont resident, had bought Devil's Mountain, the small, abandoned ski resort, a decade ago and had made something of it. The ski resort's property abutted Ezra's place and the inn Hannah owned with her sister, and Henry wanted to knock down Ezra's house and build a road and condos for the resort.

Cheating Chad was a realtor and property owner. He simply knew an opportunity when he saw it. He'd been drooling over Ezra's considerable land and its views of Devil's Mountain ever since the fire, no doubt seeing it as easy pickings for a new Main Street short-term rental property.

But Ezra didn't want to sell to any of them. Period. He'd made that perfectly clear to Hannah, Moose, and anyone else who'd listen.

"Ezra, of course *I* don't want to buy your property. I couldn't afford it even if I did." Hannah sank down into one of the only dining-room chairs not covered with books. "This is where I tell you as a friend that you're being stubborn and foolish. You need to do *something*. Fix the house, or at least the wiring. Tear the house down and build a smaller one, a place you can manage. Or sell the house and move. You can live on the inn's property if you'd like. We can build you a tiny house."

"Does it look like my stuff would fit in a tiny house?" He gestured toward the clutter lining the dining room and met her gaze with watery eyes before looking quickly away. "The vultures want me to go into a nursing home."

"You're a free man. You can do what you want."

"Not to hear them talk."

Ezra took the seat opposite Hannah, easing himself down on a stack of Sierra Club magazines that covered the chair's wooden surface. He opened the red gingham napkin that lined the basket of food and removed a slice of sourdough bread. Munching on one end, he stared off into the living room, a faraway look on his weathered, wrinkled face.

"Come for dinner," Hannah repeated. "Reggie will be there. You can talk about housing options with her. She knows real estate."

"I can't. I'm busy." He looked into Hannah's eyes, and she got a glimpse of the gentle young man he'd probably once been. "But thank you for the offer. I know you're just trying to help. Tell Peach she still owes me a game of checkers." Ezra swallowed his mouthful of bread. "I'll beat her. I always do."

"She's six. I hope you beat her."

Normally that would have elicited some snappy comeback or a hearty chuckle, but today Ezra just sat there holding his bread and looking gloomy.

"How can I help you?" Hannah asked. "I know this is getting to you. Your family, the house."

"I'm fine."

"You're not fine."

"*Campanulastrum Americanum*," Ezra said, changing the topic. "American bellflower. Your problem is simple. Those flowers are getting too damn much sun. A little sun is fine. Too much, and they burn."

*   *   *

The bike ride back to Hummingbird Hollow took only fifteen minutes. Hannah just had to ride down Main Street, take a right on Snowflake Lane, and another right onto the aptly named Dirt Road. She lingered, though, in front of Ezra's house.

Main Street in Jasper was not like a big-town main street. Aside from Ezra's property, which was deep but narrow, jutting off Main Street like a crooked finger, a half-dozen small residences, and Brian Lewis's big house next door, there was a quirky general store, a church, a bakery called Breaking Bread that shared space with a bike shop called Breaking Trail, two ski shops—one high-brow, one low-brow—Benny's Diner, a post office, a used bookstore/brewery, and a large horse farm—all spread out over more than half a mile. Devil's Mountain loomed behind the town, its rugged, wooded peaks streaked with ski trails and a lone ski lift. On the other side of Main Street, behind Ezra's place and next to the ski resort, were miles of Green Mountain National Forest, with Hummingbird Hollow and Devil's Pond nestled in their midst. Beyond Devil's Mountain were more trees, more peaks, and a natural world still mostly unmarred by humans.

Today, the town was summer-quiet. Hannah watched as a pair of road cyclists pedaled down Main Street, their attention on Ezra's property. One cyclist pointed at the disheveled house, and the other shrugged in response. A car came down the road going twice the speed limit, and Pastor Kendra Birk, who was outside watering the church's flower gardens, yelled at them to *slow the hell down*. The general store was having a sale, and a table lined with soaps, lotions, Vermont-made pottery, and maple syrup sat unattended on the sidewalk. The only sounds were the occasional car engine, Pastor Kendra's hose, and the low hum of a tractor on the horse farm.

Hannah was about to start pedaling, her mind on Ezra, when she looked up to see Brian Lewis staring at the back of Ezra's property. From the edge of his own treated and manicured lawn, he was frowning at Ezra's oversized, ramshackle barn and the small pond that merged into the forest behind it. When he caught Hannah watching him, he scowled, shook his head back and forth as though she had done something offensive, and stormed back toward his house. He was gripping a pair of binoculars in one hand and a large brown envelope in the other.

Hannah waited until he was inside before taking off again.

"That's all he does," Kendra said to Hannah as she was passing the church. "He's obsessed with Ezra and that house. I see him out there, staring at it, every time he's in town."

Hannah hopped off the seat of her bike. "Maybe he'll sell his house here and leave."

Kendra laughed. "Maybe, but I doubt it. He's as stubborn as Ezra. In fact, if that fire hadn't been caused by electrical wires, I'd have thought Brian set it himself."

Hannah smiled, but she didn't find the idea funny at all. Brian Lewis *had* looked irate, and Ezra had clearly had enough. *Vultures*. Ezra's house was an eyesore, but he was a quiet old man who never hurt anyone. As Hannah turned down Snowflake Lane, she wondered why Brian needed binoculars—and what was in that envelope?

Chapter Two

Hannah returned to the inn just as the sun was at its highest point in the sky. The August day was pleasantly warm, with a gentle breeze and cloudless sky. She biked into the inn's small parking lot and spotted Ash Kade's truck sandwiched between a blood-red Porsche Cayenne and a silver Infinity. As she placed the bike in the barn, she scanned the property for signs that Ash had begun planting the conservation meadow. She was hoping her landscaper would finally get to the muddy field toward the back of the property. Chad had considered it fallow and insisted on leaving the field mowed and empty. Hannah wanted to create a water-friendly native habitat, with water-loving native wildflowers, shrubs, and a rock garden for drainage—plus a wooden bridge that would lead to Devil's Pond—but her vision would never come to fruition if they didn't get started soon. Once October arrived, all bets were off—the snow would be close behind.

For now, Hannah took pride in how far the inn had come. The old Victorian was surrounded by flower gardens brimming with native plants hand chosen for their ability to attract pollinators. The gardens were designed so that flowers bloomed all season long, from late April through early October; and in May and early June, the height of the season, the grounds were alive with bees, butterflies, moths, hummingbirds, and other pollinating insects and birds. Even in late autumn, service berries, winter berries, and beautyberries offered a lingering, rich food source for birds and other wildlife. She had other ideas, too, but as she entered the inn, she reminded herself that she needed to get the place operating at a profit first.

"Hannah?"

Hannah spun around to see Ezra's niece, Maura Hamilton-Saunders, standing by the inn's front desk. The empty coffee mug in her hand and the scowl on her face told Hannah all she needed to know. Hannah's trip to Ezra's had been ill-timed; Maura needed her third pot of coffee. Even though the inn was designed so that guests could be self-sufficient, some guests—like Maura—preferred a more personal touch.

"Did Rebecca leave?" When Maura looked at her blankly, Hannah took the mug. "Give me five minutes and I'll have a fresh pot brewed."

Maura nodded. She pushed straight black hair back from her high forehead. Unlike her cousins, Maura had Ezra's liquid-brown eyes and hooked nose, but like her cousins, she lacked her uncle's patience. She followed Hannah into the inn's communal kitchen, her posture that of a cat ready to pounce.

"So, how do you know my uncle?" she asked Hannah.

Hannah looked up from washing the coffee pot. She'd been silently cursing her assistant innkeeper and gardener, Rebecca Folly, under her breath for leaving early without warning, and the question caught her off guard. "We're neighbors. One day he and Moose wandered over here during their evening walk. We started talking. He may be the only person in Jasper as obsessed with plants and pollinators as I am."

"That's a weird thing to be obsessed with."

"Is it?" Hannah fell silent as she ground the coffee. When the beans were done, she opened the lid, inhaled deeply—freshly ground coffee was her favorite scent—and added the grounds to the coffeemaker. "Considering that we have pollinators to thank for our food, and even your beloved coffee, I'd say it's strange *not* to be obsessed with their survival."

Maura's eyes crinkled in amusement. "Touché." She leaned against the island while the coffee brewed. "Hummingbird Hollow, a Bee and Bee. Interesting name for an inn. Bees I get, but hummingbirds aren't insects. Why birds?"

Hannah smiled. She loved it when guests asked questions. Loved it even more when they showed an interest in the inn's mission. "Both hummingbirds and bees are pollinators, as are bats and butterflies and a lot of insects. We're just starting out, but eventually our goal is to completely cover the grounds with native plants and flowers, making this inn a haven for all sorts of animals and pollinators." Hannah poured coffee into two mugs and handed Maura one. "Oat milk is on the refrigerator, turbinado sugar is on the counter, if you need them."

"I take my coffee black." Maura took a steaming sip, closed her eyes, and smiled in satisfaction. "Thank you. I know I could have done this myself, but somehow, it's better when you make it." She took another swallow and said, "A long time ago, this used to be the Jasper Inn. I remember staying here when I was younger, when my mom was alive. It's changed quite a bit."

That's an understatement, Hannah thought. The Jasper Inn, with its fussy Victorian façade, lace doilies, and floral wallpaper-vibe, had been Chad's baby—so much so that he'd had an affair with its innkeeper, Karen May. When Reggie was awarded the inn as part of the divorce proceedings almost three years ago, her sister knew that changing it dramatically would be a kick in the you-know-whats to her ex-husband. She'd thought Hannah, who'd been running a small inn at a Massachusetts farm-animal sanctuary, seemed the perfect choice—both to operate the business and to rebrand the inn—and Reggie had offered her the job.

At first, Hannah had said no. Reggie was eleven years older than she, and while they were close in their own way, her sister had trouble viewing Hannah as an adult, even at age thirty-three. But Reggie had sweetened the deal. One, she would give Hannah a forty-nine percent interest in the business. Two, Hannah got to make the inn distinguishable from the Jasper Inn. And three, Reggie would give Hannah seed money to start the remodeling. How could Hannah refuse? She'd moved back to her hometown the next month, and a partnership was born.

"The Jasper Inn was a bit more . . . traditional than this place," Maura continued. She glanced into the open dining and sitting area before shifting her attention to the patio outside. "You've really hippyfied the property."

Hannah took this as a compliment. Once, these rooms had been crammed with overstuffed antiques, but now they had a sparse, Scandinavian feel—with a Vermont twist. Hannah had traded the fox-hunt pictures for paintings by a diverse array of New England artists; she'd torn up dusty rugs and put down reclaimed hardwood floors; she'd replaced high tea with healthy snacks and an optional afternoon group hike; and she'd swapped the antiquing pamphlets for skiing and mountain-biking guides. To Hannah, the place felt homey and whimsical and connected to the outdoors. It didn't sound as though Maura agreed.

"Don't get me wrong. I admire what you've done." Maura said, as if reading Hannah's mind. She drained the mug and held it out to Hannah, who poured her another cup. "It just seems like a lot of effort for bugs."

Just then, Ash came in the backdoor. Maura eyed him sideways. "Does *he* work here too?"

Hannah caught the landscaper's eye. He smiled in amusement. "This is Ash Kade. He's doing some work for the inn."

"Oh, interesting." Maura stood up, put the coffee mug on the island, and straightened the front of her black linen pants. She smiled warmly and held out her hand. "Maura Hamilton-Saunders. Although I could probably drop the Saunders." She smiled again, but this time the expression seemed forced. "Been divorced for almost a year."

Ash held up his dirt-stained hands. "I don't think you want to shake my hand right now. But it's nice to meet you just the same." To Hannah, he said, "Have a few minutes?"

Hannah left Maura with the rest of the pot of coffee and her gaping face. She was used to seeing this reaction to Ash. With his well-muscled shoulders, tousled, wavy black hair and soulful, thickly lashed brown eyes, he had that effect on women. Hannah didn't share their fascination. Ash had been one of the first contractors she and Reggie hired, and over the two-and-a-half years since they'd begun this project, he'd pushed more than a few of her buttons. She would have fired him a dozen times if it weren't for the lack of available landscapers in the area.

"Can't be done," Ash was saying. "It's too damned wet."

He was standing on the stone veranda overlooking the back gardens, the soggy field, and the trees beyond. From here, Hannah could see the refurbished Airstream that she and Reggie had purchased as a tiny-house addition to the inn. Ezra's nephew, Rob Long, and his wife Simone were staying there now, and Bob Marley's "No Woman, No Cry" blared through the open windows.

Hannah said, "We agreed that if we planted the right trees, flowers, and shrubs, we could do something with that field."

Ash threw up his hands again. "Mud, Hannah. Mud." He shrugged. "Nothing but mud after those rains. Don't blame me. I'm not a wizard."

"The whole point of planting a conservation meadow is to plant things that *like* moisture. Do I need to get the sketches? The contractors are starting on the wooden bridge and path soon, so—."

Ash squinted up into the sun and let out a sigh. "Then we'll do the planting after they finish their work so nothing gets trampled."

Hannah could feel her face getting hot. "Their work will be down there." She pointed toward the wooded path that led into the forest and Devil's Pond beyond. "You can plant on the sides of the fields. You won't be anywhere near the bridge construction." She chewed the inside of her lip. He was stalling. "Why are you being so difficult?"

Ash ran a hand through his hair, pushing it back away from his face. His three-day-old shadow was beaded with sweat, and he wiped at his eyes with the back of a tanned arm. He looked at her but stayed silent.

"Spill it, Kade," Hannah said.

"You know that guy with the big house next to Ezra?"

"Brian Lewis?"

Ash nodded. "He called me. He wants me to do some work for him in the coming weeks."

"Let me guess. He made you an offer you can't refuse?"

Ash shrugged. "You know I've been trying to move out from under my dad's business. His offer would give me the capital I need."

Hannah's head began to throb. She was counting on Ash to get this work done before winter so they could open the back area next summer. She and Reggie planned to put in a tree-house hangout and a kayak storage rack near the path to Devil's Pond. If they had to wait another year, the field would just get swampier, the worker harder and more expensive. "You want to put off my work so you can switch to his." She shook her head. "Really, Ash? And I thought we were friends."

"Hannah—"

The inn's landline was ringing, and Hannah took advantage of the excuse to get away from Ash. Finding contractors was hard enough in Jasper; the pickings were slim and expensive. But she'd thought she had this work lined up, and now she'd either have to wait or go back to square one. There was only so much she and Rebecca could do themselves.

She opened the French doors that led inside.

"If you don't want me to take it," Ash was saying. "I won't."

Hannah paused, her hand on the door, and took a calming breath. Hadn't she been trapped in a dead-end job herself? Didn't she relish the freedom that came with owning her own business? How could she deny Ash a similar chance? Maybe if the offer had come from anyone other than the Lewises she'd have felt more generous. She pictured Brian on his lawn today, holding those binoculars and that envelope and staring at Ezra's land. *Vulture.* She had a feeling that whatever he wanted Ash to do was related to the contents of that envelope, and she resented Brian for it. She also resented Brian Lewis for upsetting Ezra, and it felt like Ash was taking Brian's side. Only Ash didn't know any of this, so how could she blame him for wanting to take the job?

"Hannah, please don't—"

"Do what you need to, Ash. It's okay." She meant it. Hannah ran inside to get the phone. She heard Ash calling out behind her, but she ignored him.

She grabbed the phone and heard, "Hannah?" It was Ezra's voice.

"What's up, Ezra?" Hannah took the handheld phone into the kitchen and began pulling fruit out of the refrigerator for the afternoon guest snack. "Did you change your mind about dinner?"

Ezra paused. "No, but I do need to talk to you."

His voice sounded tense, and Hannah stopped what she was doing. "Do you want me to come over?"

"I'll come to you. Later this evening."

Ezra hung up abruptly, and Hannah was left staring at the phone in her hand. From the bowels of the house, Maura's voice carried, high and insistent—something about Jasper's godforsaken remoteness. Hannah walked to the front desk, replaced the phone in its cradle, and took another deep breath. The sun was shining through the picture windows, illuminating the counter and enveloping her in warmth. The inn's cat, Turnip, lay in her bed by the stone fireplace, her eyes closed in contentment. It *was* a beautiful, sunny day, Hannah reminded herself—the perfect Vermont summer afternoon.

Then why do I feel so chilled?

She shrugged off the pressing feeling of dread and headed back to the kitchen. *Just nerves*, she thought, as she sliced into ripe, red strawberries. She nicked her finger with the knife, and blood beaded across her nail. Running her hand under cold water, she cursed her clumsiness. *Just nerves*, she repeated to herself. *Just my silly nerves.*

Chapter Three

Reggie stopped by the inn a little after six with dinner for herself, Hannah, and Peach. She spread pita, hummus, roasted vegetables, and a variety of sides out on the table in the small private apartment Hannah inhabited at the back of the inn. Reggie's daughter, Peach, whose given name was Telulah—a spirited six-year-old with wide brown eyes, a mop of cinnamon curls, and a spitfire attitude—stared at the food sullenly, arms across her chest.

"I'm not eating that."

"You need to try it, Peach."

Peach grunted.

Reggie glanced from Hannah to her daughter, and Hannah shrugged. Unlike Peach, who was a mini-me version of her aunt, Reggie had long, straight, dark hair streaked with gray that she always wore pulled back into a neat ponytail. Also unlike her daughter, Reggie was always impeccably turned out—with matching clothes, pristine posture, well-scrubbed skin, and with a reserved disposition to match. As a result, her patience for Peach's histrionics and stubbornness frequently wore thin, a fact that amused Hannah. *Like today*, Hannah thought.

Reggie put some roasted peppers, hummus, and a small pile of lettuce on a plate and slid it toward her daughter. "Eat, Peach."

Peach turned her face the other way and clenched her jaw tight.

"Not looking at me doesn't mean you can't hear me."

Hannah held back a laugh. Eyeing Peach's pink tutu, rainbow-striped leggings, red rain boots, and yellow halter top, she said, "Peach picked out her clothes this morning?" Her niece resembled a ballerina clown—but Hannah gave her props for originality and *chutzpah*.

Reggie's mouth was a pinched, disapproving line. She dished some food onto her own plate and sat down across from Peach. "She can wear a parka for all I care. I pick my battles. Clothing? Fine. Dinner. No way." She glared at her daughter. "You can pick three of the things on this table to place on your plate, but you must eat what you choose, Peach."

Hannah watched as Peach begrudgingly chose roasted broccoli, tabouleh, and a piece of whole-grain pita bread—none of which were on Reggie's plate.

The trio ate most of their meal in silence. When they were nearly finished, Reggie pointed her fork at Hannah and said, "You seem distracted. What's up?"

"Not distracted."

"You keep glancing at the phone."

"It's Ezra. He said he was stopping by. I tried calling him before dinner, and he didn't answer."

"Does he ever answer?" Reggie looked up from her plate, and seeing Hannah's worried expression said, "I'm sure he's fine." She sighed. "Honestly, when you moved back to Jasper, he is the last person I thought you'd befriend."

"He helps me with my flowers, I bring him food, he grumbles about it."

Reggie stabbed at a piece of pepper. "A match made in heaven."

"You always see the worst in people, Reg. Anyway, he's kind to me in his own way, and he seems lonely."

Reggie's eyebrows shot up. "Because he pushes everyone away. You were gone from Jasper for a long time, but Ezra has been alone since I can remember. He isn't always a nice man—not lately, at least. Loneliness is the natural consequence when you've walled yourself off from everyone and treat people like dirt."

"That's not totally fair," Hannah said quietly, but even as the words left her mouth, she knew there was truth in what Reggie had said. Hannah had only known Ezra as a friend for two years. When she was little, growing up in Jasper, he had been a quiet presence, eclipsed by his pretty, cheerful, friendly wife. After Molly died— before, really—Ezra withdrew even further. Her death hit him hard. He *had* walled everyone off, but now that she'd seen a softer side—a man who went out of his way to help her identify native plants, kept his wife's handmade curtains, and loved his rescue dog—she wished others could see that side of him too.

"Stop trying to save people, Hannah. People, cows, insects. *Men*." Reggie let out a frustrated groan. "I thought you came back to Jasper to focus on yourself for a change."

"I did."

"Then do it. Make something of your life—for *you* this time."

Hannah was feeling defensive, and she swallowed a mean retort. This was what Reggie always did—backed her into a corner and then got annoyed when Hannah fought back. It was a dance they'd done for years. Her sister meant well, but she wouldn't let anything go.

Hannah kept her voice even. Reggie would use any display of emotion against her. "I thought that's what I was doing here, Reggie. The inn, the business."

"You know what I'm talking about," Reggie said, her voice softer. "*Chris.*"

Hannah had known exactly what Reggie was talking about without her mentioning his name, and she resented the comment. Those were dark days, days Hannah didn't want to relive. And anyway, Reggie had never agreed with her life choices—especially her romantic relationships.

Hannah stood up. "I need some air. Leave the dishes. I'll get them when I come back."

"Where are you going, Aunt Hannah?" Peach asked.

"To the lake." Hannah held up her hand in anticipation of the next question. "I'll take you next time, Peach. It'll be getting dark soon." She glanced at her sister, who was looking at her with that maddening mixture of worry and disappointment Hannah remembered from her teenage years. "If Ezra comes by, ring me, okay?"

"You're ridiculous sometimes, you know that?" Reggie's expression softened. "But we love you."

Hannah took a deep breath. Her sister *did* love her. Although not affectionate by nature, Reggie had shown her love in a million tiny ways, not the least of which was giving her this new chance in Jasper. While Hannah knew that Reggie disapproved of the circumstances that had brought Hannah to Jasper—that had brought her to her knees, if she was being honest—she also knew that Reggie was the one person in her life who was always there for her. But her concern came with a price tag, and Hannah wasn't always willing to pay that price. Not anymore.

"I only say these things because I care," Reggie said. "You know that."

Hannah nodded. She gave Peach a squeeze. "Later,'Mater."

"Maybe, gravy."

Hannah smiled. "Close, kiddo."

Peach, who'd polished off all her broccoli and tabouleh, grinned up at her aunt. "Someday, I want to do what *you* do, Aunt Hannah."

"Oh, and what exactly is that?" Hannah asked.

"Play in the mud all day and collect bugs."

*   *   *

It was the golden hour. The sunlight warmed Hannah's bare shoulders and shimmered on the water, shattering like a million shards of glass as the kayak sliced through the lake's calm surface. This was the first nice day after a week of storms and rain, so the water level was high, and tree branches, plants, and other natural debris floated near the banks. Devil's Pond was small—only about forty acres—but the hourglass-shaped body of water was tucked into the Green Mountains with a view of Devil's Mountain and the peaks to the north. The pond sat mostly on the inn's property, with a small section bordered by national forest, a sliver on Ezra's land, and an even smaller sliver owned by the ski resort. The only area suitable for a boat launch was on the inn's side—the rest of the pond was bordered by marsh or forest—so Hannah normally had the pond to herself, as she did today.

A stream snaked its way down the mountain and through the trees, feeding the pond a steady supply of cold water. Hannah headed toward the stream, paddling through water lilies and enjoying the reflection of the trees on the water.

A loud water slap startled her, and she nearly dropped her paddle. A second later, she saw a small brown face peeking up at her from beside a floating tree branch. The resident beaver, disturbed by her presence.

"Relax," she called out. The beaver dove underwater.

Hannah tilted her face upward, letting the sun's heat soothe away some of the hurt. Reggie's concerns had nothing to do with Ezra and everything to do with Chris, the boyfriend Hannah had left just months before coming back to her home state of Vermont. Nevertheless, Hannah had to wonder whether Reggie was right about her. She did have a habit of trying to save people and animals. But maybe it went deeper than that. Maybe she was drawn to the wounded. Her job at the animal sanctuary. Ezra. *Chris.*

Only Hannah didn't want to think about Chris. Wasn't that why she had come back to Jasper? Right now, she didn't want to think about any lost soul. She wanted to focus on the business and get back to some sense of normalcy, whatever that was.

Hannah wove the kayak through a narrow marginal passage lined with cattails, bulrushes, and sedges, and into the even narrower stream. A pair of red-winged blackbirds flew from the dense grasses and landed on a cattail, watching her. Bullfrogs croaked from the shallow banks. The air was sweet with the scent of dogbane growing along the stream banks. Another hundred feet, and Hannah maneuvered the kayak upstream, toward the beaver dam. The dam was in full regalia today, with fresh branches straining the cold stream water. The beaver had been busy rebuilding after the rain.

This was Hannah's favorite spot. The air was earthy and fresh, and the sounds of the water rushing over the dam calmed her. She felt swaddled by the forest, safe from the thousand daily pressures of everyday life, and protected by Devil's Mountain, visible in the distance. She closed her eyes, bathing in the forest sounds.

A whimper startled her, and her eyes flew open. With her hand over her eyes to protect against the sun's evening glare, she strained to see what had made the sound. She spotted a brown dog partially submerged in the marsh on the other side of the beaver dam.

Carefully, Hannah wedged the kayak against the vegetation that lined the bank and climbed out of the boat, her bare feet sinking into the muddy stream bed. She couldn't see much of the dog, and she couldn't tell if it was stuck or just scared, so she moved cautiously toward it. She climbed over the beaver dam, gripping the shrubs on the sides of the stream for balance. Then she walked upstream until she was close enough to see the dog.

It was Moose. He was sitting, immobile, staring into the thick marsh between the stream and the woods.

"Come here, boy," Hannah called, alarmed, but the dog wouldn't move. "Moose!"

Moose whined. *What was he doing out here, alone?*

The feeling of dread was back, threatening to consume her. As she reached the dog, her legs scratched and bleeding from sharp prickers, she glimpsed a piece of red material sticking up above the vegetation, tented on a cattail.

Hannah recognized the buffalo plaid.

"Ezra!" Hannah ran as fast as she could through the marsh, but her feet kept sinking deeper into the mud. A sob escaped her throat, and she moaned as she finally approached Ezra's inert form. He lay sprawled across the vegetation, face down, blood caked on his head and neck. His skin was grayish, his face was planted in the water-logged soil. Gently, she placed two shaking fingers on his neck, feeling for a pulse, but she knew it was a formality.

Ezra Grayson was dead.

Chapter Four

Hannah called 911, but it would take the police and the local medical examiner time to get to the remote location. In the meantime, she refused to leave Ezra's body or Moose, who sat by it, waiting, it seemed, for the man to get up. Hannah called Reggie from the safety of her kayak to tell her what had happened. She didn't recognize her own robotic voice. She felt like she was acting on autopilot.

Her sister offered to join her, but Hannah didn't want Peach anywhere near the pond, and Reggie couldn't leave Peach at the inn alone—especially not with strangers afoot.

"Are you sure he's —?" Reggie asked.

"Yes, I'm sure."

"How did he —?"

"I don't know." Hannah scanned the woods for movement, a weapon, anything, but the forest was still. "I don't want to disturb the scene. There's blood. It looks like . . . well, like maybe he hit his head. Hard." She paused. "Or someone else hit it."

Reggie hesitated. "Why was he back there, Hannah? It doesn't make sense."

"No, it doesn't. If he'd been coming to see me, he would have taken the road. He never comes through the marsh."

"Maybe he was walking Moose?"

Hannah shook her head, then realized her sister couldn't see her. "Ezra was paranoid about ticks. No way he would have walked Moose back here."

"Maybe Moose bolted, and Ezra followed."

"Maybe." But Hannah knew that was unlikely too. The tall man and the big dog had been inseparable since Ezra had adopted Moose, and Moose was obedient. He wouldn't have run away.

Neither spoke for a moment. Then Reggie said, "Let me stay on the phone with you, Hannah. At least until the police get there."

Hannah was about to refuse, always her knee-jerk reaction when it came to Reggie's suggestions, but as she looked around the pond and surrounding forest again, she felt a rising sense of panic. It wasn't just being alone with a dead body. She didn't know what had happened or why Ezra had been out here—or whether someone was still lurking in the woods.

"Okay," she said softly. "Just until help arrives."

They didn't say much after that, but the sound of Reggie's breathing was a reminder that Hannah was not alone.

* * *

Sirens in the distance signaled police progress, but because there was no easy access to this part of the pond without a boat, Hannah wasn't sure which route they would take to get to Ezra. Moose was the first to hear the officials arrive. The dog sat up straight, his head cocked in the direction of the ski resort. A few moments later, Noah Booker and several others came tramping through the woods, their arms and backs laden with lighting equipment and medical gear. A man and a woman carried a stretcher between them. Moose stood protectively in front of Ezra's body, growling and whining.

Noah waved when he saw Hannah before pointing at the dog. "Is he friendly?"

"Normally."

Noah eyed the dog warily. He was a tall, slender man with a neatly trimmed beard and shaggy brown hair that he wore pushed back behind his ears, away from a hungry, angular face. Hannah had gone to high school with his younger sister, and despite Noah's present status as a detective, to her he would always be the same gangly, moody boy who'd made fun of her. She watched him carefully now, worried the police would do something to trigger the already agitated dog.

Noah asked, "Will he listen to you?"

"He hasn't really noticed me. He's too focused on Ezra."

One of Noah's team members said, "If he doesn't stand down, we'll have to call Animal Control."

"Let me try," Hannah said.

Hannah didn't want Moose taken to Animal Control—the idea was unthinkable—so slowly, carefully, she made her way back through the marsh toward Moose. By now the sun was setting; soon darkness would fall. She needed to be back across Devil's Pond before dark or it would be nearly impossible to navigate the water without a light. Seeing Ezra's limp form and the loyal, distraught dog was almost too much. Hannah's reserve started to crumble. She got as close as she dared, and, holding back angry tears, she extended a hand to Moose.

"Come on, boy," she crooned. "You know me."

The dog whined. He lowered his head, ears back. Hannah squatted down so they were eye-to-eye and said his name again, more firmly this time. Finally, she saw recognition in his scared eyes, then Moose bounded over the few feet of swampy vegetation that separated them, his whine louder.

"Good boy!" Hannah rubbed his head. When she was sure the dog would allow it, she gently grabbed his collar. "I'll coax him back to the inn with me. He can squeeze into the kayak."

Noah nodded. "Appreciate that. Don't bathe him or anything, just in case. We'll check him out after we take care of the body." Noah's gaze swept over the area, lingering on Ezra's inert form. He barked a few instructions to the patrol officers, then turned to Hannah. "Anything you can tell me now?"

Hannah repeated what she'd told the 911 operator. "Nothing else to share."

"You didn't move his body?"

"I felt for a pulse. That was it."

"You know we'll have questions for you." Noah sounded apologetic. "No way around it."

"Come to the inn when you're done. You'll find me and Moose there."

*   *   *

By the time Hannah paddled across Devil's Pond, put the kayak away, and brought Moose to the inn, it was nearly nine. Hannah snuck into her living quarters through the back entrance, conscious of her muddied, scratched legs and tear-stained face. She wanted to get cleaned up before she saw her guests, and to be sure they'd heard about Ezra before seeing Moose.

Reggie had put Peach to bed on Hannah's couch, and her niece was snoring softly in the apartment's small living room, her sweet face cherubic as she slept. Moose sniffed the little girl before curling up on the hardwood floor next to her, his massive, jowly head resting on his paws. Hannah wanted to towel him off, but heeding Noah's request, she just knelt on the floor beside him and stroked his head until his eyes closed.

"Sorry, boy," she whispered. Of all the creatures in the world, Moose would be most impacted by Ezra's death. Hannah was hoping a family member would take the dog. For now, she decided, he could stay with her.

After a quick shower and a shot of espresso, Hannah found Reggie in the inn's kitchen making yet another pot of coffee for Ezra's niece, Maura. Maura was sitting at the island staring morosely into an empty mug. Her cousin, Rob Long and his wife Simone were on a couch in the communal living room. Simone held a balled-up tissue to her red, swollen face, and Rob sat beside her, rubbing her back. No one was talking.

Hannah looked at Reggie, who shook her head warningly back and forth. She hadn't told them about Ezra—so why the long faces?

Rob looked up. His dark eyes were wide and moist. "A man named Noah Booker called a few minutes ago. He told us about my uncle."

"*Our* uncle," Maura said.

Simone shot her a look.

Rob said, "Sorry, Maura. *Our* uncle."

"I'm so sorry," Hannah said. "He was a good man."

Simone sobbed, and Rob whispered something in her ear that made her sob louder.

Maura looked up from the fresh cup of coffee Reggie had poured for her. "Do you know what happened to him?" she asked Hannah.

Hannah shook her head. She wasn't sure how much Noah had told them, and she didn't want to be the one to blow any confidential information. The third Grayson cousin, a surly debt trader from New York City who had rented two adjoining rooms at the inn for himself, wasn't there, so Hannah asked, "Has Waylen been told yet?"

Maura and Rob exchanged a cryptic look. Maura said, "We don't know. No one has seen him since this morning."

"Seems a little odd, don't you think?" Rob said. "*He* disappears and Ezra turns up dead."

"*Rob*," Simone said in warning. "I'm sure Waylen has a perfectly good explanation for where he's been."

"A good explanation or a good excuse?" Rob muttered.

Simone sniffed before shifting over with a huff, so she was no longer leaning against her husband's side. Hannah eyed the pair while she busied herself wiping down the counters. They seemed an unlikely couple. Rob was a handsome man in a casual, outdoorsy way. Broad and muscular, he had pleasant, even features, a generous mouth, and thick blondish hair that he wore closely cropped to his head. He seemed at home in jeans and a T-shirt— Hannah had never seen him in anything else. His wife Simone, on the other hand, looked like she'd just walked out of a New York salon. Straightened, blonde-streaked hair in a shade not seen in nature. Long, squared-off manicured nails painted deepest crimson. A black leopard-print silk pantsuit, the sleeveless blouse cinched with a wide, black-leather belt. And Hannah's favorite— three-inch spiky Manolo Blahniks in the same color as her nails.

Completely impractical outfit for this corner of Vermont, Hannah thought. No wonder Simone stayed in the Airstream all day.

"Do you want something to eat?" Hannah asked. "I can make you sandwiches or heat up some vegetable soup."

All three declined.

Maura said, "Do you have any liquor? I wouldn't mind a shot in my coffee."

Simone murmured something that sounded like agreement.

"Sorry," Hannah said. "We're not licensed to serve liquor."

"You must have a stash in your apartment back there," Maura said.

"Sorry—nothing."

Simone elbowed Rob, and he said, "A store nearby? Somewhere that sells beer or wine? It's called for in a situation like this, don't you think?"

Reggie shook her head. "I'm afraid there's nothing open at this hour, at least nothing within forty minutes of us."

Simone scowled. "And your uncle refused to move? Why would he want to stay in a town where the stores close by nine?" She let out a low moan. "And what kind of inn is dry? This whole town is on my last nerve. No wonder Ezra went crazy. Some kind of rock fever, if you ask me—"

"And no one has," Maura said under her breath.

Ignoring Reggie's warning look, Hannah opened her mouth to say something sharp in response to Simone, but the sound of the front door opening stopped her. Moose barked loudly from the apartment. Noah strode into living room, his face grim.

The inn's guests eyed him warily. Hannah watched as he sat down among them.

Reggie touched Hannah's arm and whispered, "I'm heading out. Call me later."

Reggie retreated into the apartment to collect Peach, and Hannah felt suddenly very alone.

"What can you tell us?" Maura asked Noah. "Did he have a heart attack? Or maybe he fell? I told him he was too old to hike alone. At his age, it just takes one bad fall."

Noah glanced from one face to another. Finally, heavily, he said, "We're not so sure this was an accident."

"What's that supposed to mean?" Rob asked.

Noah said, "It means—"

"How can you know anything definitive this soon?" Simone asked.

The glare Noah gave her could have curdled milk. "*It means Ezra's death is being investigated as suspicious.*"

"You think Uncle Ezra was *murdered*?" Maura asked, eyes like saucers.

Noah didn't answer, but the solemn set of his mouth told Hannah all she needed to know.

Chapter Five

"They're impossible," Noah said later. He tossed his hat on Hannah's table and knelt in front of Moose. While he gave the dog a thorough once-over, he prattled on about Ezra's family.

"Ezra called them 'the vultures,'" Hannah said.

"I can see why. Taking statements from them had something in common with feeding lions at the zoo." Satisfied, Noah stood up. He stretched his hands over his head and yawned, which made Hannah yawn.

He said, "Am I keeping you up?"

"A little." She *was* tired, but Noah promised if she gave her statement here, tonight, he wouldn't make her leave the inn. "Want some tea or coffee?"

"Nah." Noah waved a hand. "Let's get your statement over with." He sat at the apartment's small kitchen table and pointed to the seat across from him. "I know you went through it before with Officer Gupta, but I need you to repeat everything one more time. At the pond—and earlier, at Ezra's house." Hannah sat, and he squinted in her direction. "Are you sure you're okay? Finding Ezra must have been a shock."

"Hanging in there."

"You and Ezra were friends."

The way he said it—with matter-of-fact kindness and none of the surprise or judgment everyone else, including Reggie, showed—tugged at the dam she'd built to hold back her emotions, and tears pooled in her eyes. "He *was* my friend. I can't believe he's gone."

Noah stood and grabbed a paper towel, which he handed to Hannah.

She dabbed at her eyes. "You must be used to this," Hannah said finally. "Emotional people, I mean."

"You never, ever get used to it." He sat back in the chair, his steady, empathetic gaze on her face. "I meant what I told the cousins. It looks like Ezra was hit in the head from behind with a blunt object. We'll have confirmation soon, but it's being treated as a crime. That means your statement is especially important, so please take your time."

Hannah took a deep breath before going through it all again: the afternoon visit, the call, the trip across the pond. "And then I called the police—and you showed up."

Noah was writing notes in a black binder. He glanced up. "What do you think he wanted?"

"I have no idea."

"He didn't give you *any* indication?"

Hannah shook her head.

Noah said, "Why did you go out to the pond if you knew Ezra was coming over?"

"I needed some air."

Noah tilted his head. "Why?"

Hannah sighed. "Reggie was here."

"*Ah.*"

Hannah tapped her nails on the table, thinking about the order of events. "She said she'd call me when Ezra arrived. Honestly, I thought maybe he'd forgotten. It was getting late."

They sat in silence for a moment. Hannah watched as Moose paced restlessly around the small space. The dog finally plopped down by the back door with a loud huff.

"What are you going to do with *him*?" Hannah asked.

"Animal Control, I guess."

"And then what?"

Noah shrugged. "Unless Ezra's family claim him, he'll be left at the shelter. Maybe he'll get adopted or a foster agency will take him. But considering his size and age—" Letting the obvious hang between them, he studied the large dog, whose graying jowls were hanging down over his front paws. Moose snored softly, his rear legs twitching. "We went over to the house. It looks like the dog got excited and pushed his way through a screen door to get to Ezra."

"That makes sense. If someone tried to hurt Ezra, I'm sure Moose would have attacked, which means he didn't get there in time."

Noah nodded. "The screen is pretty demolished, and there are scratches around the doorframe, as though Moose became increasingly agitated. We think he heard Ezra and got protective."

"But he was too late."

"Unfortunately."

"That's odd."

Noah tilted his head. "That the dog would be protective?"

"That Ezra would have gone out without closing the main door. He was paranoid about bears. He didn't trust screen doors to keep them out."

Noah sat back, his brow creased in thought. "What are you suggesting?"

"Maybe he was just going outside to check on something. A quick trip—the kind that wouldn't require him to close up the house."

"Maybe." Noah watched Moose snore for a few moments before saying, "Or maybe someone else was with him, and the other person left the door open." Noah tapped his phone. "I guess I should give Animal Control a call. It's late, and I'm sure you're anxious to put this day behind you."

Hannah said, "What if he stayed here for a few days—at least until you talk with his family?"

"Do you really think that's a good idea? He's a big dog, and you're running an inn."

Hannah said, "It's a better idea than sending him to a shelter."

Noah chewed on his bottom lip. "I don't suppose it's a problem."

Realizing Moose hadn't had a drink since he'd arrived a few hours ago, Hannah rose to get the dog some water. While she filled a large bowl at the spigot, she turned to look at Noah. He was watching the dog with a pensive expression on his face.

"Funny," Noah said, "Aside from the killer, Moose may be our only witness to a murder."

* * *

When running out of the room wasn't an option, Moose made his distaste for the bathtub clear by lying down on the floor in front of it and refusing to move.

"I know, big guy," Hannah crooned. "But you need to take a bath if you're going to stay."

When pleading and treats didn't work, Hannah finally gave up. He was too heavy to lift on her own, and she figured Moose had had a rough day and deserved a little space. Other than being a little damp, he wasn't dirty, and he seemed happy enough to sleep on the floor. Hannah left him there while she checked on the inn, then got ready for bed. She was finally climbing under her blankets when the inn's buzzer sounded. Hannah muttered a few expletives, but she crawled back out of bed, threw on her robe, and left her apartment, Moose padding behind her.

She found Maura standing in the dark in the inn's kitchen. Her small frame was engulfed by the inn's hemp robe, her arms wrapped tightly around her torso in a self-embrace. Even though the woman had at least a decade on Hannah, she looked like a lost child standing there, and Hannah felt a wave of sympathy.

Maura swayed back and forth before reaching out to steady herself against the wall.

Hannah flipped on the kitchen light. "Are you okay?"

"How could I be okay?"

Hannah glanced at the oven clock. It was after midnight. "What can I do for you, Maura?"

Maura glanced down at her bare feet. She seemed surprised to see she'd forgotten to put on her slippers. "I wanted to talk to you alone." She looked nervously toward the steps that led upstairs to the guest rooms where Waylen was also staying. "Is there somewhere we can go for more privacy?"

Hannah led her through the common rooms and into the small sunporch off the side of the inn. She pulled up a chair, but Maura just stood there, arms still across her chest. She eyed Moose, as though seeing him for the first time.

"Is that Ezra's dog?"

"Yep."

She frowned. "Why is he here?"

"Where else would you like him to be?"

Maura shrugged, sighed, and finally sank into a chair. With a wary glance at Moose, she straightened the hem of her robe and said, "I saw you disappear with that cop. What did he tell you?"

"Nothing new."

Maura studied her nails. "*Nothing?*"

"He just took my statement."

"He was in there for a long time if he was only taking your statement."

Hannah shrugged. "What can I say? That's what we discussed. Is that all you needed? Because if so, we should probably both get some sleep."

Maura was silent for a moment, and Hannah noticed the new chips and chew marks on her manicured nails. "Your sister—Reggie is her name? Reggie Solace?"

Caught off guard by the sudden shift in topic, Hannah frowned. "What does my sister have to do with Ezra?"

"Nothing, nothing at all. I just recall that she and her husband used to own this inn, and I was wondering what she's doing these days."

Hannah's frown deepened. *Maura had all night to ask about Reggie's life, and she decides to do it now?* "Reggie is still in real estate, but she spends a lot of her time in property management."

"She must do well. With all the tourists and all."

"She does okay."

Maura pressed her lips together and raised her eyebrows. "And she was friendly with Uncle Ezra too?"

"Not particularly." *Not at all.*

"*Uh-huh.*"

Hannah stood up. "Maura, I'm so sorry you lost your uncle. I lost a dear friend today, so I understand your pain. I can assure you that Reggie had nothing to do with Ezra—in life or otherwise, and I don't understand your questions."

Maura didn't move. She sat there, frowning, her eyes narrowed in distrust.

Finally Hannah said, "What's really bothering you?"

"I followed Ezra today. I wanted to talk to him about moving . . . well, that doesn't matter . . . he wouldn't give me the time of day. I got curious. What did he do all day? I followed him when he left his house on that old bike of his. It's a miracle he didn't die in a car accident, the way he rode that bike." Maura took a deep breath. "He rode to a really nice house a few miles outside of town."

"So?"

"*So* the name on the property was Solace." Maura raised her perfectly tweezed eyebrows. "Maybe your sister and my uncle were friendly after all."

"That's not my sister's house. She lives in a smaller home near town."

"Then whose house is it?"

"There are a lot of Solaces around here, Maura. The Solaces go back generations. We have streets named after us. I don't even know them all."

Maura looked ready to argue, but she got up with a deep groan.

"Getting older sucks." She tightened the robe's belt and, leaning with one hand against the wall, said, "It wasn't your sister Reggie he was going to see?"

"Afraid not."

"Do you think the police are right?" Maura asked. "About Ezra's death being suspicious?"

Hannah thought about the scene she'd witnessed. The blood. Ezra's submerged face. She shuddered. "I don't know."

"I mean, who would want Ezra dead? I just can't figure it out. He was no peach, that's for sure, but he didn't hurt anyone."

"I'd like to know too, Maura. It just doesn't make sense."

As they made their way through the inn, toward the stairs leading to the second-floor guest quarters, Maura said, "You should get to know the other Solace. Looks like they've done well for themselves. Huge house on the mountain, big barn. I think I even saw a pool." She touched Hannah's arm. "Aren't you even a little bit curious?"

"I'm too tired to be curious."

Hannah said goodnight to her guest and thought about the lie she'd just told. Hannah had no need to be curious. As soon as Maura described Ezra's destination, Hannah had known exactly where he was going. The six-bedroom house on the hill overlooked the town of Jasper on one side, looked up at Devil's Mountain on the other, and had the best view for miles around. It did indeed have a pool—a rarity in cold Vermont—as well as an indoor sauna, a tennis court, a climbing wall, and a guesthouse. Hannah knew the house well. She also knew the man who owned it.

Hannah went back to her small apartment to call Reggie. Her sister would be asleep, and Reggie guarded her sleep like a food-aggressive dog guards its bowl, but this was important.

"We have a problem," Hannah said.

"What now?" Reggie muttered, her words sleep-slurred and anger-edged.

"I may not have been the last person to have seen Ezra after all."

"Really, Hannah? Why couldn't this wait until morning?"

"Ezra went to see Dad."

"Oh," was all Reggie said, suddenly sounding wide awake.

Chapter Six

Two days went by before Hannah could get over to her sister's house.

"I thought that whole thing was settled years ago." Reggie stared into her coffee mug, frowned, and swallowed the last of it. "What could Ezra have wanted with Dad now?"

Hannah shrugged. After laying out coffee, homemade granola, and fresh fruit for her guests, she had driven to Reggie's to talk about what to do next. Now she sat back in the Windsor chair in Reggie's breakfast nook and contemplated their situation. Hearing that Ezra had visited her father had been a real jab to the windpipe. Nothing good ever came of getting John Solace involved in anything.

Hannah said, "Whatever feud they had, I thought it was over years ago."

"Me too."

Hannah reached down and patted Moose's head. The dog rewarded her with a giant paw in her lap. He'd looked so forlorn that morning that she'd decided to take him with her, and now he sat glued to her side.

Hannah asked, "Do we tell Noah?"

"Didn't you say Ezra's niece Maura followed Ezra to Dad's house? Seems to me she should tell him."

"She thought she was following Ezra to *your* house."

Reggie snorted. "I hope you set her straight."

"I sure did."

Other than in passing, Hannah hadn't seen their father since their mother's funeral four years before, but as much as she resented her father, she knew Reggie's anger ran deeper. Their lukewarm relationship had chilled completely when Chad cheated on Reggie with the manager of the inn and John had taken Chad's side in the ensuing divorce, blaming Reggie for being too cold and too career focused. Reggie had never forgiven their father. To Hannah, John Solace's behavior came as no surprise. He'd shown his true colors years ago when he'd sold out their family.

Hannah looked up to find Reggie staring at her.

Reggie rubbed her face and said, "On second thought, I think we should tell Noah about what Maura saw. Otherwise, they may think you were the last person to have talked with Ezra before his death. Noah should know it was Dad."

"What if Maura was mistaken? What if Ezra was just going for a leisurely bike ride and happened to ride by Dad's estate?"

"Think about what you just said. Have you ever known Ezra to purposefully ride near Dad's estate?" Reggie waved her hand dismissively. "No, something was up between them."

"You're not implying that *Dad* was responsible for what happened? The man barely leaves the house to golf much less to tromp through the woods. How could he have hurt Ezra?"

"We both know Dad has the money to hire someone." Reggie glanced around, checking, Hannah knew, to make sure Peach wasn't nearby. "Besides, I think Dad will do anything to protect his property and his money."

"That would be pretty extreme."

"Dad *is* pretty extreme."

"Why would Ezra have rehashed all of that now? It's been decades," Hannah said, shaking her head. "It just doesn't add up."

"You said yourself that the vultures were closing in. Ezra's house is a mess, lots of folks want to buy his property, his neighbor was reporting him for every perceived violation under the sun, and his niece and nephews were all but forcing him into a retirement home. Maybe Ezra decided the money Dad owed him would fix everything. Maybe he went seeking his due."

Hannah thought about what Reggie was saying. It was true that Ezra had been under a lot of pressure. Maybe more pressure than Hannah realized, and she felt bad about that. But reviving a twenty-year-old dispute didn't seem like Ezra's way. "We don't even know if Dad owed him money," Hannah said. "We don't *really* know much about what happened back then."

Reggie stood, placed her dishes in the sink, and called for Peach. Over her shoulder, she said, "We know that Ezra sold Dad lots of land, Dad got filthy rich, and Ezra lived in a hovel—"

"It hadn't always been a hovel."

"You know what I mean. They made some sort of deal, Dad reneged, made a fortune, and Ezra ended up with nothing. Ezra carried that chip for years and years. That kind of anger can fester. Maybe Ezra went to confront Dad, and Dad reacted."

"Dad's a lot of things, but he's not a murderer."

Small footsteps on the stairs made Hannah stop talking, but she caught the smirk on Reggie's face.

"Sure," Reggie said. "Whatever you say."

"I'll tell Noah." While Hannah didn't think for a second that her father had killed Ezra, Noah deserved the truth. She eyed her sister, normally the rational one, with surprise. Reggie wasn't a petty person, but this felt petty—and in the wake of Ezra's death, it seemed especially so. Unsupportive father to homicidal criminal felt like a heck of a leap. "Come on Moose, time to go home."

"That dog needs a bath," Reggie said. "He smells."

"Try telling him that," Hannah said.

A sleepy Peach entered the kitchen, curly hair sticking out every which way like a mini Medusa. She rubbed her eyes, yawned, and started to whine about being tired—until she saw Moose. Just like that, she grinned and threw her arms happily around the dog.

"Peach!" Reggie said. "You don't know that dog. Get off him."

"He's a sweetheart," Hannah said. Moose was wagging his tail and licking Peach's cheeks. Hannah laughed. "Relax," she told Reggie. "It's just a little dog saliva. Right, Peach?"

"Right," Peach said between giggles.

"Telulah Mae, go wash your hands and face," Reggie said. "*Now.*"

"Uh-oh, she's breaking out your real name," Hannah whispered to her niece. "You'd better get washing."

"You know I can hear you," Reggie said, but a smile was playing with the edges of her lips too. "I need to get to work, Hannah. Call Noah. Wash that dog." Any trace of smile disappeared. "And be careful. One way or another, we may have a *you-know-what* on the loose in Jasper."

"I'll be careful," Hannah said. The thought of a *you-know-what* in Jasper *did* scare her. Of course it did. But the fear was not as strong as the anger she felt at whoever had caused Ezra's untimely death. His murderer would pay. She just hoped justice would be doled out quickly.

*   *   *

"Need a hand?"

Hannah was wrestling with the hose outside, struggling to move Moose and the hose close enough to one another to actually get the dog clean, when she looked up to see Ash standing over her with that maddening, bemused grin on his face. She looked down and realized that she was soaked, the ground was soaked, and the towel she'd brought outside to dry Moose with was soaked, but the dog was still dry.

Ash said, "You missed your target."

"Haha. Very observant. Yeah, he's as stubborn as Ezra was." Hannah stood up, pushed wet strands of hair out of her face, and placed her hands on her hips. "Are you here to work?"

"I'm here to check on you. I heard what happened to Ezra." The bemused expression was gone, and his eyes softened with concern. Ash and his family hadn't been friendly with Ezra, but in a small town like Jasper, everyone knew everyone else, and deaths were mourned, even if it meant differences had to be set aside. "I'm sorry."

"Thanks."

"I know you two had become close." They stood there, staring at one another in uncomfortable silence, and after a few seconds Ash said, "Why don't you let me help you with the dog? I'll hold him and you wash."

Together, Hannah and Ash worked quietly for the next fifteen minutes, wetting, washing, and rinsing the big dog until any hint of swamp smell was gone. Once Moose knew he was cornered, he was mostly cooperative, and Hannah had to admit that Ash was good with the dog. He held him gently and talked to him softly while Hannah used warm water to rinse Moose's fur clean. Afterward, they both watched as Moose ran around the yard, shaking indignantly.

"Where will he go now?" Ash asked.

"Here until someone from Ezra's family claims him."

"Think that's likely? I met that bunch. They don't seem . . . altruistic."

Hannah smiled at Moose's antics. "You're probably right." Then it dawned on her that when Ash had been here the day before, the only Grayson at the inn had been Maura. She glanced at him sharply. "You mean you met Maura?"

"No, I met them all, and I definitely don't see Waylen or Rob's wife as the dog-loving types."

"When did you meet the rest of Ezra's family?"

Ash used the hose to rinse off his hands. "They were at Ezra's while I was at —.

He let his voice trail off, but Hannah knew he was going to say "Brian's."

"When was that?" She fought to keep her tone nonchalant. She had no right to be angry. He could run his business the way he saw fit. Still, the fact that they had all been at Ezra's was news.

"Two days ago."

The morning of Ezra's death, Hannah thought. "And you're sure you met all of them—Maura, Rob, Simone, *and* Waylen?"

"That's how they introduced themselves. Why?"

"Do you remember the time?"

Ash frowned. "What's with the inquisition?"

"No inquisition. I was there around lunchtime, and the family acted as though they hadn't seen Waylen since the morning. Just seems odd that he was with them at the house. Can you pinpoint the time?"

Ash pulled a calloused hand through his wavy hair and slid his glance away, toward the house. His dark eyes squinted against the glare of sunshine on window glass. "I got there early. Around eight."

As she watched Moose roll around in the grass, Hannah considered the timeline. By the time she'd arrived at Ezra's he was already agitated. If his nephews and niece had been there in the morning, they could have set him off. *The vultures.* That didn't explain the discrepancy over Waylen's presence, though—unless Ash was wrong.

"And you're sure all three cousins were there?"

"At some point that morning, yes. I'm positive."

"Anything weird about their interactions with Ezra?"

"Ezra wasn't there. It was just the cousins."

"Where was Ezra?"

Ash shrugged. "No idea. When I got to Brian's, the cousins were outside in Ezra's yard. They seemed to be walking around the property, checking out the place. One of them had a notebook. They'd been talking to Brian, which is why I got introduced."

Hannah needed to grab a fresh towel for Moose, but Ash had her attention. Why had they been at Ezra's without him present? Suddenly everything seemed suspicious. She reminded herself that some things *were* just coincidental.

"Everyone was getting along?" she asked.

Ash rubbed at his mouth. "Now that you mention it, Brian seemed angry, and the one cousin, Rob, seemed cross—although maybe that's how he always is. Anyway, I couldn't tell you what they were discussing. When I arrived, the conversation stopped."

"You mentioned Rob. Was the other cousin talking to Brian too? The older one, Waylen?"

"Yes, but not until after the others left."

"Do you remember what time Waylen arrived?"

"No, Hannah, I don't."

"Then it's possible he arrived after the others left?"

"I guess."

"Did he seem agitated?"

"I don't recall."

"Did you see anything in the notebook?"

Ash rolled his eyes. "Seriously, Hannah? Did Noah deputize you?"

Hannah pushed aside her frustration. He was right, of course. Noah and his team would get to the bottom of Ezra's death. They didn't need her poking around. Anyway, she had enough to do here.

Ash wound the hose back up and took his time placing it back on the holder. Hannah looked out onto the inn's rear grounds—at the chopped-up field and the muddy area near the path to Devil's Pond. *Devil's Pond. Ezra's body.* Would she ever want to go back there again? She could only picture Ezra as she had found him. Prostrate. Unresponsive. *Dead.* Right now, nothing else seemed to matter.

"Want some iced tea?" she asked Ash, feeling guilty about quizzing him. And if she were being honest with herself, she didn't relish the thought of being alone right then.

"I'll have to pass."

Ash turned to leave but stopped short. With his back to Hannah, he said softly, "I've decided not to take the job, Hannah."

He was going to turn Brian down. "No?"

"No."

Hannah watched Ash walk back around the inn, toward the parking area, his broad shoulders stooped like a man carrying the world on them. Part of her was happy he would refuse the Lewises' offer, but she also felt bad. Clearly the decision had had been hard for him to make.

She wondered why he'd said no.

More than that, she wondered what the Lewises had wanted him to do—and whether it was connected somehow to Ezra and his vultures.

Chapter Seven

N oah called later that afternoon. "No one is claiming the dog. I'm afraid you're stuck with him for now—unless you want him to go to the shelter."

Hannah looked down at Moose, who was sleeping under her feet with his head on one sneaker. "He's no trouble. Besides, I kind of like having him here." She was finishing some accounting for the inn, trying hard to figure out how they could keep going without additional income or another loan from Reggie, and the analysis was making her head hurt. She closed her file and pushed it away. "Any new leads on Ezra's death?"

"Nothing new."

"The police have talked with his family?"

"Working on it."

Hannah paused, debating how to tell Noah about Ezra's trip to see her father, when he beat her to it.

"Moose isn't the only reason I called." Hannah waited, and finally Noah said, "Ezra visited your father yesterday. Did you know that?"

"Maura told me. She followed Ezra there."

"Do you know why Ezra went to see John?"

"Couldn't say. I haven't spoken to my father in years."

"*Years?*"

"Since Mom passed."

"Do you have a *guess* as to why Ezra might have gone to see your father?"

"Not really."

With barely veiled anger, Noah said, "Come on, Hannah. We've known each other since forever. I can tell you're holding out on me."

"Why don't you ask my father?"

"We will, but I want to hear your thoughts."

After a beat, Hannah said, "They had a dispute over land, but that was years ago."

"What kind of dispute?"

Hannah stood up from her desk and stretched. She wandered to the window and looked outside at the back of the inn's property. Rob was walking along one of the flower gardens. Every so often, he bent down to smell a flower or look at something on the ground. He seemed lost in thought. Simone wasn't with him.

"Ezra owned family property on Gallows Hill Road," Hannah said. "Acres and acres of prime real estate with fantastic views. He sold it to my dad. My father built that development up there— Green Mountain View Estates. Made his fortune." Hannah returned to her desk and started shoving papers back in file folders. The thought of her dad sitting on an ill-gotten fortune while she was stressing about paying the electricity bill made her even more agitated. "That's all I know."

"You were Ezra's friend. Didn't he tell you anything more?"

"Ezra wasn't exactly the sharing type."

"Maybe your mom told you something?"

"No one in my family talked about it. Dad made a killing, our lives changed forever, and Mom seemed happy enough to move into that big house. I was a kid when we moved. Maybe Reggie knows more." Hannah paused, thinking of the abrupt shift in her childhood that had occurred when she was still young. The family had gone from living in a two-bedroom chalet to a large estate, from scrimping to spending lavishly. It had changed her life—and not always for the better. The money had altered her father and eventually created a rift between her parents. Hannah knew she sounded entitled and naïve, but if she could have gone back to the chalet days, she would have done so in a heartbeat. At least then her family would have stayed together.

"If I had to guess," Hannah said, "I'd guess Ezra felt cheated. Dad walked away with Ezra's land, which, knowing him, I'm sure he bought for less than its value, and then built those massive homes and made a killing. I'm sure he hid those plans from Ezra. They should have been partners." Hannah readjusted the phone against her ear. "How could Ezra have been anything but angry?"

"Is it possible Ezra went to your dad's house to settle things?"

Hannah wandered from the office to her small apartment kitchen. She reached for a glass and placed it on the counter. "*Ezra* is the one who's dead, Noah. Even if Ezra had gone there to cause trouble, he was found hours later by Devil's Pond. How would my father have gotten there? The man is a couch potato, or at least that's what he was when I last saw him. If Ezra's murder was premeditated, he would have had to hire someone. The timing seems off. Why wait twenty years?"

"Unless there's more to this than meets the eye."

Looking at the glass made Hannah's mind flash to another glass, another kitchen. With a shaky voice, she said, "I'm afraid

I don't have any answers for you. You'll have to talk to my father."

*   *   *

"He was there. How did I miss that, Reggie? He was there. At Ezra's house."

"Slow down. I have no idea what you're talking about."

Cradling her cellphone between her shoulder and her ear, Hannah watched Rob meander down the path toward Devil's Pond. "Dad," she hissed. "Dad was at Ezra's."

"How do you know that?"

"The bourbon."

"Hannah, you sound hysterical. Please, please slow down and explain yourself."

Hannah leaned against the wall, tilted her head back, and took a deep breath. "Dad was at Ezra's. About two weeks ago, I stopped by to bring Ezra some salad greens—which he didn't eat, of course. Ezra hated vegetables—"

"Stay with the story, Hannah."

"Yeah, yeah, Dad." Hannah took another deep breath, closed her eyes. "Anyway, when I went into the kitchen to put away the greens, I saw an empty bottle of Whistle Pig and a single shot glass on the counter. I mentioned it to Ezra, but he just waved me away."

"Maybe because it was his."

"Ezra was sober, Reggie. He hadn't taken a drink in years."

"Maybe he broke that streak. Or maybe he'd been lying to you all along."

Hannah widened her eyes. "No, Ezra was peculiar, but he wasn't a liar. And if he'd fallen off the wagon, I would have known. It wasn't his bourbon. I didn't think much of it at the time, not until speaking with Noah about Ezra's bike ride to Dad's house, but now I'm sure."

"Maybe one of Ezra's nephews or his niece had been drinking at his house. Sheesh, lots of people drink Whistle Pig."

"Two weeks ago? They weren't in Jasper. Plus, it was Boss Hog V. I just looked it up. Boss Hog V goes for hundreds—even thousands—of dollars. Who else do you know who drinks bourbon *that* expensive?"

Quietly, Reggie said, "Just Dad."

*　　*　　*

Rob entered the inn's kitchen just as Hannah was putting the afternoon snack out on the island. Amid tortilla chips and fresh vegetables sat bowls of guacamole, salsa, and bean chili, and to this spread she added a heaping plate of homemade cornbread.

"It smells amazing in here."

"Help yourself."

"I think I will." Rob placed his backpack on one of the island stools and grabbed a plate. "I'm famished."

"Maybe Simone would like some?"

"She's asleep. I'm heading up toward Stowe to do some hiking, so I'm going to let her go on sleeping."

Hannah filled a pitcher with ice water and placed that on the island too. "You know, we have rooms inside the inn if Simone would be more comfortable here." She didn't seem the RV type, so when she and Rob had chosen the refurbished Airstream, Hannah had been surprised. "I can match the price you're paying."

"We're good," Rob said between bites of cornbread. "Waylen and I aren't exactly besties, so I thought it'd be better this way. Distance, you know. Besides, Simone is heading back to New York soon for work, so I'll have the trailer to myself."

"Oh," Hannah said, surprised. "What does she do?"

Rob stopped chewing. He seemed taken off-guard by the question. "She's in the fashion industry." He shrugged. "Probably better she's not here. We'll have a lot to do with wrapping up Ezra's estate. Boring stuff. By later this week, we should know the terms of his will. Waylen's going to reach out to Ezra's lawyer." His easy smile faded into a frown. "We all know who the executor will be, and we all know he'll make sure *he* gets every cent he can."

"*He* meaning Waylen?"

"Who else?" Rob put his second piece of cornbread down on his plate and looked pointedly at Hannah. "I sound like an ass. I'm sorry. You must think we're *all* greedy asses. Some of these resentments run deep. Waylen wasn't the nicest cousin growing up. He used to bully Maura and me relentlessly, and we were forced to take it. Now that we're adults, it's kind of hard to forget."

"Why would Ezra choose Waylen to be the executor? Your uncle was actually a pretty good judge of character. If what you say is true, I can't see him picking Waylen."

"I don't know that Uncle Ezra was such a great judge of character, but even if he was, Waylen was good at playacting when he wanted something. In fact, when I was here last year, Uncle Ezra said Waylen had been up to see him too. He complimented Waylen's *fiscal management*. That's how he put it." Rob smiled wistfully. "Once you've been given a role in a family, it's hard to break free of it. At least that's what my therapist says."

"I can see that."

Rob dipped a chip in guacamole, his expression thoughtful. "Maura was the good girl, reliable but high strung. Waylen was the golden child. Football player, A-student, handsome. And now, apparently, a financial whiz kid."

"And you?"

Rob looked down at his mud-splashed cargo shorts and frowned. "C-student, crappy at team sports, troublemaker. The middle cousin, destined for mediocrity. No matter what I did later in life, that's how my family saw me. And Uncle Ezra was no exception." He looked up and flashed her a dimpled smile. "It took me a long time to see myself through my own lens."

Hannah nodded. She understood. Hadn't she spent her life playing court jester to Reggie's queen? Her parents had viewed her as the rebellious troublemaker, and even when she did well at something, they'd focus on the negative. Coming back to Jasper had been an act of faith. It had been her own attempt to see herself through a new lens.

When Hannah looked at Rob now, she didn't see any of the things he had described. Rob had the kind of J. Crew catalog good looks that many women went for. He'd told her when they met that he owned his own business, and from the looks of his car and his wife's wardrobe, they were financially well off. She found it hard to believe he hadn't overcome his family's view of him, and she said so.

"Some people like to perpetuate that old image of me. When my parents were alive, no matter what I did, Waylen would remind them that he was more successful. I try to see past that, but it's hard."

"You make Waylen sound pretty awful."

Rob snorted. "Have you met Waylen?"

"Only in passing."

"Spend some time with my cousin, Hannah. Then you'll understand."

* * *

54

Hannah didn't have to wait long to spend some time with Waylen. She'd just put away the last of the afternoon spread and was getting ready to pick blackberries with Moose when Waylen came sauntering into the common area. His full cheeks were red—whether from exertion or anger, Hannah didn't know—and he was mumbling something under his breath.

"Waylen," Hannah asked. "Are you alright?"

"Do I look alright?"

"You look like someone who could use a cold glass of tea and some down time."

Waylen scowled. "Have you seen Robert?"

Hannah studied him while filling a glass with iced tea. "He was here a little while ago. Said he was going hiking in Stowe."

Waylen huffed. "This late?" He took the glass from Hannah with a curt nod and chugalugged the tea. After slamming the glass down on the island, he sank down onto a stool and busied himself fixing the collar of his yellow polo shirt. He seemed to be deep in thought, although the scowl never softened.

"Can I get you some food?" Hannah asked.

"Not hungry."

Hannah nodded. "I'll be outside if you need—"

Waylen's hand shot out and grabbed Hannah's wrist. Moose sat up and fixed his stare on Waylen. Waylen seemed to realize what he'd done, and dropped Hannah's arm as though it were molten metal. "I'm sorry," he grumbled. "I'm afraid . . . well, it's been a rough day." As though seeing Moose for the first time, he said, "What's he doing here?"

"He's staying with me."

"The police know that?"

"They left him here."

Waylen stared into Hannah's eyes, but she got the distinct feeling he was looking *through* her, not *at* her. She wondered what had him so distracted. Although his cheeks were less inflamed than when she'd first seen him, the puffy, ruddy skin on his face, neck, and arms remained bright pink, as though he'd been in a sun a little too long without sunscreen, and a streak of mud ran the length of his cream belted shorts. Welts crisscrossed his wrist and his calf, right below a bug bite he'd scratched until it was bloody raw. He looked, Hannah thought, as though he'd intended to go golfing that morning but ended up wrestling wild pigs in the forest.

"My cell service isn't great here," he said finally. "I'm waiting for a call from Ezra's attorney, Teddy Smith. I gave him the inn's number. I'm going to head upstairs and shower. Will you fetch me if he calls?"

Fetch me? "Of course."

"Right away. Pound at my door if I don't answer. It's rather urgent."

"I will."

Waylen stood, stumbled, and steadied himself against the island, nearly knocking over his empty glass. "And if Robert gets here, please send him to my suite."

"Of course."

Waylen looked as if he was about to walk away, but paused and turned back toward Hannah. "Did Robert say exactly where he'd be in Stowe?"

"I'm afraid not."

"Are you sure that's where he was headed? Could he have been visiting Ezra's attorney himself?"

"I wouldn't know. He didn't say."

Waylen's wooly eyebrows shot up. "Is Simone with him?"

"Last I heard, she was napping in the Airstream."

Waylen snapped his fingers. "She'll know where he is. I'll ask her." He snapped his fingers again. "If Robert didn't take Simone, he's probably at Smith's office. He wouldn't want to bore his wife with matters like Ezra's estate. I know him. Unbelievable. He could have waited for me, right?"

"I don't know that Simone hikes."

"I don't know that Robert hikes."

Hannah had the distinct impression that Waylen was talking more to himself than to her, so she didn't respond. Teddy Smith was the town's only attorney, and he handled everything from estate planning to real-estate transactions to dog-bite claims. A notorious partyer, his hours were very *c'est la vie*, and it was possible that *was* where Rob had headed. It was none of her business though, so she waited while Waylen flattened the pleats on his shorts and walked toward the inn's entry hall. Just before he opened the door to head back outside, the inn's landline rang.

Waylen jumped and spun back around, saying, "Aren't you going to get that?"

Hannah walked slowly toward the front desk and picked up the receiver. "Hummingbird Hollow, how can I help you?"

A deep male voice said, "I'm looking for Hannah Solace."

"This is Hannah. With whom am I speaking?"

"Teddy Smith. I didn't recognize your voice, Hannah. You sound so grown up."

"Teddy," Hannah said, relieved that Waylen would get what he wanted and would be out of her hair, "That's because I *am* all grown up. Waylen Grayson is right here. He was waiting for your call—"

Hannah began to hand the receiver to a hovering Waylen when she heard, "No, no, Hannah. It's not Waylen Grayson I want. It's you."

Returning the receiver to her own ear, Hannah turned around, away from Waylen's prying stare, and said, "*Me?*"

"Yes. I'm afraid we need to talk. Here, at the office. It's about Ezra."

Confused, Hannah said, "Why do *we* need to talk about Ezra?"

"I'm the executor of Ezra's will." He paused, and Hannah heard him take a hard swallow. She pictured a stiff drink—maybe a Manhattan or gin and tonic—gripped in his thick-knuckled hand. "And you, Hannah, are his heir."

Chapter Eight

Teddy Smith lived along one of the town's few paved roads, in a stately two-story white Colonial with forest-green trim. His law office took up the back portion of his house and was reachable through a separate side entrance. Giant hostas lined a brick pathway from the driveway to the door, their lavender flowers in full bloom. Hannah walked slowly up the walkway and let herself into the office, ignoring the "Closed" sign hanging from the knob.

"Hannah, come in, come in," a voice called from a half-open interior door. "I'm back here."

The office space was divided into three parts: a spare, square waiting-room area with an empty receptionist's desk and three wooden chairs, a book-lined conference room large enough to seat eight around a sleek maple table, and a tiny study crammed with books, skiing photographs, and piles of file folders stacked neatly on an oak Mission-style desk. Smith's law offices hadn't changed much since she'd last been there, but the man behind the oak desk had changed a great deal.

Teddy said, "Been a while, Hannah, and you look nothing like the defiant teenager who walked into this room so long ago." He flashed her a crooked smile. "Then again, I imagine I look nothing like the attorney who defended you back then either."

"A lot can happen in seventeen years."

"Indeed."

Teddy was a fixture in Jasper, known as much for his heavy drinking and womanizing as his sharp lawyering skills. When she'd last seen him, he had been an imposing figure, both in stature and demeanor—a great hulk of a man with a thick head of auburn hair and a vein-laced, reddened nose. This Smith was softer—thinner, but paunchy, white-haired, and slightly stooped. Instead of holding an afternoon cocktail, his hand clutched a large glass water bottle. She saw the medical alert bracelet on his arm and raised her eyebrows questioningly.

"The old ticker," he said. "About three years ago, while skiing on the Devil, my body decided it'd had enough of hard living. Thankfully, the folks there acted quickly, and I lived through the ordeal—but only barely." He lifted the water bottle. "I'm a changed man, Hannah. No more booze, lots of water and veggies, and I actually get my eight hours every night. It looks like you're a changed person too."

"Well, I haven't been charged with loitering or reckless driving again, if that's what you mean."

Smith laughed. His laugh was still hearty. He stood, grabbed a single file folder, and motioned for Hannah to follow him into the conference room. An elderly golden retriever emerged from under the desk and padded after him. "Ezra must have thought you'd changed. He seemed to put a lot of faith in you." Smith's voice lowered. "I'm sorry. About Ezra, I mean."

Hannah nodded. Smith placed the file on one side of the table and sat down. Hannah sat opposite him. The dog settled on the floor under the table, near Smith's legs, and immediately began to snore.

"That's Ernie. Ever since my heart attack, he's been glued to my side. Funny how animals know, isn't it?"

Hannah nodded. Most days, she'd rather be around animals than people. While she felt badly that Smith had gone through such an ordeal, she liked this version of him better. The snarky, cruelty-tinged sense of humor she remembered from her teenage years seemed to have been replaced with something kinder and humbler. She wondered if he and her father were still friends.

Smith sat back in his chair and clasped his hands across his stomach, leaning backward. "Based on your reaction earlier, I take it you didn't know Ezra had named you in his will?"

"I had no idea. Why would he do that? He had family—his niece and nephews."

"Ezra wasn't one to waste words. You would know that. He directed me, and I followed his directives. This is what he wanted." Smith shrugged. "He had his reasons."

"That's not good enough." Hannah thought about Waylen, the way he'd waited impatiently for that phone to ring. She had had to lie about the reason for Teddy's call to get him off her case. "His family won't like this at all."

Smith moved his hands to the table and drummed his fingers on the wooden surface. The light shining through the window hit the silver portion of his medical alert bracelet, and Hannah saw her father's name listed as a contact. *I guess that answers that question*, she thought. Once upon a time, her father and Smith had been best buddies, which was why Smith had defended her when she was arrested for reckless driving as a teen. He'd managed to get the charges dropped, and his actions back then only made her parents more beholden to him—and more embarrassed by Hannah.

"Maybe Ezra didn't want to show favoritism by choosing someone from his family as his heir. He could have done it to avoid family conflict," Smith finally added, "Or perhaps he didn't like his nephews or niece—but he did like you." He leaned forward, softening his gaze. "In his own gruff way, he seemed to think of you as the daughter he never had. And Ezra didn't like a lot of people."

"True," Hannah said, touched.

"Aren't you curious about what the will actually says?" Smith asked. "That's always the first question people ask."

Hannah shifted her attention to the small set of windows at the far end of the room. Outside, a red squirrel was jumping from tree branch to tree branch, and she followed its progress until it ran out of sight. "Ezra had nothing, Teddy. Just that house, which is a mess."

Smith was silent, and he was never silent, so Hannah suddenly felt uncomfortable. She turned toward him.

His mouth acquired a slow half-smile. "Is that what you think?"

"It's what I *know*." At the thought of Ezra, Hannah could feel the hot sting of tears again, and she took a deep breath, willing them away. "We talked nearly every day for the last two years. His kitchen cabinets were usually empty. I think he spent more on Moose than on himself. He wore the same clothes, walked or rode his bike everywhere. He lived simply."

"He did live simply, and clearly what he did have he wanted to go to you."

Hannah thought about the people clamoring to buy Ezra's property—his neighbors, the ski resort, even Cheating Chad. She thought about the three cousins now staying at the inn. She would have to sell his house just to pay whatever debts Ezra owed—and she knew the cousins would not go quietly. Exhaustion descended, making her feel tired and irritable. She was trying to get her head above water at the inn. Losing Ezra and taking care of his estate felt like a double whammy, one she was having trouble processing. But it was what he had wanted. She'd do what he wanted.

Smith reached across the table and touched her arm. "Hey, are you okay?"

"It's just a little overwhelming."

"I can help you. Reggie will help you."

Hannah nodded, unconvinced. "Did the will mention Moose?"

"There was a separate provision for the dog. Ezra asked that you care for him and left you funds to help with his care."

Hannah smiled. It was so like Ezra to put the dog first. "I don't need the funds. Moose can stay with me. He's with me now."

When Hannah glanced up, she saw Smith staring at her, an odd look in his eyes. "He left twenty thousand dollars for the care of the dog."

Hannah stiffened. "I don't think I'll need that much." *And I didn't think he had that much.*

"I don't think you get it. Ezra left you the house, which is admittedly a pigsty, but the land it's on will net you well over a million dollars. And on top of that, he has a bank account worth seven figures—"

The color drained from Hannah's face. "What did you say?"

"Ezra was a wealthy man. He lived simply, true, but he died without much debt and with a lot of assets. And they're all yours."

Hannah looked at Smith for signs he was teasing her, but she saw only genuine concern reflected in his eyes. Her head felt foggy, her hands were shaking. The inability to process what was happening had worsened, and she shook her head vehemently from side to side.

"There's some mistake, Teddy. Ezra wasn't rich."

Smith sighed. "Like I said earlier, Ezra had his reasons for the things he did, and I can't tell you what they were. I just know he had money." Smith tilted his head to meet Hannah's gaze. "And now you will have money too, Hannah. It's what Ezra wanted."

Chapter Nine

H annah drove away from the law office in a mental fog. Teddy Smith had shown her the terms of Ezra's will, and she'd seen Ezra's simple directives expressed in his typical terse language: the entire estate to Hannah Solace, including care of Moose, with twenty thousand dollars set aside in trust for Moose's care, the remainder of which would go to Hannah after Moose's death, and Teddy Smith named as executor of the estate. There was no doubting the will's authenticity. The question was *why*? Why would Ezra leave it all to her, and why the hell did he have so much money? The house was in disarray, he'd worn old, threadbare clothes, and he didn't even have a working car. His ancient Buick sat in a ramshackle barn on the back of the property. Hannah had never even seen him drive it.

It was more than that, though. Ezra had never given her any indication that he thought of her as more than a friend. Sure, they'd gotten closer over the last two years, but she sometimes felt like her concern for his well-being was unwelcome to him. It was as though he wanted to be left alone and her attention was a bother.

None of it made any sense.

*   *   *

Hannah pulled into the parking lot of Reggie's office at 3:48. Her sister hadn't answered her phone, so Hannah went right to the source. She saw Chad's Suburban parked next to Reggie's Subaru and thus knew the reason for her sister's unresponsiveness. Reggie and Chad were like ice cream and vinegar. Each was fine on its own, but you never wanted to experience them together.

When Hannah walked into the spare, clean office of Solace & Little Realty Management & Sales, the first thing she noticed was Reggie's administrative assistant, Luke, sitting in the corner with headphones on, trying steadfastly to stare at his computer screen rather than the two adults hurling insults at one another.

"Get out," Reggie was saying quietly. Her eyes were closed, and her fists were clenched. Hannah cringed. When Reggie used her inside voice, you *knew* you were in big trouble.

"Reggie, be reasonable," Chad said. "Come on. You can't do this."

"I can, and I am, and you lost any right to have input into my actions when you dipped your wick in that pot of wax."

Hannah cleared her throat before her sister could torture any more metaphors. From across the room, Luke caught Hannah's eye and raised his eyebrows in a *Good luck with that* gesture.

"Get out, Chad," Reggie said again. "I neither want nor need you here."

Chad's already ruddy face was now tomato red. His straight black hair, normally pushed back with some goopy hair gel, hung in his face in sweaty ropes. He was at least a foot taller and a hundred pounds heavier than his ex-wife, but his ruffled demeanor in the face of Reggie's unerring calm in that moment made him seem smaller.

"Regina Emily Solace, you have no right to sell that storefront right out from under her, and you know it's wrong." Chad's voice descended into a whine at the end. "Come on."

This time, Hannah whistled—loudly. Reggie turned to look at her sister as though seeing her standing there for the first time.

"Reggie," Hannah said firmly. "Finish whatever squabble you're having with Chad. We need to talk."

*   *   *

It was another twenty minutes before Chad finally left, and not before he and Reggie had locked themselves in the small kitchenette to continue their argument. When Reggie finally emerged, she looked vindicated—almost happy. Reggie rarely looked happy, so Hannah wasn't surprised to observe that Chad seemed distinctly *unhappy.*

"What'd you do to him this time?" Hannah asked her sister.

"What makes you think I did anything?"

"He walked out like a scolded puppy, tail between his legs."

Reggie shrugged. "I have an offer on the Mayfair building. Chad wants me to tell the owner to turn it down."

"He should be happy. That building's been around forever."

Reggie slid into the chair behind her desk and began straightening already perfectly straight stacks of paper. "The buyer wants to put a cute little pottery shop in there. Guess who else is planning to open a cute little pottery shop?" Reggie arranged and rearranged her lips, but she couldn't hide the vengeful smile.

"Karen," Hannah said.

Reggie nodded. Besides being the prior innkeeper of Hummingbird Hollow, known then as the Jasper Inn, Karen May had been one of Reggie's closest friends. She was also the woman for whom Chad had left Reggie, and Reggie, Hannah knew, would never forgive Chad or Karen. Reggie wasn't exactly the forgiving type, and while she avoided public displays of contempt, she found her own tiny ways to make the couple suffer. Reggie Solace was the queen of paper cuts—always had been.

"Why are you here and not at the inn?" Reggie asked. "It's nearly dinnertime. I know how you like to organize evening sunset hikes and paddles."

"The only guests right now are Ezra's family members, and other than Rob they're not exactly the outdoorsy types, and Rob went hiking in Stowe. Plus, with Ezra's passing and all, it seemed like bad form to even offer." Hannah flopped down on the armchair facing Reggie's desk. She pointed at Luke. "Can you send him somewhere?"

Reggie glanced at her watch. "He's not done with work for twenty-four minutes."

"Seriously?" Hannah folded her arms over her chest. "This is important. I'll wait twenty-four minutes."

Reggie shot Hannah a frustrated glare. She waved until she got Luke's attention, and when the younger man had pulled his headphones away from his ears, said, "Today is your lucky day. You can leave now, but I expect to see you twenty-four—nope, twenty-three—minutes early tomorrow."

"But I have—"

"Good-bye, Luke."

When Luke had left the building, Reggie sat back in her chair, and frowning, asked, "What is so important that I needed to let Luke go early?"

"I can't believe you're making that kid make up the time."

"When I want HR input from you, I'll ask." Then, with apology in her voice, she added, "Tell me."

Hannah described the call from Teddy Smith and her subsequent meeting with him. "I'm mentioned in Ezra's will."

"Lucky you. What did he leave you? His stacks of old magazines? Maybe his rusty farm equipment?" Reggie looked smug, but when she saw Hannah's despondent expression, the smugness disappeared. "What's the matter, Hannah? Is it the dog?"

"The dog stays with me."

"Then why do you look like you spent a night in a haunted hotel and woke up spooning a ghost?"

Hannah took a deep breath. Just saying the words was hard. "Ezra made me his sole heir. I get Moose, Moose's inheritance, and everything Ezra owned."

"Moose's inheritance? Who leaves stuff to a dog?"

"It's not an inheritance, exactly. More like money set aside for Moose's care."

"What, like five hundred dollars? How much could a dog need?"

"Twenty thousand, according to Ezra."

"Dollars?" Reggie shook her head as though trying to clear it. "Ezra *had* twenty thousand American dollars?"

"Apparently. There's more."

Reggie pushed a stray hair back from her face with an impatient swipe. "Come on, Hannah. You're being coy. What else did Smith say?"

"I inherited the house."

Reggie stood up, began to pace, and Hannah could see the accountant wheels turning. "The house has to be torn down, but the land is worth a small fortune. The ski resort wants it, the neighbors want it, even my cheating bastard of an ex wants it. Assuming Ezra didn't mortgage it to the max, that will be a tidy sum." She shook her head again, and her neat ponytail bobbed behind her. "Wow!"

"There's more, as in a fat bank account. A seven-figure bank account."

Reggie stopped moving. "No."

"I know, right? Why would he have all that money and let the house go? He could have fixed it up long ago—"

Reggie held up a hand. "That's not what I mean. He *can't* have had a fat bank account. Dad cheated him, remember? Ezra had *no* money. In fact, I remember Pastor Birk asking me if I had a property Ezra could stay in after his house caught fire. She was organizing a charity event for him." Reggie resumed her pacing. "And how many times have I heard down at the town clerk's office that Ezra wasn't paying his property taxes on time? Why else would he be delinquent? He couldn't afford the jacked-up taxes on the land."

"If Ezra was so poor, then where did the money come from?" Hannah asked, thinking of Ezra's trip to see their father the day he was killed and of the empty bourbon bottle. An unwelcome thought ran through her mind, and she hunched forward, trying to shake it off. It was starting to feel like homey little Jasper was a town full of secrets.

Reggie circled the room one more time before stopping in front of Hannah. She sat down on the edge of the desk. "Good question. Before you accept a cent, Hannah—before Smith doles out a cent—we should know how a land-poor man became a multimillionaire seemingly overnight."

Chapter Ten

Hannah didn't go straight home. The thought of seeing Waylen and his cousins now that she had the information about Ezra's will made her feel physically ill. There would be questions— questions she wasn't ready to answer— and she was in no mood for a fight. She checked the inn's message line to make sure there were no new guest inquiries or requests from the current guests and then headed into the center of town, toward the Jasper United Congregational Church.

Pastor Kendra Birk wasn't outside tending to the church's small vegetable or flower gardens, nor was she in her office. Hannah walked around to the entrance of the church hall and heard hammering coming from inside. She stuck her head in and was surprised to see Kendra's husband, Jay, nailing a picture hanger into the hall's white wall.

"I don't think I've ever seen you doing physical labor, Dr. Birk," Hannah said, trying to hide a smile. The bespectacled older man looked startled, and nearly dropped the hammer he he'd been gripping as though his life depended on the task at hand.

A slim, well-dressed man in his sixties, Dr. Jay Birk ran the closest thing the town had to an urgent care, and while Hannah had seen him about town at restaurants and shops, she'd never seen him wearing anything less formal than pressed khakis and a starched button-down shirt. Today, though, he looked downright casual in dark jeans and a Penn State T-shirt.

"I assume you're looking for my wife."

"She around?"

"She took off on that godforsaken motorcycle of hers to grab more picture hangers. She has it in her head that the hall lacks warmth." He pointed to a stack of framed photographs. "Somehow, lining the walls with pictures of the very mountains we see out our windows will provide *warmth*."

That godforsaken motorcycle was actually the pastor's e-bike, a wide-seated cruiser Kendra had decked out with an oversized basket lined with a brightly colored sunflower material and a rear rack. She could be seen riding that thing all over town and beyond, and clearly her husband, cautious by nature, didn't approve.

"Good of you to help her with the pictures."

Jay frowned, but his bright eyes betrayed his affection for his wife. "I assure you, I had no choice in the matter."

Just then, Hannah heard the buzz of the e-bike, and a few seconds later, Kendra floated into the room carrying a packet of picture hangers. When she saw Hannah, she smiled broadly, a smile that reached and crinkled her vibrant brown eyes.

"Hannah, great to see you. What brings you here this afternoon?" Kendra's expression darkened. "I'm so sorry to hear about Ezra."

"Thank you, Pastor."

"A million times, Hannah, call me Kendra." Kendra glanced at her husband, who was eyeing the hammer in his hand in much the same way he'd look at a burning cigarette. "Jay, can I leave you to this?"

"It depends. Do you want these pictures to be straight?"

Kendra laughed, dismissing her husband's protestations, and led Hannah back outside. "Are you okay?"

"I want to talk to you about Ezra."

"You must be feeling awful. It's understandable. You two were close."

Kendra was her husband's opposite in nearly every respect. Whereas Dr. Birk was cautious and reserved, Kendra was friendly and open. At least a decade younger than he, her thick, graying hair cascaded to her shoulders, framing her handsome, sun-weathered face. Her first reaction to any request was always an ebullient "yes." Known for taking in stray people *and* animals, she allowed dogs at Sunday service, organized town clean-up days, donated bikes to kids in need, and hosted a monthly food-pantry party where anyone could take from the church's well-stocked cupboards, no questions asked. What Kendra Birk *didn't* abide were mean people, litterers, and cursing. How she had gotten along with Ezra, Hannah had no idea.

"I am, Pastor—er, I mean Kendra. But that's not what I want to talk with you about."

Kendra tilted her head. "Why don't you come into my office. We'll have some privacy there."

Hannah glanced around. No one else was on Main Street at that moment, and other than Jay in the church hall, no one was at the church. Nevertheless, Hannah followed Kendra into the front entrance, through the small vestibule, and into Kendra's office. It was large and neatly organized, with shelves full of worn bibles, children's storybooks, and self-help guides lining one wall, and metal and wooden bins of toys and crafting materials along another. A refurbished pine desk stood proudly in the center of the room, and three yellow upholstered chairs faced the desk. A large, simple pine cross hung on the wall behind the desk, its worn patina adding warmth to the rest of the room.

Kendra sank into one of the upholstered chairs, Hannah into another. "Grief is a process, and under the circumstances in which Ezra died—"

Hannah held up a hand. "I'm not here for counsel, Kendra. Maybe that will come later. Right now . . . right now, I'm just trying to understand some stuff."

Kendra looked momentarily confused. "I'm happy to help, but I didn't really know Ezra that well. He wasn't—well, let's just say he didn't see much need for church."

"But you helped him out anyway."

Kendra tilted her head, causing a strand of hair to flop in front of her eyes. She tucked it behind her ear and stayed silent. But her gaze was piercing, patient.

"When his house burnt down," Hannah said, "you organized a charity event for him."

"As we would for any parishioner who suffered a catastrophic loss."

"He wasn't a parishioner."

"He was once, when Molly was alive." Kendra sighed. "You as well as anyone should know that you don't have to be a parishioner to worship here—or to receive assistance. All are welcome, especially in their time of need."

Hannah had no need to be reminded. As a teen, she had stayed in the church's spare quarters more than once, depending on Kendra and Jay for support when her father kicked her out of the house. Kendra had always been there for her, despite the fact that her parents had never once attended the church or made a financial donation, at least to Hannah's knowledge. But that was Jasper. People rallied when one of their own was down.

"Did Ezra accept your help?"

"He took the food, but when we offered him a temporary place to stay, he declined," Kendra said. "He claimed Moose wouldn't like it. By Moose, we both knew he meant himself."

Hannah smiled. It sounded like Ezra. "Did you get the sense that Ezra *needed* help?' Hannah frowned, searching for the right words. "Was he, you know, struggling financially?"

Kendra's brow creased. "He'd had a house fire—"

"Right, but did he do or say anything that made you *think* he had nowhere to go, no money?"

Kendra shook her head, a small smile playing on her lips. "Hannah Solace, what are you trying to say? Out with it, please, because your line of questioning has me wondering what you're really asking me."

Hannah took a deep breath. "You're a pastor, so what I tell you stays between us, right?"

"Of course."

Hannah told her about the will. "Between the property and the bank accounts, Ezra was well off, even by today's standards."

Kendra sat back in her seat, eyes wide, the empathic and patient counselor expression now replaced by stark bewilderment. "You got me. He didn't act destitute, never asked for a cent, but I certainly thought he could use some help financially. His clothes, that house. His bike." She stood, walked to the end of her office, opened the door, and glanced outside, into the vestibule. When she sat back down, she was frowning. "And he left you everything?"

Hannah nodded.

"That's going to bring you trouble. You understand that, right?"

"You mean because of his nephews and niece?"

"That's part of it. His family will complain, may even dispute the will. You just came back two years ago. The timing doesn't look great." Kendra took a deep breath, as though shoring herself up for a difficult conversation. "I try to see the good in people. You know that, right?"

"Of course."

"Well, when there's money involved, people get stupid. Money corrupts. The Bible is clear on that point." Hannah started to protest, and Kendra stopped her. "I'm not saying it will corrupt *you*. I'm saying that once people find out Ezra had money, and they see he left it to a young woman who'd befriended him in his later years, they'll make certain assumptions."

Hannah covered her mouth, horrified by what Kendra was implying. "How could anyone think that? He was my *friend*."

"I understand, Hannah. And *you* know that. But even in a small town like Jasper, where everyone has known everyone else since they sported diapers and suckled from their mothers' breasts, there will be raised eyebrows and insinuations. And maybe worse."

"Worse?"

Pastor Kendra glanced at the cross on the wall to her left. She steepled her fingers and affixed her counselor's gaze back on Hannah. "Ezra was murdered."

It took Hannah a moment to understand what she was saying. "Oh God," she moaned. "You think—"

"I think no such thing." Kendra reached across the divide and grabbed Hannah's stone-cold hand. Her touch was warm and gentle. "What I do know is that you will need to be strong. Lay low, don't listen to people's nonsense, and whatever you do, don't tell anyone else about Ezra's will."

*   *   *

Hannah climbed into her car in a daze. Clouds were creeping along the edges of the sunny sky, and the early evening air now felt soupy and suffocating. Across from the church, the coffee/bakery/bike shop was closed, but four people had congregated in front of the store. She recognized Ash. He was speaking to Emma, the shop's co-owner, and Henry Yarrow, the owner of Devil's Mountain Ski Resort. The fourth person had his back to her, but when he turned sideways, and Hannah saw the prominent Roman nose and tousled hair, she realized the trio was talking animatedly with Noah Booker, the detective on Ezra's case.

Hannah stuck a hand out of the window, waving to them as she passed. Their gazes followed her as she made her way down the street, toward the inn. Only Emma waved back. *Is it my imagination*, Hannah wondered, *or did Noah and Henry exchange a guilty look? I'm just letting Kendra's words get to me.*

Against her better judgment, Hannah slammed on her brakes. She pulled the car over, parked along the road in front of one of the ski shops, and climbed out. *So much for lying low.* She walked in the direction of the group.

"Hannah," Henry Yarrow said with a smile that was a bit too jovial. He was a short man, trim and wiry, with a bald head and a neatly groomed gray mustache that sat like a hairy caterpillar above his thin upper lip. "Good to see you. How's the inn faring? Quite a face lift you've given it."

Hannah thanked him. "All good, Henry." She acknowledged Ash and Emma before turning to Noah. "Do you have news?"

"News?" Noah's forehead creased. "You mean about Ezra?"

"No, Noah, about the price of diesel at Manny's Pump and Go. Yes, about Ezra." Impatience spurred her on, and she said, "I thought maybe you'd know something by now."

"I just spoke to you this afternoon," Noah replied. "I'm not *that* good."

"You must be crushed, Hannah," Emma said. "Ezra was *such* a *nice* man."

Hannah turned to Emma, incredulous. Emma Wakely and Nadia Taylor co-owned Breaking Bread and Breaking Trail, and while Emma handled the bike part of the business, her business partner Nadia ran the coffee and bake shop. Over the years, Emma had complained to the town office repeatedly that Ezra's property was an eyesore, petitioning for zoning rules that would allow the town to force a clean-up. Ezra had responded by piling up old, rusty bikes outside his home, with a "Free to anyone except Emma" sign in front of them.

Somehow, Hannah didn't think Emma had found him particularly *nice*.

"He'll be missed," Henry said. He shook his head. "Imagine something like that happening here, in Jasper. Inconceivable."

Hannah looked from Henry to Noah to Emma, resting her gaze on a very quiet Ash. "I interrupted something," she said. "Sorry about that." Her tone said she wasn't the least bit sorry.

It was Henry who waved away her words. "Don't be silly. We were just talking about Ezra's house. What will happen to it, that sort of thing." His eyes flitted to the right, steadfastly avoiding contact with her own. "You know, now that his family will decide its fate."

"Hoping to buy it from them, Henry?" Emma asked. Hannah thought she heard a twinge of annoyance in the woman's tone, but Emma covered it quickly with, "I wouldn't blame you. Would make a nice spot for another resort entrance and maybe some condos."

Henry nodded solemnly. "Interesting possibility."

Weasel, Hannah thought. She knew full well he'd been asking Ezra to buy that property for years for that very purpose.

"Have you spoken to Ezra's lawyer?" Emma asked Henry. "I bet Teddy can tell you whether the nephews and niece are willing to sell."

"It's too early for the estate to be settled," Noah said, holding up a large hand. "That'll take time. Months, likely longer, given the investigation. Anyway, Henry, it sounds like you'll have to get in line. Lots of interest in that land. Prime piece of property."

Ash frowned. Quietly, he said, "It's also a prime spot for grouse, turkeys, frogs, and I've even seen a moose or two back there. Ezra once saw spotted turtles in that tiny, untouched pond he has behind the barn." He looked pointedly at Henry. "They're endangered."

Henry flashed Ash a broad, reassuring smile. "Don't get ahead of yourself, son. Even if we did buy that land, I'm sure we could work something out. Save the turtles and all that."

"I think we're *all* getting ahead of ourselves," Noah said. "The land isn't the issue. We obviously have a larger problem here." He let his words hang there before glancing over at Hannah. "Can I talk to you before you head back to the inn?"

Henry's eyebrows arched in amusement. "Someone's in trouble."

"I guess," Hannah said to Noah, ignoring Henry. "Now?"

Noah nodded. "We can take a walk." To the group, he said, "Call me if you think of anything. Anything at all." He fixed his gaze on Henry. "Especially if your recollection of that day comes into sharper focus, Henry. I mean it." Noah touched Hannah's arm. "I'll walk you to your car." When they were farther down the road, he added, "Away from prying eyes."

Chapter Eleven

"Why don't we head down to the park?" Noah said when they arrived at Hannah's car. Henry and Emma were still standing outside the bike shop, whispering to one another while glancing over at Hannah and Noah. "I promise not to keep you long, but I want to make sure there are no unintended participants."

"I guess. If it'll help."

The park was wedged between the national forest and the post office. It covered only an acre of land, most of which consisted of a grassy rectangle used for town picnics, the farmers' market, and the odd concert, but in one corner, a seesaw, a small, curved slide, a large swing set, and two picnic tables had been centered inside a square of wood chips. A soccer ball sat abandoned next to one of the picnic tables, and Noah kicked it out into the grassy field.

"Still got it," he said, smiling.

"Still *think* you've got it."

"Hey now." Noah slid onto a seat at one of the picnic tables and folded his hands in front of him. "Who are you to talk?"

"I was a decent athlete in my time."

"All I remember is you playing with Polly Pockets and Beanie Babies."

Hannah slid into the seat across from him. "Because I was a kid. Not the same."

Noah scrunched his features into a fake grimace. "I'm pretty sure you were, like, sixteen."

Hannah laughed. When she was sixteen, Noah had been her biggest crush. They both knew that at that age she was sneaking gin and vodka from her parents' liquor cabinet and staying out all night—not playing with toys. But for a moment, Hannah let herself enjoy their easy camaraderie. She'd lost touch with his sister, but memories of the time spent with their family were good ones. Unlike her own parents, the Bookers had always seemed happy to have her around.

Noah's face darkened. He glanced toward the forest, swallowed visibly, and said, "Had Ezra seemed different to you before he died?"

Hannah considered the question. "Different in what way?"

"In any way."

"The man was eccentric, Noah. You know that. He was always *different*. You'll have to be more specific."

"You didn't notice a decline in the last weeks or months? Confusion? Forgetfulness?"

"No. He was as sharp as ever." Hannah tilted her head questioningly. "Why are you asking?"

"Just doing my job."

Hannah tried to read the expression in Noah's eyes. "Did someone else say Ezra had been acting oddly?"

"No. In fact, quite the opposite. A man is dead, and no one seems to have noticed anything—that's the problem." Noah rubbed at his temples and sighed. "Ezra's state of mind is important because someone could have used that to their advantage. I need to figure out who served to benefit from Ezra's death."

"Motive."

"Lots of people had opportunity, but who had motive?"

Hannah studied the trees lined up along the edge of the park like soldiers guarding a fort. She knew she was on dangerous ground.

"Those who thought they would inherit when he died? I imagine you can get a copy of Ezra's will."

"We're working on that."

Hannah nodded. She watched Noah trace a seam in the table, back and forth, over and over. She figured he hadn't just wanted to ask her about Ezra's state of mind. He knew more than he was saying.

"I'm the beneficiary, Noah."

Noah looked up sharply, surprised. "You know?"

"Teddy just told me today."

Noah's hand stopped moving. "Yeah, he told me today too. He didn't sit on that news for long." He chewed on his lip and seemed to be mulling over his next words. "You had no idea? Before now, I mean. Ezra never told you that was his intention?"

"Absolutely not."

"You never suggested that you be his beneficiary?"

Hannah sat there, stunned. How could Noah even think that of her, much less ask the question? She considered Pastor Kendra's warning. *Tell no one.* And seeing the suspicion and embarrassment in Noah's eyes, she understood why.

"Of course not. I had no idea. I didn't even know he had money. I assumed he was leaving his house to his family, and that the house would come with a lot of debt." She met his gaze, her jaw tight. "Frankly, I'm pretty upset you even thought to ask."

"It's my job, and that's a lot of money."

"You should know me better than that."

Noah studied her face, his expression hardening into professional reserve. "I need to ask tough questions, Hannah. Once the will becomes public, there will be others asking the same questions. You should be prepared for that."

Hannah watched a bumblebee fly lazily from dandelion to dandelion, its buzzing the loudest sound in the park. Softly, swallowing her anger, she said, "I didn't ask for this. Like I said, I didn't even know Ezra had anything other than that house, and for all I knew, it was mortgaged. I certainly didn't ask to be his heir, nor did I take advantage of his age or state of mind."

"You understand there's only your word for that." There was no accusation in his voice, but somehow that made the sting worse.

Hannah allowed her anger to take hold again, and with iron in her voice, she said, "I'm not stupid, Noah. I know the will gives me motive. But while you're wasting your time looking at me, whoever did this will be quite literally getting away with murder."

"We have a process to follow. That's just how the law works. We can't go on hunches or longtime friendships." He searched her eyes. "Please understand that. None of this is personal."

Hannah's nod was curt, the rage building now, a coal fire in her belly. Ezra was dead, she stood to benefit, and now her friend, a man she'd known for most of her life, was looking at her with suspicion.

Hannah stood up abruptly. "Do your job, then. Investigate me all you want. Just be quick about it."

She walked away, leaving Noah alone at the table. If Noah and the police were busy investigating her, who was left to find Ezra's actual killer?

*   *   *

The inn was blessedly quiet when Hannah returned. Still nursing her rage, she slammed open the door to her apartment and stopped short when she saw Moose standing in the narrow hallway, evaluating her with those large, sanguine eyes. His great jowls drooped, the graying hairs around his mouth glistened with water dripping from his chin onto the wood floor. Recognizing her, he wagged his tail once, then sat with a huff before sinking down into a despondent crouch, his tail still.

Oh, Moose, Hannah thought. She sank down next to him and stroked his head. He eyed her with wary affection before eventually closing his eyes and giving in to her touch. They sat for a long time like that, Hannah's hand rhythmically stroking the dog's long back. As she petted Moose, she found her anger waning. *Of course Noah has to do his job*, she thought. *And of course he would have to rule me out.*

She considered Noah's questions, trying to re-create his train of thought. What else did the police know? *Had* Ezra been acting differently recently?

Moose stretched his legs and rested his head in her lap. Hannah smiled, but it was a smile laced with sadness. As she stroked the soft fur under Moose's muzzle, she thought of an interaction she'd had with Ezra a few days before he'd been killed. She had arrived, as always, with a little food offering, something he'd complained about but ultimately eaten, and a list of questions about gardening. Ezra had answered her questions in his roundabout way, providing both more and less insight than she'd asked for, and she'd written his answers on a small pad she'd brought with her. Afterward, he'd asked her to drop him off at a house quite a few miles out of town. He'd asked for rides before—there was no Uber in their corner of Vermont—so his request, while unusual, was not uncommon. What *had* been surprising was his outfit.

Before they left, he'd changed into a white button-down shirt, clean jeans, black suspenders, and a belt, a departure from his normal dirty Carhart pants and red flannel shirt. He'd even washed and combed his thinning white hair.

Hannah had made a joke—something like "She must be a stunner."

He'd responded with a sad "He is."

Hannah had been in a rush that day, so she'd dropped him off without paying much attention to his destination. All she remembered was the house—a stern Colonial blue home on a rutted dirt road—and the dark woods that surrounded it. A birdhouse had been painted to match the house and jutted gaily from a low bed of brightly colored wildflowers, a touch of whimsy in an otherwise forbidding property.

"How will you get home?" she'd asked Ezra then.

"My fairy godmother," was all he'd said before climbing out of her car.

Oh, Ezra. Hannah placed Moose's head down gently on the floor and stood up. She went to the large closet that doubled as her office and sorted through the piles of papers stacked neatly on the desk. She finally found the small notebook wedged between a Sundance catalog and an electric bill and paged through it until she found her notes from that day. Scribbled on its pages were the formula Ezra had given her for stubborn aphids (Ivory soap, canola oil, and water), tips for controlling windflowers gone wild, and directions for replanting her beautiful scarlet beebalm. Disappointed, she placed the notebook back on her desk—the address he had visited wasn't written in there.

Damn, Hannah thought to herself. She tried to remember where the house was located, but she'd followed unfamiliar winding backroads, plus Ezra had directed her there, so there was no

GPS history. Hannah glanced at Moose, now snoring contentedly on the cool wood floor, and remembered that she hadn't gone straight home that day. Instead, she'd driven from that house to the closest hardware store to buy kitty litter for Turnip. The hardware store was only a few minutes away from Ezra's destination, and its address should still be in her GPS.

Hurriedly, she grabbed her phone. She scrolled down until she found what she needed—Lucky's Hardware Emporium. If she drove to the hardware store, she bet she could retrace her steps to that house. In retrospect, Ezra's behavior that day had been strange. Whoever lived in that blue Colonial might know something about Ezra that could help. It wasn't much, but it was something.

Chapter Twelve

Hannah was late getting on the road that evening, but there was no traffic, so she made it to Lucky's Hardware Emporium in less than twenty minutes. Cellphone reception was practically nonexistent in this part of Vermont, and it took her a few minutes to scan the pre-loaded maps on her phone. She had thought if she could just get to Lucky's, she could work backward and find the mystery home from there, but now she wasn't so sure. Lucky's and a tractor repair business were the only two shops around, and otherwise, it was just woods—dirt road after dirt road meandering through the forest, with Devil's Mountain looming in the distance. She wished she'd made note of the street name at least. She felt lost.

After twenty minutes of driving aimlessly around, she was about to call it quits when something pricked at her mind, sparking a memory. A street sign was nestled in the trees, its metal band bent nearly in half so all she could see were the first three letters of the name. She remembered noticing that bent sign when she'd driven Ezra. After that, she thought, she'd come to a crossroads, and Ezra had asked her to take the road on the right.

Dark clouds were hanging low in the darkening sky, promising rain. The road was narrow and bumpy, capped by a thick canopy of trees, and it was becoming harder to see in the dim light—it would be even harder once the rain started. Hannah scanned the road, looking for the crossroads, and sure enough, she spotted the diverging dirt roads a mile down. She slowed, veered right, and followed a slightly wider dirt road past a white Cape Cod, a small cedar cabin, and, finally, to the blue Colonial. She pulled in the driveway behind an old silver Subaru wagon and killed the engine, relieved to have found the house but debating what to say when she knocked at the door.

She didn't have to debate long before the front door opened and a short, trim elderly man wearing gray wool trousers, a pressed white shirt, and blue paisley suspenders came out of the house carrying a can of what looked like bear spray. Despite the heat, he had a fedora on his head, and tufts of bristly white hair stuck out below its wool brim.

The man walked down to the lawn, cocked his head sideways, and said evenly, his voice a surprisingly deep baritone, "You're not here on purpose, I presume?"

Hannah climbed out of her car and smiled. "On purpose, I'm afraid." Eyeing the bear spray, she said, "I'm Hannah Solace. I was a friend of Ezra Grayson's."

The eyes behind his wire-rimmed glasses were friendly but wary. "*Was* a friend. I take it you know, then?" He stood taller, pulling up his petite frame and pushing his shoulders back. When Hannah nodded, he said, "Then you also know Ezra was murdered."

"I do. In fact, that's why I'm here."

The man seemed to be considering these words when thunder cracked overhead and fat raindrops started to fall, slowly at first but gaining momentum. "Come in," the man said finally, apparently deciding the rain was more of a threat than Hannah. He waved the can of bear spray. "But know I'm armed."

Hannah laughed, hoping he'd meant to be funny. The image of the small, dapper man waving the bear spray reminded her in some tiny way of Ezra's occasional minor acts of bravado, like the time he insisted on going outside first after a bear sighting. With an ache that throbbed hard and unexpected, she found she missed her friend, and that ache propelled her forward, into the odd man's home.

Despite the plain exterior, the inside was anything but boring. Yellow walls, bright white trim, wall-to-wall bookshelves, antiques, vibrant nature paintings, and ornate tapestries lit up the interior, and even a small model train wove through and around the living room, its miniature cars tooting and chugging along a miniature track. Half toy store, half hobbit house, the home was cinnamon-scented and welcoming in an almost childlike manner. Hannah felt herself grinning despite the grim circumstances.

"You like it?" the man asked matter-of-factly. "When my wife died, I decided life was too short to live like an American Gothic painting. I wanted sunshine and birdsong, so I brought it in here." He eyed her up and down, his gaze resting on her Hawaiian print Vans. "What did you say your name was?"

Hannah told him again. "I own the Hummingbird Hollow Inn. Ezra and I had been friends for a while."

"I'll try not to hold that against you." The man glided over to a stool shaped and painted like a mushroom and sat down. "Why are you here, Hannah-friend-of-Ezra? And sit, please." He waved toward a matching mushroom stool. "My dear friend made these. How could I turn them down? They're so very *Alice in Wonderland*."

Hannah had to agree. She sat down on one of the stools and said, "I'm trying to retrace Ezra's actions in the weeks before he died."

"You mean the weeks before he was killed. Don't sugarcoat it. Someone wanted Ezra dead, and they took it upon themselves to make it happen." The man's face was grave when he spoke. He stroked his tufty beard with a clean, well-manicured hand. "So then, you're trying to find his killer. Are you with the police?"

Hannah hesitated. "No."

"You're doing this on your own, a vigilante of sorts?"

Hannah hesitated again, but she decided honesty was the best path. "I guess."

The man clapped. "How absolutely brilliant! I'm not a fan of the police. Not since they pulled me over and ticketed me for missing a taillight. How am I supposed to know a taillight is out? It's not like I can see the back of my car." He smiled, displaying perfectly white, perfectly even teeth. "Jasper's own Nancy Drew."

"I wouldn't say that—"

"It suits you. Your hair is a bit curly and unruly, and of course you're too old to be Nancy, but you'll do."

"I really just want to know—"

"Why Ezra was killed." The man frowned, and in a voice dripping with suspicion, asked, "What does all this have to do with me?"

Hannah smiled again, amused. The man's reference to *Alice in Wonderland* wasn't too far off. With his scattered thoughts and abrupt shifts in topics, he reminded Hannah of the White Rabbit. She studied the bookshelves and saw fantasy novels, historical mysteries, antique editions of various novels and treatises, and even a full set of the *Encyclopaedia Britannica*. He was as different from Ezra as peanut butter was to jelly, yet Ezra had worn his Sunday finest to come here for a reason.

"Ezra visited you a few weeks ago. It was a Tuesday afternoon, sometime around four. I know because I dropped him off."

"So what? Surely Ezra visited lots of people."

"Not really. And this visit stuck out in my memory because Ezra got dressed up—or at least dressed up for Ezra."

The man's small mouth settled into a resigned "o." "I see. I was wondering when the police would get around to coming by. I didn't expect Nancy Drew." The train's whistle screamed loudly, startling them both. The man stood up slowly, walked to the train, bent down, and turned off the engine.

When he returned to the stool, he gave Hannah another once-over and said, "My name is Louis Driver. Ezra was my brother-in-law."

Hannah felt momentarily confused. Ezra's sisters and brother had all moved away. One died in Pennsylvania, one in New Jersey, and the last one in Florida. That much she knew because Ezra had complained about them all. Then it hit her. "You were his wife Molly's brother?"

"No, no. Molly's sister, Anita, was my wife. Anita passed away three years ago." He glanced toward the window, and Hannah saw the shadow of grief pass over his features. "You say you and Ezra were friends?"

Hannah nodded. "It was an odd friendship, I guess, but we had come to rely on each other. The bond of outsiders, you could say."

Louis gave Hannah a knowing smile, and something about him softened. "Ezra came to Anita's funeral, and I'm afraid I turned him away. You see, Anita never forgave Ezra for what happened with Molly. And although I never quite understood my wife's anger toward the man, I felt obligated out of loyalty to follow suit."

Hannah shook her head. "Molly died of natural causes."

"It wasn't her death that angered my wife, it was her withdrawal before her death. Anita had been a fiercely practical and serious woman, but underneath it all, she loved her sister. As sisters go, they were day and night—Molly was lightness in the face of Anita's stern world outlook. But then, one day, that all changed, and Molly just seemed to fold in on herself. Anita blamed Ezra."

Hannah thought of the Molly she had known. She'd been kind and sweet and generous, the happy foil to her husband's dour personality. "Hadn't Molly been ill?"

"That was what everyone thought, but even an illness wouldn't have quelled Molly's joyful nature. She wouldn't have let it. Plus, she would have told Anita about an illness. Why hide that from her sister? No, she was depressed."

"Depression *is* an illness. Why would your wife blame Ezra?"

Louis shrugged. "She thought Ezra was making her miserable, I guess. Keeping her holed up in that house, keeping her from her family. You see Ezra and Anita had never been close. My wife felt he wasn't good enough for Molly, and Anita was free with her opinions. Ezra, I'm sure, felt Anita was a meddling shrew, and that man couldn't hide his feelings if he tried."

Hannah could concede that. Ezra hadn't had much of a poker face. She said, "Ezra didn't seem like the controlling type."

"No?" Louis studied Hannah's face, his sharp, blue-eyed gaze unflinching. "Then I query how well you actually knew the man."

"I'd known him pretty well for the last two years, and during that time he seemed to . . . well, give up any façade of control."

Louis's smile was one more of pity than condescension, but Hannah experienced it as a mixture of both.

"Well, I knew him *pretty well* for the thirty years before that and I can say he was quite controlling—of Molly, his properties, his money, you name it. Don't fool yourself into thinking Ezra was some saint, because he very certainly was not."

Hannah was surprised by the vehemence in the man's tone. "Why did he visit you now, after all that time?"

Louis took a moment to study the hand holding the bear spray. He flexed a few fingers, sighed, and said, "He wanted to make amends. It was that simple."

"Why now, after all this time?"

Louis looked up, and Hannah saw sadness reflected in his eyes. "Because he was dying."

The rain had stopped, and silence descended upon the room.

"Dying?" Hannah said finally.

"Cirrhosis of the liver. He didn't have long to live."

"That can't be true." But even as she said it, she knew she was wrong. She remembered his wan appetite, his slightly yellowish eyes and complexion. She had rarely seen him drink, but rumor had it that he'd drank his grief away after Molly's passing—and then some. She'd chalked his physical symptoms up to age, but clearly there'd been more going on—things he hadn't shared. Things she should have noticed.

Louis said, "You didn't know."

Hannah shook her head. She felt heavy with shame. If Ezra had been ill, she should have known. She could have helped him.

Feeling bruised and shaken, Hannah thanked Louis for his time and rose to leave.

"Hannah *Solace*?" Louis said softly, holding up a hand to stop her. "As in Regina Solace's sister?"

Hannah nodded, surprised he knew Reggie.

"Your sister talked me out of selling this house when Anita died. She said not to make any major life decisions for a year, and I'm grateful for her sage advice." His eyes flashed. "Instead of leaving this godawful place, I turned it into the home I'd always wanted. Anita is probably doing somersaults in her cremation urn, but that's okay. I loved my wife, but she was as controlling as Ezra. Probably the real reason they never got along." He walked toward the kitchen. "Come on, I have something for you before you leave."

Hannah followed Louis outside and around to the back of the house. She saw that he'd been digging up a flower bed, and a dozen purple irises sat in a plastic milk crate, their bulbs thick-knuckled and dirt-covered.

"Take them," he said. "I think I read that you and Reggie are trying to build a native garden for pollinators. You could use these. Irises are a solid flower for attracting butterflies and hummingbirds."

"They're beautiful," Hannah said. "Don't you want them?"

"These were Anita's. She was fond of monochromatic flower gardens." His frown told her what he thought of monochromatic flower gardens. "I want to plant something fresh and different. If you have any ideas, let me know." Louis smiled. "I'm partial to a nice wildflower mix. You never quite know what you're getting. Surprises keep us young."

"Ezra was good with flowers. He helped me a lot."

"Ezra used to be botanist. Did you know that?" Louis handed her the crate, his chest puffed out beneath the suspenders. "He was also a master gardener in his day. Inspired me." Louis smiled. "I can tell by the look on your face that you had no idea. There's probably a lot about Ezra you don't know."

"Maybe you can share. I'd love to hear some old stories."

Louis looked suddenly tired. "I'd probably like that more than I'll admit. Now get going before it rains again and good manners force me to ask you in for supper. I only have one meatball and a small container of penne, so I'm afraid we would both spend the night hungry." His said the words lightly, and Hannah saw a twinkle beneath the fatigue. "Go forth, Nancy Drew, and find the person responsible for what happened to Ezra."

Hannah put the flowers in the back of her car, then stopped short of climbing behind the wheel. "So did it work out?" she asked softly. "Did you and Ezra make amends?"

Louis rubbed his bearded chin with one hand. He'd left the bear spray inside, and the other hand now dangled by his side. It clenched into a fist at the mention of Ezra. "After three years, I realized I'd been holding onto Anita's grudge, not my own. I told Ezra there was nothing for which to make amends."

"He must have been relieved."

Louis's eyes narrowed, remembering. "He seemed almost disappointed."

"*Disappointed*?"

Louis nodded. "He acted deflated when I told him there was nothing for which he had to apologize. I think maybe part of him wanted me to let him have it." Louis held up a clenched fist. "Really let him have it."

"Like he was looking for a physical fight?" Hannah tried to hide her surprise. The thought of the two old men duking it out was simultaneously amusing and horrifying.

"Not exactly," Louis said. "More like he was looking to *be* punched."

"That's odd."

Louis shrugged. "That was Ezra. Anita used to say he was an enigma, and about that, at least, my wife was one hundred percent correct."

Chapter Thirteen

Later that night, Hannah sat in the quiet of her apartment at the inn and thought about her conversation with Louis Driver. *Because he was dying.* The words replayed over and over in her mind. She recalled the last few discussions she'd had with Ezra about things that had seemed innocuous at the time but now resonated with the meaning bestowed by hindsight. There was the day he'd explained the complexities of the old plumbing system. And the time he'd asked for her help changing a blown fuse—how patient he'd been while showing her how to find and manage the fuse box. And the very strange day he'd led her to his study, a restricted, surprisingly neat inner sanctum on the second floor, so she could take his mail to the post office. In his own strange little ways, he'd been grooming her to take over his property.

Then there were all the times he'd relinquished care of Moose to her, allowing Hannah to take the dog outside or feed him. *He was testing me,* Hannah thought, *and letting Moose learn to trust me.* Hannah closed her eyes, saddened by the thought that Ezra had held his illness secret, that he hadn't felt he could tell her about it. Tears seared her eyelids. How alone he must have felt.

It wasn't the first time I missed the signs, Hannah thought. *It wasn't the first time I let someone down.*

The inn's buzzer rang, and Hannah stood up shakily. Her guests needed her, and she had to get herself together. As she splashed cold water on her face, the buzzer rang again insistently. She could hear Maura calling her from the other side of her apartment door— Maura, who seemed so clueless about her uncle's life. Of course, his family had no idea their uncle was dying.

Or did they?

Who had Ezra told aside from Louis? Maura? Rob? Simone? Waylen? Had any of them known their uncle was ill? If they had known, it would explain their mad rush to Jasper, each one falling over him- or herself to be Ezra's favorite. And based on Ash's account, lining up buyers for the property before Ezra was even gone. If they believed they were Ezra's beneficiaries, then maybe one of them—or all of them—had reason to murder their uncle to get a rush on that money.

Had they known how wealthy he was?

And what would happen once they found out that *she* was his heir?

Hannah stared into the mirror, her heart thumping against her ribcage. She could be harboring a killer *here*, at the inn. Maura pushed the buzzer again, and Hannah jumped. Suddenly the door between the inn and her apartment didn't seem so sturdy. She glanced at Moose, who sat alert in the hall, watching the entrance into the inn. *Good dog*, she thought, and let him walk beside her to meet her guest.

* * *

"Well, someone did it," Maura whined. "I figured it was you."

Hannah examined the broken door into Maura's room. The handle was dented, and someone had tried to wedge the door open, as evidenced by the gouges in the doorframe.

"Why would I try to break into a guest's room when I have the master keys?"

Maura crossed her arms over her chest and harrumphed. "How should I know. If it wasn't you, then who did it?"

Hannah shook her head. "I don't know, but whoever did this wasn't very good at it. Or they were interrupted." She turned to face Maura, who was looking warily at Moose. "When did you find your room this way?"

"Right before I came to get you."

"Just now?"

Maura's face reddened. "Yes. I just got back."

"When you left, there was no damage?"

"None that I noticed."

Hannah asked, "What time was that?"

The pink flush deepened. "Around lunchtime."

"Were Rob and Waylen with you?"

Maura shook her head. She glanced down at her black wedge heels and shuffled her feet. "I was alone."

Noticing Maura's obvious discomfort, Hannah said, "Where did you go?"

Maura broke eye contact. "Just some sightseeing."

"Huh." Hannah didn't believe her, but she opted not to press. She opened the door to Maura's room and looked around inside. The bed, chair, and desk all looked undisturbed. In fact, the bed looked completely undisturbed—as though Maura hadn't slept in it during her entire time in Vermont. Most guests wanted the daily cleaning service, but Maura had opted out. Maybe there was a reason.

Hannah asked, "Did you notice anything missing?"

"No."

"Any reason someone might want to get into your room?"

"Not that I know of, but a thief could have targeted me randomly."

Hannah spun around, facing Maura. "The only people staying at the inn right now are your family members, Maura. There's a keypad to get in and out of the inn's front door, and the other entrances are kept locked from the inside, so it's highly unlikely a stranger wandered in, made it upstairs unnoticed, and tried to get into your room—or any room."

Maura wrapped her arms around her chest. "Highly unlikely doesn't mean impossible. What about that contractor of yours? The hot one."

"Ash?" Hannah almost laughed at the thought. "He generally stays outside." Hannah glanced at the door again. "Look, I'll change your room if you'd like. I can put you closer to Waylen, or give you a room downstairs, near my apartment. Would you like that?"

Maura nodded. "Downstairs, near you and that dog." She pointed at Moose.

"I'll also let the police know what happened, in case they want to come over and make a report."

Maura's eyes widened in panic. "I don't think that's necessary. The report, I mean." She waved a hand at the door. "The person didn't even get inside the room. For all we know, they thought this was their room and did this by accident. No need to involve the cops. Not now with everything else that's going on."

The change in Maura's tune didn't surprise Hannah. She'd seemed embarrassed by the fact that she'd been gone all day, alone, and clearly, she hadn't been spending her nights at the inn. Whatever questioning the police would do would only serve to highlight her absence—something Maura clearly did not want. Hannah's curiosity was piqued, but she decided to play it cool.

Hannah took Maura downstairs and showed her to a room near the common space. It was a smaller room with less privacy, but Maura seemed fine with its size and location.

"We don't need to mention this to my cousins," Maura said.

"They may have been the ones who did that. Don't you want to ask them? It could put this whole thing to bed."

Maura shook her head vehemently back and forth. "Everyone's on edge already. No need to make it worse."

Hannah didn't respond to this right away. Instead she handed Maura fresh towels and led her to the kitchen for a cup of late-night decaf.

"I'm surprised Waylen wasn't roused by our discussion in the hallway," Hannah said offhandedly. "It's after ten o'clock."

Maura was busily staring at her nails. Hannah noticed the chips in the blood-red paint, the worry lines around her mouth, and the dark circles under her heavily made-up eyes. Hannah wanted to attribute these things to grief, but she suspected heartbreak over Ezra's death was not what was weighing most heavily on his niece.

"Do you want to talk about it?" Hannah asked, placing the steaming cup on the island in front of Maura. "Innkeepers are a lot like bartenders. All ears."

Maura's smile was pained. "Thanks, but there's not much to talk about."

"If you're worried about the room, my guess is that it was an honest mistake. Someone thought the room was theirs and got frustrated when their key-card wouldn't work."

"Someone as in Waylen?" Maura stirred her coffee listlessly, "He does like his scotch. Maybe he'd had a few too many."

"Exactly." Hannah rinsed out the coffee carafe and wiped down the counters. When she was finished, she placed the plates out for the next morning's breakfast. "How did your uncle seem to you this trip?" she asked casually while working. "Before he passed away."

"What do you mean?"

"Did he seem like himself?" Hannah asked, repeating Noah's line of questioning.

"The police asked me the same thing, and I'll tell you what I told them. He was no stranger than usual. Uncle Ezra didn't really talk to me, so I'm not sure I would have noticed if he had been off. He mostly grunted answers at me." She continued: "I don't know how you became friends with him. I'm sad he's gone, of course, but the truth is I never felt close to him."

"Did you see a lot of him growing up?"

"Christmas, Thanksgiving, occasional birthdays or weddings."

"How about your Aunt Molly? Did you spend time with her?"

Maura tilted her head, thinking. "My mom and Molly got along well. Molly was always nice to us, but she died when I was in my early twenties."

"How about Ezra—was he close to your mom?"

Maura nearly spit out her coffee. "My mother—Ezra's sister— was a gregarious woman with a big heart. I'm not sure how our grandfather chose Ezra over her—or my aunts, for that matter."

Hannah stopped folding napkins and turned toward Maura, surprised by the outburst. "Chose in what way?"

"My grandfather inherited *his* dad's land and money. He, in turn, left everything to Uncle Ezra. Unless Ezra squandered it, there should have been a pretty sum in his name. As the eldest male child, he got it all. Crazy sexist and old-fashioned, right?"

Hannah let the implications of what Maura was saying sink in. That meant Maura *had known* Ezra had money. That meant they *all* knew Ezra had money—or at least could have had money.

As breezily as she could manage, Hannah said, "And Ezra's heirs are the three of you?"

Maura's laugh was more of a snort. "Seriously? It would be nice to think he split it between the three of us as his closest living heirs, but my and Rob's guess is that Waylen got it all, and Waylen's guess is that Rob got it all." Maura raised her eyebrows. "I was nobody's guess."

"That's awful."

"You're damn right. Now we just get to wait for the official word." Maura drained her coffee and pushed the empty mug toward Hannah. "Thanks for the joe. I'm going to bed."

Here? Hannah wondered as she watched the other woman disappear into the guest quarters. *Or wherever it is you've been for the last few nights?*

*   *   *

Hannah made two calls before going to sleep herself. The first was to Reggie to fill her in on the day's events, but her sister didn't answer the phone. The second call was to Noah. He didn't answer either, so she left a brief message informing him of the damage to Maura's door. She still felt angry toward him, and figured it had either been an accident or Maura had done it herself, but she decided safe was better than being a suspect.

As Hannah drifted off to sleep, her mind kept wandering back to Louis Driver and his final description of Ezra. *Disappointed. Deflated.* Like a man who *wanted* to be punished.

What kind of man *wants* to be punished?

A man seeking penance for something he'd done in the past?

"What could you possibly have been seeking atonement for, Ezra?" she said aloud. The only answer came from Moose, who thumped his tail against the floor and kept it wagging long after she'd finished talking.

Chapter Fourteen

H annah crawled out of bed at 5:38 AM, twenty-two minutes before her alarm was set to go off. Her mind was a whirling, twirling vortex of worry, and she needed to clear it if she was going to do anything productive that day. She fed Moose and took him outside, then brewed a pot of coffee for her guests, none of whom were up. After drinking three cups of the coffee herself, she decided to go for a paddle.

She walked out toward the simple wooden structure that housed the boats, and realized she couldn't do it. At the thought of getting into—or even looking at—the water where she'd first seen Ezra's body, her insides clenched and her hands began to shake. She wasn't ready to face the pond where Ezra had died. Frustrated and annoyed at herself, Hannah hauled the smallest of the boats to her car. She hoisted it on the rooftop boat rack, secured it, and threw her paddle and gear into the trunk. If she couldn't kayak on Devil's Pond, she'd go somewhere else.

It was a stunning late August morning, sunny and sleepy and cool, and Hannah decided to head to the small but scenic Sugar Hill Reservoir in Goshen. She texted Reggie her intentions and asked her to stop by the inn later that morning. The drive was an easy thirty minutes down Route 73, then down a few back roads. Once there, she unloaded her boat and carried it down to the boat launch area, as she had a dozen times before. It was still early, and she had the small lake to herself, so she took her time paddling into the open water.

A fine mist rose in gossamer tendrils from the lake's surface. The fog, the trees, and the few cotton-candy clouds reflected on the water, and Hannah felt like she was meandering through two mystical worlds as she paddled her way into the center of the lake. To the east, Worth Mountain and Gillespie Peak rose through clouds of white mist, and beyond them, Devil's Mountain stood taller than the rest. Crows called to one another from the trees overhead, and a family of ducks puttered along the edge of the reservoir, one behind another. Hannah took a deep breath of the clear, sweet air, and once again she sensed the harbingers of autumn—scattered clusters of maples and birch trees just beginning to turn, squirrels scurrying about on the shoreline, filling their winter larder, and a trio of loons, the one offspring dressed in its juvenile brown plumage.

As her paddle sliced through flat water and the morning sun warmed her face, Hannah thought about Ezra and his death at Devil's Pond. Her conversation with Louis still bugged her. If Ezra had been looking for absolution, that implied he'd done something wrong. Was it as simple as Anita's misplaced frustration with Molly's condition, as Louis had implied? Or was it something else, something more sinister—something linked to his death?

One of the loons hooted, and Hannah turned to see the trio dive under water nearby. The juvenile loon surfaced just a few feet from Hannah's boat, and she stayed still while it swam away, careful not to get closer or make any sudden movements that might scare it or its parents. Her attention still on the loons, Hannah thought about her own parents and her life before the family moved to the big house. While John Solace hadn't been a regular fixture in the home, her mother, Reggie, and Hannah had spent many days hiking and canoeing around Jasper. Bev had given her daughters a love of the outdoors. Bev and her few close friends were always spending time with them outside.

Friends like Phyllis Katz, Hannah thought.

She hadn't seen her mother's best friend since her mother's funeral, and she and Phyllis weren't on the best of terms. Phyllis had lived next to Ezra and Molly, though, in the days before Brian Lewis bought the place and added three thousand ostentatious square feet to the original fifteen-hundred-square-foot home. Phyllis had moved into one of the area's few townhomes, but in the years she lived near the Graysons, Phyllis had been close to Molly. Hannah remembered all three of them—Molly, her mother, and Phyllis— spending summer days at Lake Dunmore and winter days skiing at Devil's Mountain. Maybe Phyllis could fill in some blanks.

The sun had burned off the last of the mist, and Hannah decided it was time to go. She had guests who'd want their breakfast, and she hoped her sister would come by. As Hannah neared the shoreline and the boat launch, she saw a man standing by the water's edge, looking out at the water—and at her. Hannah held her breath, the grip of fear clutching her gut, and tried to make out his features, but it was fruitless at this distance.

She paddled forward, gripping the handle tightly. *You're being ridiculous,* she told herself. *He could just be someone here to fish or enjoy the early morning mountain view.* Only she knew deep down that wasn't the case, a suspicion confirmed as she neared land and recognized Chad's lumbering form waiting impatiently two feet from the water.

"What are you doing here?" Hannah asked as she climbed out of the kayak. She lifted the boat out of the water and started carrying it up the hill toward the car.

"I need to talk to you."

"Here?" When she reached her car, Hannah started hoisting the kayak over her head, and Chad grabbed one end, lifting while trying hard not to let the water drip onto his Tommy Hilfiger blue button-down shirt. "This feels a little like stalking."

"Don't act crazy," Chad snapped. "I needed to speak with you in private, and Reggie told me you'd be here."

"You drove thirty minutes to have a private conversation with someone who lives six minutes away, and I'm the crazy one?" Hannah tossed the kayak strap over the boat and secured the clasp. "I'll ask you again. What do you want, Chad?"

Chad rocked back on his loafered heels. Despite the coolness of the morning, sweat stained the fabric under his arms, and a thin sheen of sweat had collected on his brow. "I need your help."

Hannah was midway through securing the second strap, and stopped what she was doing. "Normally when people need a favor, they at least try to be nice."

"I could be sweet as a peach pie and it wouldn't matter."

Hannah pulled the strap tight, tied a knot, and tugged on the kayak to make sure it was firmly in place. Finished, she threw her life jacket and paddle into the car's hatch.

"Hannah?"

"I heard you, Chad, but you wasted your time coming here."

"You don't even know what I want."

Hannah leaned on the car, arms crossed. "You're right. What *do* you want?"

"I know Ezra's family members are staying at the inn. I was hoping you could put in a good word for me as they decide what to do with that property." He eked out some semblance of a smile. "I'll offer them the best deal, if they'll just hear me out."

"No."

"I don't need you to give them the terms. They've been talking with Henry and Brian Lewis, who'll take advantage of them. I just need you to convince them to talk to me. Level the playing field."

Hannah opened the car door. "No."

"Come on, Hannah. We were family. Do this for Peach's future."

Hannah shook her head. "If you were worried about family or Peach's future, you wouldn't have left my sister for her best friend."

Chad's face was turning the color of fall maple leaves. "Hannah, come on. Just do this one thing—"

"Bye, Chad."

"You'll regret this.

As Hannah drove away, windows down, she heard the long, slow wail of the loons. It was a haunting sound that echoed through the canyon. Chad followed behind Hannah's car and waved a clenched fist in her direction. Hannah reached her hand through the window and gave her former brother-in-law a friendly wave. She'd keep this visit from her sister. Preventing another Solace-Little battle was one thing she *could* do for Peach.

*   *   *

"You summoned?" Reggie swung into the apartment kitchen, ponytail flying, and tossed a loaf of bread onto the counter. "Complements of Nadia. She said to tell you it's a new flavor—orange cranberry walnut. No eggs, no milk, no butter."

Hannah accepted the offering with a halfhearted smile. Nadia, the owner of the Breaking Bread half of the bike/coffee/bakery shop on Main Street, had been a physicist in her prior life. She had retired to Vermont at the tender age of fifty-five and had been trying to convince Hannah and Reggie to offer her goods at the inn ever since they had met. Each time Nadia came up with a new recipe, she sent some to the inn. Hannah hadn't caved on a contract yet, but her waistline was starting to suffer from the bribes.

"Are you just here as Nadia's messenger?"

Reggie sliced herself a piece of the bread, threw it on a plate, and sliced another for Peach, who was stalking the inn cat, Turnip, across the room. The cat saw her coming, though, and sprang up on all fours, leaping over Peach and onto an end table before disappearing down the hallway.

"Turnip, come back!" Peach yelled.

"Well, we won't see that cat until tomorrow," Reggie whispered snidely to Hannah under her breath. "Peach honey, come and eat something before camp."

"No."

Reggie rolled her eyes at Hannah. "Enough with the judgment. Before you say a word, *you* try telling her and see what happens."

Hannah said, "Peach, come and eat something before camp."

"Like what, Aunt Hannah?"

"Like an orange and a piece of toast."

Peach shrugged. "Okay. I like oranges and toast."

Hannah hid her triumphant smile behind a mug of coffee. Her niece's sparkly green tank top and pink leggings peeked out from beneath a ragged Superman cape, and she spun around, watching as the cape flared around her. She was gripping a wand between her chubby fingers and aimed it at the toaster.

"I don't think that'll do it," Hannah said. She put a slice of Nadia's bread in the toaster and pulled some jam from the refrigerator. Then she started to peel an orange.

As Peach took a seat at the island, she said matter-of-factly to Hannah, "I have science camp today. We're learning about frogs, so you should come."

"That sounds like a lot of fun. Are you sure I'm allowed to crash your camp?" Hannah asked.

"Everyone can go." She glanced at Reggie with a supersized scowl. "Except you, Mommy. They said no parents."

Reggie shook her head. "Did your camp counselor really say that, Peach? It's important to be honest."

Peach shrugged again, tossing the cape behind her, and said, "Nope. I made that up."

"*Well then*." Hannah placed a plate of toast and orange sections in front of her niece and said to Reggie, "At least she owns up to her actions. More than I can say for some people."

"Speaking from experience?"

"Indeed."

"Scoot, kiddo." Hannah sent Peach into the living room with her food so she could share the strange happenings from the day before. Hannah told her sister about her conversation with Noah, Louis Driver's revelation that Ezra was terminally ill, and Maura's discovery of the damaged door.

Reggie frowned. "Someone damaged the door to Room 4?"

"With everything I just told you, *that's* what you're worried about?"

Reggie slid into a chair at the table. "That and the fact that Ezra was ill. You had no idea?"

"None whatsoever. And I feel awful that he didn't feel he could tell me."

Reggie was quiet for a moment. She picked at a piece of the bread but didn't put any in her mouth. "I saw him walking along Main Street one day, and he stumbled. Kendra ran out of the church and helped him up, and by the time I got there, he seemed fine. In retrospect, I did notice a yellowish cast to his skin, but I didn't think anything of it at the time. I feel bad that I never said anything."

Hannah nodded. She had no comforting words to offer—she was still grappling with her own shame.

Reggie said, "What about this Louis Driver? I thought I knew everyone around here, but that name doesn't ring a bell."

"He was Ezra's wife's sister's husband. He lives outside of town. He knows you. In fact, he said he consulted you about selling his house after his wife died, and you suggested he sit on a decision for a while."

Reggie's eyes brightened. "Short man, well dressed, a little finicky?" When Hannah nodded, she said, "I do remember him. It was a few years ago. He'd been recently widowed and wanted to sell his house right away. I always tell people in that situation to give it some time."

"He appreciated the advice. Ended up staying in his house."

Reggie nodded. "Good, I like it when people listen to me. Now if only my daughter would do the same."

They both laughed. Reggie said, "He runs the vintage clothing shop in Rochester."

"I'm not familiar with it."

"I don't think he's there much. Semiretired."

Peach wandered back into the kitchen with her empty plate and slid it onto the counter.

"Ate everything?" Hannah asked, noting the way Moose was following Peach closely. Both dog and child wore guilty expressions.

Peach opened her mouth to speak, glanced at Reggie, and answered, "It's all gone."

"That child is going to be a lawyer," Reggie said when Peach had returned to the living room.

"She could do worse." Hannah took the seat opposite her sister and thought about how to broach the next topic. She decided candor was the best option and said, "I need you to help me with something."

Reggie's expression darkened. "Are you okay?"

"I am, Reg, but I'm worried. Noah made it pretty clear yesterday that he thought the person with the most motive to hurt Ezra was me—"

"That's ridiculous."

"I know, and while he and the police are investigating me, whoever did this will get away with what they did—or worse."

Reggie's eyes narrowed to slits. Hannah didn't have to explain what *or worse* meant. "Do you want me to talk to Noah?"

Hannah shook her head. "No. Let him do his job. But in the meantime, maybe we can poke around a little." Reggie started to protest, and Hannah said, "Let me explain, okay? The way I see it, someone may have killed Ezra in the heat of the moment during an argument. If we can figure out who he was with later that day, it may lead to the person who did this."

"*Heat of the moment* would mean Ezra was willingly out at the pond. Why would Ezra have been out at Devil's Pond?"

"Think about it, Reggie. Ezra was a complicated man with a lot of frenemies. Multiple people wanted to buy his property, and he wouldn't let them." *Including your ex-husband*, Hannah thought. "He complained daily about the constant inquiries and, in Brian's case, threats. Maybe he'd decided to entertain one of those buyers. The pond abuts his property. It's possible he and whoever killed him had hiked out there to discuss a possible sale. Go for a friendly walk around the property, an argument ensues, things turn ugly, and bam!"

"But he told you earlier that same day that he would never sell."

"He also led me to believe he was fine physically."

Reggie nodded slowly. "I see your point, but there's an alternative."

Hannah's brow furrowed. "Ezra's will."

"Right. Someone knew he had money, believed they would inherit, and wanted the money sooner rather than later."

"With his illness, they would have gotten it sooner anyway."

Reggie stood and placed her and Peach's plates in the dishwasher. "Not necessarily. Maybe they didn't know he was sick. Even if they did, just because what Ezra had was terminal doesn't mean he would have died quickly. He could have lived for months or even years, needing expensive medical care or a nursing home."

"Care that would have drained his accounts." Hannah gave a slow, disbelieving shake of the head. "And all the while, the house gets more decrepit and the big estate dwindles."

"Exactly. Whoever did this may have viewed Ezra's untimely passing as a way to preserve their inheritance."

"That's assuming they knew he was sick."

"And assuming they knew his property wasn't mortgaged to the max."

"If we're right," Hannah said, "The people with the strongest motive are his own family members."

"All of whom are staying here." Reggie lowered her voice "Which brings us back to the damaged door. Why don't I go have a look while you help Peach gather her things?"

Hannah glanced into the living room where her niece was watching cartoons with one arm around Moose. "I guess you want the easy job?"

Reggie flashed a half-smile. "For today, anyway."

Reggie disappeared for ten minutes while Hannah finished tidying up the kitchen and Peach's belongings. When Reggie returned, she announced that it did indeed look like someone had been trying to force their way into Maura's room. "Why, I don't know. If someone thought it was their room, they might have been trying to enter by mistake. Otherwise, you have an intruder."

"It was just me, Rebecca, and the guests yesterday," Hannah said. "And the guests have codes for getting into the inn."

"Maybe one of them shared the code. Did you check the security footage?"

Hannah felt her face flush. "It doesn't record."

"Of course it records."

Hannah waved her hand breezily, turning away from her sister. "Only if you have the subscription."

Reggie threw her head back in exasperation. "Seriously, Hannah? Why do you have cameras if you're not going to pay for the subscription?"

Here we go, Hannah thought. She'd been avoiding any discussions about money for months. If Reggie knew the inn was operating in the red, she'd question every penny Hannah spent. Instead, Hannah had tried to make do with what she had on hand, scrimping and reusing and growing whatever vegetables she could at the inn. She wished she had a bigger safety net, but she was managing— and the guest experience wasn't suffering. Besides, no one in these parts locked their doors. Why should she pay for a security subscription service if she didn't need one?

"Hannah, answer me."

Hannah spun around. "Do you see this place? We have four guests. *Four.* That's barely enough to keep the place going much less pay for unnecessary services." Peach peeked around the kitchen wall, and Hannah lowered her voice. "No security footage for now."

"Then we won't know who entered the inn."

Hannah threw up her hands. "Look, the easy thing for Maura to do would be to ask her cousins. That's how normal families act."

"They don't exactly seem normal, do they?" Reggie's voice had the low-pitched, steely tone that told Hannah she would drop the topic—for now—but Hannah shouldn't think for a moment that it was dead. "I need to go. Peach needs to get to camp."

"Before you leave, I have something to ask you." Hannah shifted her eyes away from her sister's. "When was the last time you spoke to Aunt Phyllis?"

That stopped Reggie mid-step. "Not for a long time. Years. Why the random inquiry about her now?"

"She used to live nextdoor to Ezra and Molly. She could have some insight into Ezra's past. You said yourself that I shouldn't accept a penny until I understand why he had the money. I can't find out where the money came from without knowing more about his life."

"That was a long time ago, Hannah. I doubt Aunt Phyllis remembers much about Ezra and Molly."

"She's sharp. Aunt Phyllis remembers everything. And she and Molly were friends."

Reggie's eyebrows rose upward. "Are you sure that's the only reason you want to see her? You know how Phyllis can be."

Phyllis was a retired judge. Despite the fact that she wasn't a blood relation, they'd called her "aunt" since Hannah could remember. Maybe it was because she'd never had kids of her own, or maybe it was because she and Hannah's mother had been friends for so long that it was a title of respect. It didn't matter—neither Phyllis's aunt-ness nor her judge-ness were of interest to Hannah right now. She just wanted to know why Ezra had been feeling penitent, and she hoped Phyllis could offer some insight. Still, Hannah hadn't seen Phyllis Katz in years, and the last time they'd been together hadn't gone well. Hannah said, "What choice do I have?"

"You could hire a private investigator to look into Ezra's past."

"And what, pay him in zucchini? I just got done explaining our financial situation."

"You're about to become a millionaire."

Hannah felt the weight of those words like a slam to her shoulders. "I'd give it all up happily to have Ezra back."

Reggie reached a hand out and touched her sister's shoulder. "I'm sorry. I shouldn't have said that." She paused. "Would you like me to go with you to see Aunt Phyllis?"

Hannah brightened. "I thought you'd never ask."

Reggie glanced at her watch. "Let me take Peach to camp and check in at the office. How about if I pick you up after lunch? Say around two? I'll call ahead to make sure she'll be home."

Hannah thought about her schedule. She had work to do in the gardens, but nothing that couldn't wait, and a few orders to place, which she could do now. "That works. Rebecca's here for a few hours this afternoon, so she can handle the afternoon snack."

"Prepare yourself," Reggie warned. "Let's not have a repeat of the funeral."

Hannah didn't need a warning. Phyllis Katz was the only person as good at pushing Hannah's buttons as her father was. *I've matured*, Hannah told herself—*and I'll make damn sure Phyllis knows it.*

Chapter Fifteen

They found Phyllis on the deck of her townhome, reading a thriller and drinking iced tea out of a pink-plastic Disney princesses cup. When she saw Hannah and Reggie standing by the banister, she took her time finishing the page she was on before inserting a bookmark, taking a long sip of her tea, and gesturing toward the two empty lounge chairs. Reggie perched on the edge of one and Hannah sprawled across the other.

"It's been almost four years," Phyllis said flatly, a hint of her native Boston accent bubbling under the surface. There was no accusation in her tone, but Hannah read accusation into it anyway. "What brings you girls here now, after all this time?" She held up her novel and waved it at them. "No, no—let me guess. You came to tell me I was right all along."

Seriously? Hannah wondered what had made her think Phyllis would be civil. Hannah shimmied to the end of the lounge and was just starting to propel herself upward and off the seat when Reggie caught her eye. The look she was giving her said *sit your ass back down*, and Hannah did. No use angering her sister more than once today.

"We're not here to—," Hannah started to say.

"We need your insights." Reggie cut Hannah off. "I'm sure you've heard about Ezra Grayson's murder."

Phyllis smoothed back her chicly styled short white hair. "I did."

"You used to live next to him," Reggie said. "Him and his wife Molly."

Phyllis glanced from Reggie to Hannah and back again, her intelligent eyes studying each of their faces in turn. "I did, but what does that matter now?"

"We thought you might be able to shed some light on Ezra's past," Hannah said. "Who knows? Maybe that will lead to a break in the investigation."

Phyllis's mouth twisted in amusement. "Are you working for the police now, Hannah?"

Hannah met Phyllis's gaze head-on, no longer able to hide her annoyance. Reggie's 12-gauge stare was only fueling her own impatience.

"Enough with the snide comments," Hannah said to Phyllis. "Can you just let it go?"

"I'm afraid I can't."

Hannah said, "It's been four years."

"And in those four years, you haven't said a word about what happened."

"I'm sorry—is that what you want to hear? I should have listened to you. Do you think I don't feel guilty every time I think about my mother?" Hannah stood up. "Every time I think of her, your words echo in my head. So yes, you were right all along, and I'm a terrible daughter." Hannah bit her bottom lip, wiped her eyes with the back of her hand. "Happy now?"

Phyllis at least had the decency to look chagrined. She put her Disney princesses cup down on a small table and disappeared through a pair of French doors, returning a minute later with two glasses of iced tea and a box of tissues.

"Here," she said, handing Hannah the tissues. She placed the iced teas on a cast-aluminum dining table and pulled three heavy chairs out for them to sit. "My tea has a healthy dose of Long Island in it, but yours are plain." She gestured toward the chairs. "Join me, girls."

Hannah caught Reggie's eye and was surprised to see empathy there. Her sister disliked displays of emotion, angry outbursts—anything that could be viewed as dramatic—which is, Hannah knew, why she hadn't wanted Hannah to come here in the first place. At the core of Hannah's bitterness toward her mother's best friend was her own guilt at not having gone to see her mother before she died. Reggie knew that. Sheesh, even Hannah knew that. She didn't need constant reminders of how she'd failed her mother.

Reggie said, "Aunt Phyllis, neither Hannah nor I want to rehash what happened when my mom got sick. As Hannah said, she's dealing with her own guilt. We want a relationship with you, but it's not fair to constantly remind us of what you lost. It was our loss too."

Phyllis smoothed her clothing, and without making eye contact, gave Reggie a quick nod. Her sharp, hard eyes and aquiline nose were softened by a generous mouth and a fleshy, round face, but when she was angry, those piercing eyes took over—like now. When Hannah was younger, she had always been struck by how different Phyllis and her mother seemed. Phyllis was athletic and stocky, with a confident swagger and the air of someone who believed she'd earned her place at the table—whatever table she happened to be sitting at. In contrast to Phyllis, Beverly seemed like a stray dog asking for table scraps. Thin to the point of frailty, kind-hearted, generous, and conflict-averse, she had trouble standing up for herself, much less for anyone else—including her daughters. When Bev was first diagnosed, Phyllis had been by her side at every doctor's appointment and every treatment. She'd argued with doctors and insurers on Bev's behalf, even threatening a lawsuit over medication costs. She'd stayed by Bev's side throughout the illness and was there alongside Reggie when Bev drew her last breath.

John Solace had been out golfing—a fact Phyllis was unlikely to forgive. Hannah Solace had been in Massachusetts, tending to goats—a fact Hannah *knew* Phyllis would never forgive. Phyllis had called Hannah the night before Bev passed. "Come home, Hannah, or you will regret it for the rest of your life. I don't know why you're so angry at your parents, but now is the time to swallow your pride. She doesn't have long."

Hannah had heard that before. Bev's last year had been near miss after near miss, false alarm after false alarm, but on that weekend, her mother's heart had decided she'd had one treatment too many. She passed away at 11:22 the next morning.

Hannah knew the time down to the second. She knew because Phyllis told her. She also knew that she was an easy target for Phyllis's attempts at imposing guilt trips. Phyllis's real anger was toward John, whom she had never liked; but he was as impervious to guilt trips as he was to feelings of loyalty. Phyllis couldn't move that rock, so she focused her energy on this one.

Hannah expressed none of this. She drank the tea and sat waiting until her vision had cleared and her breathing returned to normal.

Changing the topic, Reggie said, "This place is nice." She looked back at the large, three-story townhome behind them.

Phyllis frowned. "Thank you. I hate it."

Reggie laughed. "Are you ever happy?"

Phyllis opened her mouth to argue, but instead her face broke into a wide grin, and they all laughed. When their laughter had subsided, Phyllis said more quietly, "I haven't been truly happy since your mother died."

Hannah glanced at Phyllis, stunned by the rawness of her tone. That simple sentence was full of grief—even after four years. Suddenly, Hannah saw their friendship in a new light. Phyllis had loved Bev truly and deeply. It explained her anger toward Hannah and John, it explained her frustration with the doctors, and it explained her continued grieving. Perhaps it wasn't a romantic love—or perhaps it was—they'd probably never know. In any case, there was a reason she was *Aunt* Phyllis. Hannah couldn't do anything to change how she'd treated her mother that last year of her life, but she could give her mother this—acceptance of her best friend.

"I'm sorry," Hannah whispered. Then, more loudly, "I'm sorry I wasn't there for my mother or for you. I should have been there, and you were right. I will regret it for the rest of my life."

The three women sat around the table, silent. At a nearby townhome, someone was grilling, and the scents of cooking meat and lighter fluid filled Hannah's nostrils. Two boys were playing catch on the community's open lawn, and a lifeguard's whistle shrilled from the pool located somewhere on the grounds. It was an idyllic afternoon, and the sounds of others having fun only underscored Hannah's own sense of loss.

Eventually, Phyllis said, "You wanted to talk about Ezra?" She reached over and squeezed Hannah's hand. "Let's talk about Ezra."

* * *

"What can I say? The man was a crab, but he was devoted to his wife. Anyone could see that."

They'd settled inside Phyllis's living room, and Phyllis was sitting in the lotus position on her spotless white couch. She stretched tan arms over her head, extending silver ring-clad fingers toward the ecru wall behind her. "Molly seemed to adore him right back."

"There was nothing you remember from that time period? Maybe a big blow-up with a neighbor, or a fight with Molly's family?" Hannah asked, thinking of Louis and his wife Anita. "Anything?"

"We're going back twenty years, Hannah. It was a rough time for me—the divorce, my own health issues." She shrugged. "I didn't pay that much attention to Ezra and Molly."

Reggie sat forward, resting her elbow on her knee and her chin on her palm. "That was around the same time that my dad bought Ezra's property. Considering how much that changed my parents' lives, I would have thought my mom would have talked about it."

Phyllis unfurled her legs. "Sure, that was a game changer for your parents, but in a good way. They finally had money. It solved a lot of problems."

"It also created a lot of tension in the long run," Hannah said. "Between them—and, especially, with Ezra."

"We think Ezra accused our dad of cheating him," Reggie said.

Hannah added, "Dad bought the land cheap, then developed it for millions, effectively cutting Ezra out of the deal."

"I don't know anything about that," Phyllis said quickly.

"You're a lawyer. Surely my parents talked to you about the sale," Reggie said.

"I'm not that kind of lawyer. Plus, it's no secret that I'm not your father's favorite person. Never have been."

Through the sliding-glass doors Hannah watched a neighborhood cat run across Phyllis's banister and leap onto one of the lounges, making itself at home. Once, Phyllis hadn't been so different from that cat, Hannah thought. She had been at their house all the time, a companion to her mother and an aunt to them, treating their home as her own. She wondered whether the reason her father hadn't liked her was jealousy. Perhaps he'd resented Phyllis's constant presence in their house and in his wife's life. Hannah decided to approach the question in a different way.

"Was my mom upset about the deal?" Hannah asked. "She never liked conflict."

"Your mom was an honest woman. She wouldn't have taken part in anything underhanded."

"Not knowingly," Reggie said.

Phyllis didn't answer this, but she didn't deny it, either.

"Do you remember Molly's illness?" Hannah asked. "What did she have?"

Phyllis swiveled in Hannah's direction, then slid off the couch and onto the floor, where she sat cross-legged, staring at Hannah with a quizzical look on her face. "Illness?"

"Molly died unexpectedly a year or two after the sale. We heard she'd been ill. Some people have said she withdrew socially, stopped interacting with people."

Phyllis gave her a wry smile. "Would you be happy if you were married to Ezra?"

Reggie shot Hannah a warning look, but there was no need—Hannah hadn't expected anything less. There was a reason Hannah had been Ezra's only friend. While the townspeople of Jasper were upset about his death, she knew there would be no grand memorial to celebrate his life.

"Seriously. It sounds like Molly changed. Something in her life made her withdraw," Hannah said. "The thing that makes the most sense is illness—whatever illness was her final undoing."

"*Final undoing*? Oh, Hannah, you've always loved melodrama. Molly never mentioned an illness. I do seem to recall that she was outside less often, and she stopped playing bridge at the church. But there was so much happening those days that I didn't think much of it." She scrunched her features, looking pensive. "There was this one conversation—"

"Yes?" Hannah asked, trying not to sound too eager.

"Molly was outside. She looked a bit haggard, as though she hadn't been sleeping well. Not just for one night, but for a while. Do you know what I mean?" When Hannah nodded, she continued, "I asked her if everything was okay." Phyllis looked out the sliding-glass windows, but her eyes were far away, remembering. "She said it was, and then she asked me whether Vermont had the death penalty."

"Why would she ask about that?" Reggie said.

Phyllis shrugged. "No idea."

"What did you tell her?" Reggie asked.

"I told her only if she was thinking about committing treason, but she didn't seem to find that funny. She looked at me sideways and went back inside."

* * *

"The death penalty," Hannah said on the way back to Reggie's car. "What do you make of that?"

Reggie slid behind the wheel and started the engine. "Oh, who knows. She could have been watching true-crime television and wanted to know if the killer could be executed in Vermont." She glanced over at Hannah. "I'm sorry this was a dead end."

Hannah fastened her seatbelt and sat back while Reggie backed the car out of the lot. Reggie was right, of course. Morbid curiosity, a true-crime docudrama . . . there were a lot of reasons Molly could have been asking about the death penalty, but that conversation had stuck with Phyllis for a reason.

As Reggie drove down the mountain toward Jasper, she rattled on about her business, her latest argument with Cheating Chad, and Peach's morning outburst. Hannah tried to focus on what her sister was saying, but all she could think about was Ezra's body lying there, lifeless, in the marshy area by the pond.

Her pond, her sanctuary. Ezra knew she loved that pond, that she resisted any kind of roadway leading to it out of fear that the ecosystem around the pond would be destroyed. He'd loved it too, although his waning mobility had made kayaking and even hiking a chore. Had he been trying to reach her through the forest instead of the road? If so, why?

Hannah couldn't shake this feeling that everything she had discovered so far was connected. The pond, Molly's personality changes, the sale of Ezra's properties to her father, Ezra's desire for forgiveness, her inheritance—they all led in some meandering way to Ezra's murder on that fateful day.

Chapter Sixteen

Hannah returned to the inn to find Ash digging up a fresh bed in the back field. He was shirtless, his broad, tan back rippled with muscles from the hours of landscaping, his boots and legs mud-splattered from the waterlogged field. Another, younger man worked beside him, and a dozen or so pots containing various flowers and shrubs sat in the shade of the bordering pines and spruce.

When Ash saw Hannah, he tucked the shovel handle under one arm and wiped the sweat from his brow with a rag he pulled from his back pocket. Then he took a long drink of water from a metal bottle hanging from a tree.

"Take a break," he said to the younger man. "Come back in ten."

"No muddy boots in the inn!" Hannah called after him, then turned to survey the work he and Ash had done. When she'd left that afternoon, this area had been a mess of rocks, mud, and grasses. Now a pile of rocks and boulders sat stacked in the field, and a ten-by-ten area had been turned over.

"This is crazy," Ash said, following her gaze. "You know that, right? Can't you just put up some bee houses and hummingbird feeders and call it a day?"

"Bee houses can be breeding grounds for molds and diseases. Ditto hummingbird feeders if they're not cleaned regularly. It's better to work with what we have and try to re-create a natural habitat."

"You know what else would help? Digging a big pond here."

Hannah smiled. "We have a big pond."

"I'm well aware of that." Ash was about her age, but at times he seemed younger than she and at others far older. Today he was acting like a grouchy old man. "I'm just saying that this seems like it will take years to really work."

"I choose to be positive."

"You call it positive, I call it naïve. But, hey, you're paying the bills."

Hannah shook her head. "I'm impressed you decided to come here instead of taking Brian Lewis's money."

"I know you're anxious to get this done. Besides, there was too much commotion over there today for anyone to get anything done."

"Commotion? Why were you there? I thought you were turning down the job."

"I went over there to tell him."

Hannah repositioned herself under the shade of the trees. "What was going on?"

Ash gestured toward the house. Hannah saw Rebecca there on her hands and knees, weeding a flower bed, her black curls held back from her face by an oversized barrette, her thin body ensconced in brown Carhart overalls. Other than Rebecca, though, no one was there. Even the Airstream was silent.

"Rebecca?"

"Your guests." Ash took another drink of water and hung the bottle back in the tree, tucked in the branches where it would stay cooler. "They're at Ezra's, presumably checking out their inheritance."

126

"What could they possibly be doing there?"

"When I left, they were talking to Brian Lewis. I guess he was already making his pitch to buy the place. He wants to knock down the Victorian and build a more modern guesthouse that he can also rent out. They were traipsing all around the property, even going through Ezra's outbuildings. Did you know Ezra has an old car back there?"

Hannah nodded. Ezra had three outbuildings on his property: a toolshed that housed his gardening tools, a ramshackle barn with an old tractor, a chipper, and an ancient Buick inside, and a small greenhouse, vine-covered and long since returned to nature. Ezra hadn't gone back there often, but he kept his garbage in the barn and away from bears, so Hannah had been in there a few times while helping out around his house.

"I don't get it," she said now. "Why were they at the property?"

"Laying the groundwork for a fat deal?"

"Isn't it kind of presumptuous to negotiate the sale of a property you don't own yet?"

"Well, the oldest one—Waylen?—seemed pretty intent on wheeling and dealing. Brian was laying out his vision and I heard a few figures bounced around." Ash's eyebrows shot up. "*Big* figures."

Hannah wasn't surprised. Other than Henry Yarrow, who wanted to expand the ski resort, no one local had the means Brian Lewis had. No one, that was, except her father.

"So why couldn't you have worked at Brian's?" she asked casually. "It's not like a few people on Ezra's property would interfere."

"That's what you'd think. Then Henry showed up to look at the place, and Chad followed. Soon they were all talking and drinking beer and discussing the options for that old house. They were in my way, and, anyway, I couldn't stomach it. The man isn't even in the ground yet."

Hannah agreed. It took a lot of nerve to treat other people's property that way. She felt violated on Ezra's behalf. When Teddy had first told her about the will, she thought it was strange that Ezra had chosen her as his heir over his own relatives. But if this was how his family was behaving, maybe he had known exactly what he was doing after all.

"Do you think they're still over there?" Hannah asked.

"Why, looking to cash in on Ezra's misfortune too?" As soon as Ash said the words, his eyes narrowed with regret. "Oh man, Hannah, I'm sorry. I know you're not like that. I think today just rattled me. If that was what Ezra was dealing with . . . I never liked the guy much, but his personality makes a hell of a lot more sense now." He reached a gloved hand out and touched her arm. "Forgiven?"

"Forgiven." Hannah forced a smile.

"I really am sorry. Look, we're going to head out of here soon, once we get these plants in the ground. Is there anything else you need me to do before we leave?"

Hannah said no, and Ash picked the shovel back up. On her way inside, Hannah stopped to check in on Rebecca. The older woman was weeding the hostas Hannah had inherited from Chad in the shady section of the side bed. Fat bumblebees buzzed around her, and a hummingbird hovered by a purple hosta flower just a few feet from Rebecca's head. If Rebecca noticed, she didn't let on.

"Can I get you something to drink?" Hannah asked her. "It's hot out today."

Rebecca jumped, clearly startled. It took her a moment to transition from her thoughts to the present. "No, no, thank you. I'm fine."

"Did anyone call or come by while I was out?"

Rebecca crinkled her nose apologetically. "I'm afraid not. The guests were out most of the day, so other than replacing some towels and putting out the food you prepared, I've been working out here."

Hannah looked at the beds. They were thriving under Rebecca's bright-green thumb, and Hannah couldn't be more pleased. Clearly, though, Rebecca preferred gardening to inside work. She steered clear of the human guests whenever she could, which made her less useful inside.

"I also walked Moose," Rebecca offered. "I heard him whining."

Moose. Hannah was still getting used to having a dog. It was his dinnertime, and he'd want to go for a walk that evening, keeping to Ezra's schedule. Maybe she'd take him over to Ezra's house tonight. They could take a stroll down Main Street. She hated the idea that the vultures had been on Ezra's property unattended. She hated it even more that she was already feeling a frisson of possessiveness over the property.

"Are you okay if I leave early today?" Rebecca asked. "Mark is taking me to Dorset. We're going to the theater to celebrate our anniversary."

"Ooh, congratulations. How long have you been married?"

Rebecca shrugged. "A long time."

"That's certainly reason for celebration."

Rebecca looked up from the plant she was pruning and held a hand over her eyes, shading them from the sun "Some would say so."

Rebecca had lived in Jasper all her life. She and her husband Mark once owned the little general store on Main Street, but they had sold it a few years back. Rebecca had applied for the job at the inn when Hannah first opened, and she had been Hannah's reluctant wing woman ever since she was hired. In those two years,

Rebecca had rarely talked about Mark or the general store they used to own, even in passing, so Hannah was surprised by the request.

"Of course you can go," Hannah said. "Enjoy the show."

Rebecca gave her a watery smile. "I don't see that happening. Not much into crowds."

"You can stroll around Dorset, have a bite to eat. It's a beautiful town."

Rebecca looked unconvinced, and Hannah suspected that, given a choice, she would have preferred to stay with the bees and the hummingbirds over visiting the Dorset theater with her husband, anniversary or not.

*   *   *

Hannah walked the mile and a half to Ezra's house, Moose in tow. The old dog seemed happy to be going for a walk, and he pulled Hannah down Dirt Road, trotted next to her on Snowflake Lane, and by the time they got to Main Street was moseying along behind her. As Hannah approached Ezra's house, she felt her entire body tense. The last time she'd been here, he'd been alive, and everything had been different. Although derelict, the old Victorian had had some life to it, and now it looked empty, listless, and sad.

You're attributing human feelings to a house, she chided herself. But it was true. Without Ezra, the house was a ruined shell. *Maybe a house needs people*, Hannah thought. This house seemed to be in mourning.

Legs and heart feeling heavy, Hannah climbed the steps to the front entrance. She still had the key Ezra had given her, and as she started to use it, she noticed the broken screen door was gone and the lock was shiny and new. She tried the key, and it didn't fit.

Someone had changed the lock.

Hannah and Moose walked around the outside of the house, stepping over a pile of old tires and a broken wagon along the way. The lock on the basement door was broken, and Ezra had never bothered to fix it. As Hannah drew closer, though, she noticed a padlock on the basement door too. Unless she wanted to climb a rotted trellis to an upstairs window, or drop nine feet from a basement window, she wasn't getting in. Now she knew why the vultures had been there: to stake their claim.

Hannah walked back to the porch and sat down heavily on the front steps. The air was thick with the scent of wild roses, which grew in heathen masses around the porch. Their fragrance reminded her of Ezra, who'd refused to trim the flowers his wife had planted. Night was descending, and the setting sun lit up the western sky in brushstrokes of orange, yellow, and red. The house wasn't beautiful—far from it—but there was a coziness to its place on Main Street, and the view of Devil's Mountain reminded Hannah of all she loved about Vermont.

Hannah was about to call Teddy to see who'd authorized the lock changes when Moose started to bark ferociously. He strained at his leash, lunging toward the back of the house and pulling Hannah to her feet. Hannah turned the corner to see Rob, Waylen, and Brian walking from the direction of the barn. At the sight of the dog, Brian drew back and the cousins stopped in their tracks.

"Put that dog away," Brian called. "He's dangerous."

Moose lunged toward the men, his barking loud and frenzied. Foam spewed from his open mouth. Hannah had never seen the dog so worked up. She was having trouble holding the leash.

"What are you doing here?" she asked the men.

"We could ask you the same question," Waylen responded, eyeing Moose. "This is our house."

"Not officially," Hannah said.

"It's just a matter of time," Waylen responded.

"You had no right to change the locks."

Waylen laughed. "On the contrary. We had every right to protect our property. Who knows how many keys Ezra gave out."

"Did Ezra's lawyer give you permission to change the locks? He's the executor."

Rob had the decency to look uncomfortable with the question. He mumbled something to Waylen, who nodded his agreement. The two cousins came forward, and Moose lunged again. All three men took a step back.

Waylen said, "How about we handle this tomorrow through Teddy Smith, when it's daylight and you're not holding a rabid dog? Otherwise, I may have to call the police."

"Go ahead and call them," Hannah replied. "Neither Moose nor I is doing anything wrong."

"You're trespassing," Brian said. He was practically hiding behind Rob. "You and that dog should go."

Hannah looked from one man to another. She knew she had grounds to argue with them, but she also knew that arguing would mean showing her cards, which she wasn't ready to do.

"Tomorrow, then," she said. "You'll have to remove those locks."

As she was walking in the direction of the inn, a still agitated Moose beside her, she thought about the locks, the three men, and the easy camaraderie they seemed to share. Like chummy businessmen who'd just reached a deal? Only Moose's hostile reaction to seeing them made her wonder. Was Moose simply protecting his home—or was he reacting to the man who had killed Ezra?

Chapter Seventeen

Hannah awoke early the next morning so she could get to the farmers' market before the best vegetables were gone. She grew what she could at the inn, but there was some produce she liked to can for winter—like tomatoes and pickles—and others that she overindulged in while they were in season. Today she was hoping to grab some of Jenson farm's organically grown fresh ginger, cantaloupe, and garlic. Next year would be the inn's first season for garlic, but for now she had to rely on her neighbors.

Hannah climbed on her bike and rode into town, her mind still on her encounter with the men at Ezra's house the day before. She arrived at the market, which was held at the town's small park, a little early, so she parked her bike, grabbed the basket liner that doubled as a grocery bag, and walked over to Nadia's booth where the older woman was laying out cookies, biscuits, muffins, and loaves of freshly baked bread on her signature linens from Provence. She smiled when she saw Hannah, her dark eyes crinkling.

"Let me give you a hand." Hannah reached for one of the empty baskets, and following Nadia's lead, started filling it with crisp-crusted baguettes. After that, she moved on to the cinnamon raisin scones, placing them in a yellow-fabric—lined basket. "I don't know how you do this all day and stay slim."

"I happen to think carbs are the secret to a long and healthy life." Nadia handed Hannah a thin slice of rosemary and garlic focaccia. "Carbs, eating seasonally, and small portions. Try this."

Hannah bit into the bread. "Heavenly!—making it nearly impossible to eat small portions."

Nadia laughed. "I figured you'd be here, so I made you some cider donuts too."

Hannah clapped. Nadia made the world's best cider donuts, fragrant and soft. "I'd say I'll take them all, but I don't want to be selfish. How about a dozen? I'll put them out for my guests."

Nadia wrapped a dozen donuts in parchment paper and set them aside. "Anything else?"

Hannah ordered a loaf of the cranberry-orange walnut bread and paid Nadia. "That's it for now. Off to pick up some veggies and then back to the inn. It'll be a busy day."

Hannah waited in line at the Jenson's stand, picked out her ginger, garlic, and cantaloupe, and then threw in a few Hungarian red peppers. She decided to make a tour of the stands to grab some breakfast—the focaccia had only whetted her appetite. A young man with a tufty beard, wearing jeans and a blue and black Baja hoodie, was playing an acoustic version of "Wagon Wheel" under a maple tree at the end of the market. Three white-haired old men and one older woman sat in semicircle near him, listening, talking, and eating.

The market brought not only locals doing their weekly food shopping but tourists and second homeowners as well. Children played in the playground while their parents shopped, and adults and teens milled about the various stalls, perusing art, pottery, and handmade scarves and jewelry, and sampling the food offerings. Large rattan baskets hooked over arms overflowed with fresh corn and other vegetables, and families sat on picnic blankets on the outskirts of the green lawn, eating and laughing. With the sun shining and the lush green mountains and forests in every direction, Hannah understood the appeal. This was effectively her grocery store, but for some it was a novelty. She chided herself for ever taking her hometown for granted.

"Hannah," Kendra and Jay Birk said in unison as they passed her carrying two large bags of goods.

Hannah nodded her hello. Behind them she saw Henry Yarrow standing by Mia Lopez's jewelry stand. She was about to stop to talk with him when she noticed he wasn't alone. Brian Lewis stood with him, and the two were deep in heated conversation. Hannah heard Ezra's name mentioned, but when she got closer, both men clammed up.

"Hannah," Henry murmured. He glanced around uneasily.

Brian Lewis suddenly found Mia's sterling-silver pins fascinating. He pulled a beefy hand through his salt-and-pepper hair and fumbled for his phone, moving away from Henry and distancing himself from Hannah.

"Gentlemen," Hannah said through clenched teeth. She walked on, but as she rounded a curve to visit Tom's Taco Express for a couple of barbequed jackfruit tacos, she bumped into Mark Folly, Rebecca's husband.

"Hey," she said. "Is Rebecca here too?"

"She's around somewhere." Mark smiled broadly. He had perfectly white, capped teeth that contrasted with his weathered tanned skin. His personality reminded Hannah of someone who made his living inside the DC beltway. "She sure loves working at the inn."

"The gardens love *her*."

Mark nodded. "My Rebecca has the greenest of thumbs."

Hannah had only met Mark a few times when he owned the general store, and back then he had mostly eyed her with suspicion as she and her teenage friends walked around the shop. She glanced around now, looking for a way to end the awkward conversation.

Mark beat her to it. He lifted a bag containing fresh ears of corn. "I'd better go. Take care of my wife, okay?"

Hannah agreed. As she continued on her way to Tom's Tacos, she felt the heaviness of someone's stare on her back. She turned around and got a momentary glimpse of Rebecca standing between Mia's jewelry stand and Milly's Flowers. Rebecca was watching her husband as he headed toward the parking area, but Hannah could have sworn that a moment before she had been watching her.

* * *

"Don't be ridiculous," Reggie said over the phone later that morning. "You make it sound like Moose picked the killer out of a lineup. That dog has cloudy eyes. He probably didn't know who he was barking at."

"Bullshit," Hannah said, cradling the phone to her ear. Outside, Rebecca was tending the herb garden. Hannah watched through the window as the older woman methodically drew a scuffle hoe over the earth between the plants, creating a small pile of grassy weeds that she'd throw into the compost bin. "You should have seen him salivating to get to Brian."

"Let's just say I humor you and agree that Moose was going after Ezra's killer. Why Brian? The nephews were there too."

"Brian has a lot to gain. If he tears down the house, he can build a second income property and get rid of an eyesore that's bringing down the market value of his current house. He even offered Ash a job. Preparing ahead of time."

"This is all conjecture," Reggie said.

"Not really. You should have seen the three of them walking around like they already owned the place. Rob and Waylen were clearly seeing dollar signs, and Brian looked like a fox that'd just finished off a chicken. Then this morning I saw him cozied up to Henry. Smug and happy that he would be the chosen buyer. I bet he's planning to sell Henry enough of Ezra's land to put a road in that would lead up to the resort, thereby recouping some of his outlay."

"Even if Brian and Henry are trying to work some deal, that doesn't make either of them a killer."

Hannah left the window and walked to her bedroom. While changing into a pair of work shorts and an old T-shirt, she said, "I saw Brian staring at Ezra's house the day Ezra was killed. He was carrying binoculars and an envelope. I think he'd made another offer—an offer Ezra refused. Brian looked angry when I saw him last night, and this morning he wouldn't even acknowledge my presence. What if the day Ezra was murdered, Brian confronted him, and when Ezra refused to sell to him again, he killed him."

Reggie sighed. "That still doesn't explain why Ezra and the killer were out by Devil's Pond. I don't exactly picture Brian Lewis traipsing around in the wilderness."

Hannah was about to protest, then stopped herself. Reggie was right. Brian wouldn't go into the swamp voluntarily. She'd never seen him wear anything other than loafers, and in all the years he'd owned that house, she had never seen him do anything more athletic than play golf. "How do you explain Moose? Maybe it was Waylen or Rob who got the dog so agitated."

"Or maybe it was circumstance," Reggie said. "The dog is old, his eyesight is bad. He was protecting you and his home, pure and simple."

"I'm not sure it *is* that simple."

"You have an inn to run, Hannah. Let it go."

Only Hannah couldn't let it go. Her next call was to Teddy Smith, Ezra's lawyer. Even if no one would listen to her, Teddy needed to change the locks on Ezra's house. When he didn't answer, Hannah called out the window to let Rebecca know she was going out. She would head over to the Teddy's office to talk to him herself.

*   *   *

Hannah parked in Teddy's driveway, next to a now familiar Porsche Cayenne. As she entered the law office, she heard the vehicle owner's voice, shrill and angry. She stood in the waiting room, debating whether to leave, but their conversation caught her attention.

"There is no way that's true. No damn way, Teddy."

"I'm afraid it is true."

"Who the hell else would he leave it to? It's not like he had anyone else in his life." Silence, then, "Damn it, just tell me who he left our property to."

"It's not your property. This was Ezra's property to do with as he pleased."

"Hogwash. Tell me who's inheriting. A nonprofit? That innkeeper girlfriend of his?"

Calmly, Teddy said, "The police are performing a murder investigation, and probate is just under way. Once things are settled, it will all become public knowledge."

Hannah heard what sounded like a fist slamming into a wall. The bang reverberated across the small space.

"Take it down a notch, Waylen," Teddy said, a hint of old, hot-tempered Teddy just under the surface.

"Don't tell me what to do, not while you're keeping what's rightfully mine."

"Waylen, dude, be reasonable—"

"I'll be back with my own lawyer."

Hannah heard footsteps coming toward her. She rushed back out the door, counted to five, and walked back inside, yelling, "Teddy!" as she entered, trying to look as though she hadn't just eavesdropped on their conversation; but she was rattled by what she'd heard.

Both men were in the waiting area. Teddy stood in the doorway to his office, swathed in rumpled cotton and wearing an annoyed expression. Waylen fumed by the door, fists clenched, his mouth an angry, crooked smear.

They looked at her and said, in unison, "Hannah."

Hannah straightened her spine, held her head up. "Teddy, I need to talk to you."

Waylen growled, "Get in line."

Teddy cleared his throat. "Actually, Waylen, I have a meeting scheduled with Ms. Solace, so you and I are finished for today."

Waylen's gaze ricocheted between Hannah and Teddy. After a tense, steamy moment, he opened the door and left, calling out behind him, "I'm not done with this, Smith."

Teddy made a hand-washing gesture. "My savior in wrinkled cotton," he said to Hannah, eyeing her work clothes.

"I could say the same about you."

Teddy laughed. "Touché. I imagine you're here about Ezra as well."

"I'm here about Waylen. And Brian Lewis and Rob Long. The three of them were at Ezra's yesterday, poking around the place unattended. They even changed the locks on his house."

"They can't do that."

139

"No, they can't, but they did."

"I'll have them changed again today." Teddy looked out the window as Waylen was getting into his Porsche. "That guy really believes the world owes him."

"He certainly believes Ezra owed him." Hannah paused, weighing her next question. "You didn't tell him about me?"

"Of course not."

"Why?"

"Because we don't need more trouble, and as executor of the property, it's my duty to protect the estate. Part of that means going through the probate process and determining the correct heir, which could be drawn out in this case given the murder investigation and the family." He turned toward Hannah, the lines around his eyes deepening. "You know people could find out anyway. They often do."

"I know," Hannah said. "In the meantime, though, I'd like to get into Ezra's house."

"You don't have any claim to that house until probate is complete."

"I don't want anything, Teddy. I just want to look around, see if anything . . . anything explains what happened."

"The police have already been through it."

"I know." Hannah looked out into the driveway, where Waylen was still sitting in the idling Porsche. "I thought I might see something they missed. Besides, I have Moose, and I need to collect some of his things."

Teddy shrugged his shoulders. "Well why didn't you lead with that? Meet me there tomorrow at nine sharp. I'm playing a round of golf with your—" He looked suddenly apologetic. "I tee-off at ten-thirty."

"Don't bother telling my father I said hi," Hannah said. "But I'll see you tomorrow."

"He misses you, you know. Why don't you give him another chance?"

Hannah studied Teddy's face for signs that he was being sincere. When she was young, Teddy had intimidated her. His confidence, the certainty with which he faced every decision, made him seem larger than life, and when around him, Hannah had felt insignificant and insufficient. He would defend her on some stupid charge and then act like it was no big deal, all the while making sure she knew her place in the grand pecking order. As her father's buddy, he could do no wrong, and even though he was supposed to be on her side, she always knew it was her father he was protecting.

But he no longer scared her. Standing there now in his wrinkled denim shirt and khakis, reading glasses hanging from a lanyard, she was reminded that he was human. Her father was human too. Neither one of them could make her feel small now without her consent.

"If he misses me so much, tell him he knows where I live."

Teddy sighed. "Do you need some help with him?" Teddy pointed through the door at Waylen. "It would appear he's waiting for you."

"I've dealt with worse."

Hannah left the law office and headed to her car. Waylen waited until she had her car door open before climbing out of the SUV and accosting her.

He said, "Why are you here?"

"To talk to Teddy."

"Is this about yesterday—the locks?"

"It's none of your business."

Waylen spoke through his teeth, forcing restraint. "Are you the mystery heir? Is that why you're here?"

Hannah slid into the driver's seat. "I'll see you at the inn Waylen." She tried to close the door, but Waylen wedged a thick calf between her and the door.

"Were you sleeping with him? Or maybe you just played nursemaid, pretending to care about him to get in his good graces? He was sick, you know. I just found that out from the police, but I'm sure you were already aware." He leaned closer. "What did you have to do to get him to name you in his will?"

"Back away. Now."

"Maybe he left everything to that damn dog, and you get the dog? Is that how the two of you worked it out?"

His hand was on the roof of her car, and he was leaning so close she could smell the onions he'd had with breakfast.

"I said step away, Waylen. Now. I'm warning you," Hannah said between clenched teeth. She looked up to see Teddy coming outside, but she held up her hand. She'd said she could handle Waylen, and she could. Thinking of Louis Driver and his comical attempt to protect his house, she reached under the passenger seat and grabbed the cannister of bear spray she kept in the car for hikes. She held it up to Waylen's face. "Unless you want me to use this, I suggest you get the hell back in your car."

Waylen's eyes widened at the sight of the bear spray. Hannah released the safety catch, and he seemed to deflate before her eyes. Grumbling something unintelligible, he backed away from the driver's side. Hannah waited until he'd pulled out of the driveway before returning the bear spray to its spot.

Teddy tapped on the window. She rolled it down.

"Are you okay?" he asked.

"I'm fine."

"Good move on the bear spray."

"I'll see you tomorrow, Teddy."

"I didn't tell him anything."

"I know." Once Teddy was back inside, Hannah put her head down on the steering wheel. It hurt. Her stomach hurt. Waylen was her guest at the inn, and she had just threatened him with bear spray. She imagined how that Google review would read. And then there was the small matter of the will. Uncorroborated or not, Waylen would tell his cousins that she was Ezra's heir, and then the real battles would begin.

Chapter Eighteen

Hannah spent the rest of the morning outside working in the gardens. Anger at Waylen still gnawed at her, and she knew that the best way to relieve it was through physical labor. She and Rebecca had planted a three sisters garden in the spring, and after weeding for an hour, she plopped a basket on the ground and began picking green beans off the climbing vines that were wrapped around the maturing stalks of corn.

The three sisters garden had been Rebecca's idea, and looking at it now, Hannah was grateful for her resourcefulness. A traditional Native American planting method in which corn, beans, and squash were grown together, it saved space. Each vegetable had a specific purpose. The corn gave the climbing beans stability, the beans provided much needed nitrogen for the soil, and the squash leaves covered the soil, shading roots and preventing the growth of weeds. Hannah had read about the method, but it was Rebecca who had carefully planted the seeds in the right formation, adding compost and water, and who had tended the garden until each of the three "sisters" was thriving. In addition to the baskets of food the garden would bring, the beans and corn attracted honeybees, which were now buzzing around Hannah in this sunny corner of the inn's property.

Hannah sat back on her heels, the basket nearly full. She added two yellow squash before moving on to the tomato garden. Here, too, they had used companion planting, and the sweet scent of basil filled her nostrils as she picked tomatoes and fresh herbs from between the French marigolds. The marigolds attracted an array of pollinators, including bees and hoverflies, which were busy doing their jobs—keeping away destructive bugs like aphids. She and Rebecca had created a small ecosystem that worked, and as a result she had more produce than she could use at the inn.

I'll take some to Ezra, she thought before reminding herself that he was no longer there to receive vegetables, or anything else. *Who am I kidding?*, she thought, *he would have complained anyway*. She pulled off her canvas gloves and rubbed her eyes. Ezra's passing still felt surreal, as though the man would show up any minute, cantankerous as ever.

Hannah called Moose, who'd been sleeping in a shady spot by the inn, and trudged back inside. She'd make a vegetable stew from the tomatoes, squash, and green beans, something she could serve later that afternoon with some crusty bread.

Hannah's phone rang, and she was surprised to hear Louis Driver's voice on the other end.

"If you're still investigating Ezra's death, Nancy Drew, meet me at my shop." He paused, cleared his throat, and gave her directions. "Be quick about it. I have something important to show you."

There would be no time to cook today.

* * *

A Vintage Look shared shopping space with a pottery store and a small jewelry boutique. Set back from the road, the one-story building made up for its charmless cinderblock exterior with a dark-green-and-white awning, wooden park benches, and terra-cotta pots overflowing with a candy-colored assortment of flowers. The large storefront window was lined with male mannequins wearing a variety of vintage formalwear. Outside the entrance, an antique copper urn doubled as an umbrella stand, and one bright-yellow umbrella protruded gaily from its interior.

Bells alerted Louis to Hannah's presence as she opened the door. She found him in the back of the store, pinning a three-piece pinstriped gray flannel suit onto a mannequin.

"Fall will be here before you know it," he said, talking around a pin in his mouth. "No one is thinking linen and seersucker right now."

Hannah wasn't sure any men near Jasper were thinking seersucker right now period, but she didn't say so—especially because he himself was dressed from head to toe in light-blue seersucker. Instead, she said, "Nice shop."

Louis's eyebrows shot up. "Nice? You're looking at forty years'-worth of collecting, sorting, and mending. This place is a master-piece. My retirement dream."

Hannah had to admit that the place had a certain *je ne sais quoi*. The landscaping charm extended inside, with antiques, plants, and vintage lighting used as the backdrop to some stunning and colorful men's suits. There was no musty secondhand smell—just the faintest hints of pipe tobacco and sandalwood. It was like shopping in your grandfather's study. She was impressed. She was no fashion expert, but she figured Louis would have better luck selling his goods in New York City.

"What did you want to show me?" Hannah asked.

Louis took his time pulling the last pin from his mouth and using it to secure the suit to the mannequin. When he was finished, he walked to the checkout counter, where a floral box was sitting on top of the walnut surface. Slowly, he pulled the lid off and removed a stack of envelopes from inside. They were secured with a rubber band, which he pulled off one by one with agonizing deliberateness. He sorted through the stack, selecting three envelopes.

"This box contains my dear deceased wife's written memorabilia. Love letters from me, which I shall not share, birthday cards from Molly, a few letters from her parents, and these." He handed Hannah the envelopes.

Hannah opened the first one. It was a letter from Ezra to Anita written on plain white paper. She recognized his chicken-scrawl handwriting. The message was terse: *Help your sister, Anita. She won't help herself, and she won't listen to me. If you won't listen to me over the phone, and you won't see me, I figure the only thing left to do is appeal to your better nature in a letter.* The note was undated, but the smudged envelope, yellowed with age, bore the postmark April 12, 2003.

The second letter was similar but ended with: *You know this isn't my fault. Do something.*

The third letter was a little more heartfelt, a little more pleading in tone: *The only person on this great earth she might listen to is you. I know she has a wall around her right now, but I think you can break through it. Give her that chance. Whatever you think of me, do it for her. Please.*

Hannah stared at the letters in her hand. They were postmarked within months of each other. "When did Molly die?"

"About six months after that last letter was sent."

"And you didn't know about these before?" She handed the letters back to him.

"My wife was hardly the sentimental sort. But after you visited, I decided to look through her belongings—the stuff I kept, anyway—to see if there could be some clue. I found these." He scrunched his brow. "What do you think?"

"What do I think?" Hannah threw her hands up. "I have no idea what to make of these. I think the important question is what do *you* think?"

Clearly Louis had been waiting to be asked that very question, because he took off his fedora, leaned against the counter, and stroked his beard—basically doing everything short of striking an actual thinker's pose.

"I told you Molly became withdrawn. I also told you that Anita blamed Ezra. Anita wasn't the sharing type, and she never mentioned these letters, but she did keep them, which made me wonder. Did she feel guilty for not doing more? What had happened that Molly wouldn't listen to Ezra but maybe would have listened to her sister?"

"You have no idea what happened?"

"I always assumed she was ill—mentally or physically. And that very well might have been the case. But here's the thing. No one, and I mean *no one*, went to my dear Anita for nurturing or a pep talk. She was more a drill sergeant than a grandmotherly type, if you catch my drift. If Ezra was desperate enough to ask Anita for help, he was looking for a kick in the derriere."

"Which meant that Molly was feeling bad about something she had control over."

Louis looked pleased. "Exactly. He would never ask Anita to lay into Molly over heart disease or clinical depression. Ezra was a man of science. If he wanted the big guns, it was because Molly was being stubborn."

"Did Anita comply?"

"Your guess is as good as mine, but things between him and Anita only soured further after that, until they weren't talking at all."

Hannah watched as Louis placed the envelopes back on the pile and secured everything with the rubber band. "Why are you telling me all of this, Louis?"

Louis replaced the lid and met Hannah's gaze. "Because if I told the police, they would think I was a silly, meddling old fool. But you, Nancy, are both interesting and interested, and I figured you would see this as something worth sharing."

Hannah nodded. He was right.

"What's next?" Louis asked, clearly enjoying the challenge.

"The truth is, I'm not so sure this has anything to do with Ezra's murder. At least not directly."

"Perhaps not," Louis said. "But it is interesting that Ezra came to ask forgiveness right before his murder. What was he seeking forgiveness for? The fights he'd had with my late beloved during this timeframe?" He tapped the box. "Coincidence?"

What Hannah found interesting was the timing of the correspondence. The first letter had been sent more than twenty years ago, which also coincided with the timing of the sale of Ezra's land to her father. Whether these events were related she had no idea, but she knew who might.

However, she wasn't willing to share any of this with Louis, so she said, "It smells really good in here—as though a highbrow men's salon were a scent."

Louis glanced around conspiratorially. He reached behind the counter and pulled out a diffuser. "Sandalwood." Then he led her to the small office at the back of the store. On his desk was an organic soy candle from Hazel & Bee Organics. The scent was Rose Tobacco. "I may cheat a little. It's all in the marketing after all."

"Clever."

Louis smiled. "The upside? I'm supporting a Vermont business, and no one gets lung disease. Besides, who doesn't love a vintage suit that smells like their grandfather's closet?"

* * *

Hannah drove toward the inn and thought about those letters. The timing was strange, true—and the very fact that Ezra had written the letters, clearly pleas for help on Molly's behalf, seemed out of character. Plus, if Louis was to be believed, and there was no reason *not* to believe him, the fact that Anita had held onto those letters also seemed odd.

But what did any of that have to do with Ezra's murder?

Probably nothing, Hannah thought. It would be easy to pin his death on one of his greedy heirs. They certainly had motive, and any of them could have had opportunity. For that matter, Brian Lewis, Cheating Chad, and Henry Yarrow all had motive as well—the potential sale of the land to them by the heirs, something Ezra steadfastly refused to consider. A more tenuous motive, perhaps, but motive nonetheless. And then there was the potential for a simple act of aggression brought about by rage. Ezra could be infuriating. Any one of those men could have lost his temper and might have done the unthinkable on the spur of the moment.

But this is all conjecture, Hannah thought. *And none of it explains why Ezra made me his sole heir*. Hannah had a gut-punch feeling that her situation was somehow tied into all of this. Ezra had been sick, and though he'd been trying to make amends with his brother-in-law, he had cut his entire family out of his will. *Why?*

Hannah pictured the expensive bourbon and Ezra's death-day bike trip to her dad's house. John Solace seemed as entangled in this story as anyone. Hannah sighed. *Perhaps it's time we had a chat, Dad.*

She turned the car around, dreading what lay ahead.

Chapter Nineteen

John Solace lived in what could have been a plain vanilla McMansion had it not been for his wife's good taste. Instead, timber framing graced the interior of the sprawling modern farmhouse, and the outside did its best to complement the thirty-acre rolling hill on which it resided. With a nod to New England architecture, a steep-pitched red barn was attached to the house by a breezeway, its three doors opening, Hannah knew, to allow access to three cars, not farm equipment. The doors were situated along the roofline with no protective overhang so that every winter snow accumulated in front of the doors, making it harder to get the cars out. This design flaw gave Hannah a tiny bit of pleasure.

She parked in front of the barn and sat idling for a few minutes, debating whether she had the courage to go inside. She hadn't been here in nearly ten years. When John had purchased the two-hundred-acre parcel from Ezra, he'd split it into eleven plots, keeping the best one—the one with the most scenic view—for himself. He'd sold the others as part of a development deal, and then, several years later, he'd used the considerable proceeds to build his own house. Hannah's mother had been reluctant to move out of their small chalet, but John had enticed her with promises of big budgets for decorating and a gourmet kitchen.

In the end, Bev had gotten design freedom and a kick-ass kitchen, but it had cost her in the form of John's fidelity. He'd never admitted it, but rumors can flow in a small town like the current in a raging river. John and one of the architects. John and the young archeologist assigned to study the site before they could build. And later, John and one of Bev's nurses. Some people can come into money and see it purely as an agent for change. For others, the change that occurs is in them, and that, to Hannah, was her father. As a working man, he'd been standoffish but reliable. As a rich man, he'd lost his way.

Ezra had been only one of his victims.

Hannah turned off the car engine and made her way to the front entrance. She thought about simply opening the door—*isn't that what normal families did?*—but decided to ring the bell. A woman answered on the second buzz. She was wearing black pants and a white shirt that only intensified the red of her sunburned face. She looked to be in her sixties but had the wiry physique of a runner.

"Is John here?" Hannah asked.

"Who may I tell him is calling?"

"His daughter."

Hannah watched the older woman's mouth fall open in surprise. *She doesn't know he has daughters*, Hannah thought.

But that wasn't it.

"Come in, come in. He was just talking about you," the woman said. "He'll be thrilled you're here."

I'm not so sure about that, Hannah thought, but she followed the woman into the bowels of the house whose skeleton she knew well.

* * *

John Solace was sitting in a leather recliner, a mug of something steaming on the table next to him. The room was large—what they had called the great room growing up—and a ninety-eight-inch television was displaying a golf game in full surround sound.

When John saw Hannah, he clicked off the sound but kept the picture. "Hannah," he said. His voice was calm and even—no hint of the thrill his housekeeper had predicted.

"Dad."

"What brings you here?" He moved his seat into an upright position and pushed off the throw covering his legs. He was wearing shorts, and his skin showed pale and veiny beneath. "I wasn't expecting a visit."

"I should have called first."

The words hung there, unacknowledged. They both knew Hannah would never have called first. They both knew John might not have answered if she had.

"Where are my manners? Sit, sit." He pointed at a matching recliner on the other side of the small table, which also faced the television.

When she was young, the room had been filled with over-stuffed couches and extra wide armchairs—spaces to lounge in and relax and watch television. Her mother had preferred a warm, homey environment, and she'd managed to keep the large space simple and inviting. The new decor was cold and modern. There was a U-shaped leather couch in the room now too, but Hannah suspected it didn't see much use.

She sat on the edge of the recliner.

"What can Heather bring you to drink? Coffee? Iced tea?"

"Nothing, thank you."

John dismissed the housekeeper with a curt nod. When she had left the room, he cleared his throat. "I'd like to think this is a social call, but we both know that's not the case."

Hannah agreed, studying her father. He'd aged since she'd last seen him up this close. His hair, once thick and wavy and the color of walnuts, was now a dull gray. His face was clean-shaven, and she saw that underneath the beard he'd worn for decades lurked a weak chin and a stingy mouth. His eyes darted from her to the television and back again, restless.

"I'm here about Ezra."

John's eyes widened in surprise. "Why?"

"Because he was my friend, and now he's dead."

"I heard, and I'm very sorry, but what does that have to do with me?"

"You tell me."

Hannah's curt tone must have caught his notice, because he turned his attention away from the television. "Seriously? You don't talk to me for years, and now you come here accusing me of . . . of what, Hannah? You think I killed Ezra?"

"Someone saw him biking to your house the day he died."

"So what?"

"What did he want?"

"That's none of your business."

Hannah snorted. "I know you were at his house just weeks before his death."

"I was not."

"Who else drinks Boss Hog V? No one else in Jasper can afford the stuff."

John opened his mouth and closed it again. The hand holding the remote had a tremor. "Ezra and I had some unfinished business."

"Because you cheated him?"

John's nostrils flared. "I did no such thing. Is that what he told you?"

"We never discussed you. Ever."

"Well, I didn't cheat him out of anything. On the contrary, Ezra made out like a bandit on those deals. He could hardly complain."

"*Deals*?"

Only John was no longer listening. He stood up with some effort, paced to the other side of the room, and pulled a pipe from a drawer. He stuck the end in his mouth, unlit.

"Was he going around telling people I cheated him? The bastard."

Hannah stood up as well. Her father wasn't a particularly tall man, but he held himself with regal posture, and she forced herself to meet confidence with confidence.

"Ezra wasn't telling people anything. We just assumed. given the feud between you for all those years."

John said, "*We?*"

"Me and Reggie."

"Of course." John chewed the end of the pipe and ran a hand through his hair, shaking his head. "Your sister only sees the worst in me."

"Can you blame her?"

"No." John took an audible breath. Suddenly he looked tired and defeated, older than his seventy years. "What do you want from me, Hannah? If it's to relitigate the past, I'm not interested. If it's to forge a new future, one in which you can learn not to despise me, I'm all in."

"Can we start with the truth?" Hannah said softly. "Why were you at Ezra's, and why did he visit you?"

"I didn't cheat Ezra, but he never liked the terms of the deal I struck with the land I bought from him. He claimed I didn't keep my word."

"Did you?"

"Any agreement covering land has to be in writing."

"That doesn't answer the question."

John sat heavily down on the couch, wincing as he bent his legs. "Ezra thought I was buying the two hundred acres for myself, not to develop it. He was angry. It was his family's land, and he didn't want it used that way. I figured by making huge lots, I was honoring his wishes. It's not like I turned it into ski condos or two-acre housing units." He waved his pipe. "Believe me, I could have."

"That was the unfinished business?"

"Part of it. He wanted me to petition the town to create zoning laws that would prevent the owners of the other ten houses from splitting the lots into smaller lots and building more houses."

"And you said . . .?"

"I had already built those restrictions into the deeds. Think I want to look out and see fifty houses on this hillside? No way."

"That was it?"

"Pretty much."

"You said 'deals' earlier. What other deals did you and Ezra make?"

John waved the pipe again. "There was some other Grayson land involved. Ezra sold everything off at the same time."

Hannah had a feeling that her father was hiding something by the way he was avoiding eye contact, but she knew him well enough to know how stubborn he could be. If he didn't want to tell her, he wouldn't.

"Why do you care?" He asked her. "Let the police do their job."

"I'm a person of interest in the investigation."

John swiveled around to look Hannah in the eyes. "What for?"

"Ezra died on the inn's property, and I was the one who found him."

"That amounts to nothing."

"I guess the police don't think so."

Her father was studying her closely, looking for some indication that she was lying. She knew that scrutinizing look from her teenage years and despised it. She had toyed with telling him the whole truth—that Ezra had named her as his sole heir—but she didn't trust him with the information. Her one consolation was that clearly Teddy hadn't told him either. Maybe the lawyer *had* changed.

"Do you need an attorney?" her father asked.

"No, nothing like that. Like I said, he was my friend. I want to help."

There was skepticism in her father's gray eyes. "You have your mother's heart."

Hannah cocked her head, "And her lack of judgment about people?"

John smirked. "I didn't say that. You did." He rubbed his chin as though stroking a phantom beard. "Can we get together again some time?"

Hannah rose, accepting that as her cue to leave. "Maybe."

She heard the golf announcer's baritone before she'd even left the room.

* * *

"You did *what*?" Reggie asked.

"You heard me."

"Why in the devil would you think Dad would tell you anything useful? Or true, for that matter."

Hannah turned into the inn's parking area. She surveyed the cars, as she always did—just Ash and Rebecca here right now. No other guest cars. She said, "There's always hope."

"You call it hope, I call it foolishness." Reggie murmured something to someone else in the office. "Speaking of devils, Chad's here. I need to run."

"Tell him I said hi."

"I'll do no such thing." Reggie paused. Hannah thought she'd hung up, but then she said, "If it's Dad and Ezra's business dealings you want information about, I know someone who might be able to help."

"Do tell."

"Do you remember Tilda Howard?"

"Aunt Tilda? Mom's friend, the wildlife rehabber?"

"One and the same. She's a new member of our book club. She and Mom were friends, but more importantly, she was also friends with Molly. Maybe she would have some insights about what went down between the families."

"Why would she know?"

"I'm older than you, and I seem to recall some heated discussions between her and Mom around that time. They liked to chat about other people."

"Some might call that gossip."

"And some might say, 'thank you, sis, for the investigative tip.'"

Hannah smiled, considering the offer. She remembered Tilda as a high-cheek-boned goddess, as gifted with people as she was with animals. Hannah hadn't seen her in years—not since her mother's funeral. Tilda was friendly with Phyllis, so Hannah had assumed she might harbor similar resentments.

"I can't just crash your book club, Reg."

"Ah, but we're looking for a place to hold it, so you *could* offer us the veranda at the inn. Add some snacks, and I bet you'll have Tilda singing in no time."

Hannah was starting to feel manipulated. "If that's the price, I guess we can afford it."

"Great. We'll see you tonight at seven."

Hannah shook her head. "Wait a minute. You didn't say it was *tonight*."

"Gotta go! Make sure you have some of that hummus I like on hand. The members will love it."

Hannah hung up, exasperated. She didn't feel like cooking or getting the patio ready for a bunch of hungry women, but if it helped, she'd do it.

As she got out of the car, she saw clouds gathering overhead. The day's sunny disposition was quickly changing to moody and overcast. It seemed completely appropriate to the situation.

Chapter Twenty

"Why am I helping you spray down the patio furniture?" Ash asked as he lifted a metal chair to inspect for spiders, as instructed. "Who cares if this stuff is spotless? It's outside."

"The group of women my sister is bringing over, that's who. Book club night."

"Fun." Ash sprayed down the last of the heavy chairs and pulled it up around the eight-person table. "Want the bistro chairs too?"

Hannah nodded. The table could easily seat ten. If there were more than ten, her sister could pull up an Adirondack chair.

Ash wiped down one of the wet seats and sat down. "Happy with the plantings?"

"The meadow is coming along. Thank you."

"Wildflower and red clover seeding will have to wait until next spring."

Hannah nodded. She knew the meadow would take time, but it would be worth it. She looked out over the yard. While it was a far cry from the sterilized landscape Reggie had won three years ago, it fell far short of her vision for it.

The flower gardens surrounding the house, finally a buzzing, living, colorful ecosystem, would eventually extend into most of the yard, with paths of chipped wood and seats and benches and meditation gardens. The small herb and vegetable garden on the southeastern side of the property would be expanded, with more organic offerings to supply the inn all year long, and the berry-bush border—including animal-friendly winterberries and beautyberries—would eventually extend to Devil's Pond. A rain garden would be planted on the flat land near the driveway to capture and purify rainwater and snow melt. And of course, the wet field at the back of the property would be restored to a meadow capable of absorbing water while providing a habitat for local animals and insects.

Way down the line, Hannah wanted to add solar and a rainwater capture system. For now, baby steps. She was working with a limited budget and a lack of help.

"I appreciate your working with us," she said with some latent reluctance. "We're small, but eventually we'll be mighty."

"Once you get some guests?" Ash said with a glance at the driveway. "I think what you need is a marketing manager."

"Know one who would work for free?"

Even as Hannah joked, she knew Ash was right. None of this would matter without guests, because without guests there would be no funds to bring her vision to fruition.

"Why did you come back here?" Ash asked.

"To Vermont?"

"To Jasper."

Although Hannah had known Ash and his dad for decades, they rarely spoke on a personal level, and the question was unexpected. "Reggie offered me a deal I couldn't refuse."

Ash smiled, which brought out his dimples and the laugh lines around his eyes. "Yeah, we've all heard about her vendetta against Chad."

"His loss, my gain."

"That wasn't all, though, was it?"

"No, it wasn't." Hannah sat down on one of the bistro chairs and traced the table's ornate diamond pattern with her index finger. The table had belonged to her mother: one of the few things she had taken from her childhood home. "I was engaged. It didn't work out."

Ash didn't say anything. Maybe if he had, Hannah would have stopped talking, but in the face of his silence, she went on, "His name was Chris. We broke up three years ago. I took it hard, and Reggie was there to clean up the mess." Hannah met Ash's gaze. She saw curiosity and kindness in his eyes. "My sister is very good at cleaning up messes."

"Why did you break up?"

"Why all the questions?"

Ash shrugged. "Watching you out here cleaning these already clean tables made me curious. Not many people our age return to Jasper to open an inn."

"Not many people our age stay in Jasper without ever leaving."

Ash smiled. "Ain't that the truth."

Hannah watched Rebecca as she worked in the garden. She was picking rocks out of the dirt between the rows of kale and placing them in a bucket. Her headphones were on, and there was a rhythm to her work. Hannah wondered if it matched the music she was listening to.

Hannah continued, "I was supposed to go to law school after college. That was my father's plan, but my heart wasn't in it. Instead, I started working for a farm-animal sanctuary in Massachusetts."

"To spite him or because you loved it?"

"I guess a little of both. I started out as an animal caretaker, but eventually I moved into marketing—a glorified social media position—and then eventually took over their little inn. Chris was the head gardener. It was his job to make the property beautiful so donors would be happy to continue opening their wallets, but it was also his job to ensure balance in the environment. That is, food for the animals, plenty of native plantings, watering holes, that kind of thing."

"That's where you learned about this stuff."

"Chris is a landscape architect by trade. Anyway, one thing led to another, and eventually we got engaged. The thing was, Chris was hard to know—*really* know. I thought I would be the one to crack that shell. What I didn't realize is that he has a dark, troubled side, and sometimes it leads him to do reckless things."

Hannah's gaze moved from Rebecca to her own hands, now knotted and clenched, as though of their own accord. "Three years ago, in a fit of anger toward me for something stupid, he drove down a country road going 122 miles per hour. I screamed for him to slow down, to stop. He ignored me. He crashed his car with me in it."

"Oh God, Hannah. I had no idea. I'm sorry."

Hannah nodded. "Thanks. I ended up with a broken femur, a few broken ribs, and a punctured lung. Chris nearly died. He lost his driver's license, started drinking, lost his job at the sanctuary. I stayed with him for a while until Reggie came down and set me straight." Hannah stood up and began rearranging the chairs around the table. "I broke up with him shortly after that, but I stayed on at the sanctuary. Until Reggie called again, that is."

"And here you are."

Hannah glanced at Ash to see if he was giving her that teasing smile he'd perfected, but she saw only empathy. "And here I am."

"Happy to be back?"

Hannah took a deep breath before answering. *Was* she happy to be back? "Yes," she said truthfully. "Right now, there's nowhere I'd rather be."

* * *

Reggie and Peach showed up at 6:45. "Will you watch Peach?" Reggie asked Hannah.

"Sure, she can help me serve the hummus you wanted so badly."

"You're funny. She has a project she needs to finish for science camp."

"This is feeling like a setup all around."

Reggie handed her a canvas tote. "Don't be so dramatic. She needs to draw and identify three flowers. She's already picked and drawn two—black-eyed Susans and irises. Once she finishes coloring them in, she needs one more. I figured you were the perfect person to help her with that."

Hannah set her niece up at the island in the inn's kitchen. She gave her colored pencils and left her with a plate of crackers, grapes, and hummus. She also slipped an Oreo on the plate. "Don't tell your mother."

Peach giggled. "I won't, Aunt Hannah."

Hannah went outside and placed a crudité platter, hummus, crackers, and grapes on the long outdoor table. She had brought out wine glasses earlier, and Reggie opened the two bottles she'd brought along. She slipped the bottle of white into a bucket of ice.

"We're each supposed to bring a food item or a beverage. Wait until you see how many bottles of wine we end up with. A bunch of lushes."

Hannah smiled. "What did you read?"

"Read?"

"For the *book club*? What was tonight's selection?"

Reggie waved her hand. "I don't even know. I can't tell you the last time I read the book."

"Isn't the book sort of the point?"

Reggie gave her a look that said, "Oh, naïve little one," and poured herself a glass of sauvignon blanc. A car turned into the driveway, and a tall, well-dressed woman in head-to-toe beige climbed out of a Tahoe.

"That's Fawn," Reggie whispered. "She's new. Gets the award for dressing like her name."

Hannah left Reggie to her book-club members and returned to the inn. Peach had finished coloring the iris purple and was on to coloring a black-eyed Susan the same shade of purple.

"They're typically yellow, kiddo," Hannah said.

"I like purple."

"Isn't this a science project? Aren't you supposed to be dealing with facts?"

Peach clenched the pencil harder. "I like purple."

"Fine, purple black-eyed Susans it is."

While Hannah cleaned up the kitchen, she listened to the book-club chatter through the open window. She was waiting until she recognized Tilda Howard's honey-coated voice before going back outside. What she heard, though, was Maura's nasal pitch.

"Is this a party?" she was asking someone in the club.

"A book club," someone answered.

"Ooh, the wine looks good. I'll have some of that."

Hannah shook her head. She wondered how long it would take Reggie to boot Maura out of their soiree, and sure enough, two minutes later Maura entered the kitchen carrying a large glass of white wine. By the time she came in, Hannah had a fresh pot of coffee brewing.

When Maura saw the coffee, she raised her head, sniffed, and said, "My own little slice of sanity. Let me finish this appetizer and then on to the main course." She glanced at Peach's work. "Is that a coneflower?" She said, pointing to the black-eyed Susan.

"Nope," Peach said.

"It looks like a coneflower."

Hannah said, "It's a black-eyed Susan."

"But they're yell—" Maura started to say before seeing Hannah's firm head shake. "It's lovely."

"I know." Peach pushed the two papers aside. "Ready for the last flower, Aunt Hannah."

"Give me five minutes, kiddo. Why don't you go check on Moose?"

While Peach disappeared into the apartment, Hannah poured Maura a cup of coffee. "How are you doing?"

"As well as can be expected." She studied her nails. "It all feels kind of surreal. I don't know what to think."

"How are Waylen and Rob?"

"No idea. I haven't seen either of them since yesterday. They're like their own little boys' club. Have you seen them?"

"Here? No," Hannah said, feeling only a smidgen of guilt at the omission about seeing Waylen at Teddy's office. "Maybe they went hiking or something."

"Hiking?" Maura laughed. "Rob perhaps, now that Simone is back in New York, but you'd sooner catch Waylen doing his own laundry than hiking. He doesn't "do" wilderness. He doesn't even walk across a lawn."

"What does he do for fun?"

"Oh, I don't know. Roasts and eats small children, rips apart teddy bears, throws old women off bridges. He's a venture capitalist. One of those people who never has enough money or status."

"Not your favorite cousin?"

"Can you tell?" Maura took a sip of the hot coffee, smiled, and said, "Can you come to New York to make my coffee every day?"

Hannah smiled. "Sorry." She refilled Maura's mug.

"We're not *all* awful people," Maura said. "Rob, for example, is a good guy. He and Simone have had their issues, but he perseveres, no matter what happens; he's not nasty like Waylen."

"Did the three of you spend a lot of time together growing up?"

"It was mostly me and Rob. Waylen was older and a bully. We spent time with him when our parents forced us together." Maura looked toward the open window, where the book-club discussion was clearly heating up, judging from the rise in noise level. "And now if we co-own Ezra's house, we'll have to find a way to coexist." She shrugged. "I say sell the property to the highest bidder and get out of Dodge."

The front door opened, and Rob entered the inn. "What's happening out there?" he asked, aiming his thumb toward the patio. "I want whatever they're having."

"You'll have to settle for coffee," Maura said. "I was told more wine was off-limits. Did you hear from Ezra's lawyer?"

Rob shook his head. "Waylen was going to meet with him this morning. I haven't checked my e-mail or my messages yet. Doesn't look like Waylen's car is here, so I'm assuming he hasn't returned?"

"No one has seen him," Maura said. "I tried calling, but he didn't pick up."

Rob accepted a cup of coffee before walking back toward the inn's front entrance. "I'm tired. Call me when he gets back, and we can figure out our next steps."

"Wait, Rob—did the police question you today?" Maura asked.

"They caught up to me this morning. Bunch of questions." He glanced at Hannah before his attention skirted to his cousin. "Nothing major. You?"

"Same."

Rob shook his head. "I just want all this to be over."

With Rob gone, Maura held out her mug for one more refill. "I'm going to my room too. When Waylen gets back, will you ask him to call me?"

"Of course," Hannah said, hoping he'd decide to spend the night somewhere else. She would like to have some time before the truth about the will got out. Hannah watched Maura open the door to her suite before calling for Peach. "Let's get that last flower before it's dark."

Hannah followed an excited Peach into the yard. Peach immediately made a beeline for the flower gardens, carrying a small notebook and a pencil with her. Hannah detoured through the patio to say hello to Reggie's guests.

She recognized two-thirds of them, including two women who'd gone to school with Reggie, two women who worked with Reggie in real estate, and three old family friends. She was surprised to see a man there—a fifty-something with a crew cut and sharp jaw who was watching Reggie when Reggie wasn't looking. Hannah filed that away for later. But no Tilda.

Reggie shrugged apologetically. "She said she was coming."

Hannah knew it had been a longshot anyway. She was about to leave the boisterous group to join Peach when one of the women tugged on her shirt. She recognized her mother's old neighbor.

"It's good you came back to Jasper," the woman was saying. "Bev would want you here."

"I'm happy to be here."

"How's your father? We never see him anymore. Is he well?"

Something about her tone made Hannah think that Nancy was interested in more than her wealthy father's well-being. Feeling a little dirty, she said, "He's fine."

"I always enjoyed your father's—"

"Aunt Hannah! Come look! I found something!"

Glad for the distraction, Hannah excused herself and left the book club to see what had Peach so excited. Her niece was on the edge of the forest, not far from the path that led to Devil's Pond, where a cluster of Canada lilies extended their skinny stems well above the heads of the other border plants. Peach was jumping up and down, pointing between the tall plants.

"Look what I found! A painted rock!"

Hannah joined her niece. At first, she didn't see the rock, nestled as it was among the grasses and wildflowers that bordered the forest, but once her eyes adjusted, her stomach clenched, and a wave of dread coursed through her.

"Peach, step back," she said sternly. "Now."

"But Aunt Hannah, who painted that rock? Look at it. It's a science find."

"Peach, I said step back."

This time, Peach obeyed.

"Go to your mother and tell her to come down here with her cell phone, okay? This is very important." Peach's normally stormy eyes looked hurt and wet in the waning light. Hannah knelt down so they were eye to eye. "You found something very important."

"You're mad at me."

"I'm not mad at all. I just need you to get your mother."

When Reggie was finally by her side, Hannah showed her the rock. Large, flat, and jagged-edged, it was indeed red—coated with the brownish-red of dried blood. Bits of hair and grass were stuck to the surface, trapped in the blood.

"Damn," Reggie said under her breath.

Hannah covered her mouth with her hand. She was afraid she was going to be sick. "You might want to ask your book club to leave. Things will get interesting soon."

"Indeed."

Hannah looked at her sister, who was still staring into the brush. "I think your daughter found the murder weapon."

Chapter
Twenty-One

Noah was the first to arrive. He cordoned off the area and hustled everyone inside. Hannah watched from the kitchen window as a swarm of uniformed officers inspected the gardens and woods behind the inn, trampling flowers and destroying small habitats it had taken two years to cultivate.

She felt Reggie's hand on her shoulder, then her sister's arms wrapped around her from behind. Hannah felt tears welling up, but she refused to give in. Once the floodwaters started, they wouldn't stop. It was bad enough losing Ezra. Now she was losing the very thing he'd helped her to create.

"We'll help you fix it," Reggie whispered. "Me, Peach, Rebecca. We can get Ash too. You'll see. They need to do this, Hannah. It's their job."

Hannah knew what she was saying was true. Much as Hannah appreciated her sister's kindness, she also knew there was no fixing what was now broken. Only time and attention would heal the gardens. She just hoped they didn't find anything else out there. Who knew what else they would destroy?

About two hours later, Noah came inside. Once again, he met with each guest of the inn alone, in the sunroom, before moving on to Reggie and Peach and, finally, Hannah.

"Did you find anything else?" Hannah asked him.

"I think I'm supposed to ask the questions," he said gently.

Hannah tucked a stray curl behind her ear. August nights could get cold, and the sunroom felt chilly. Hannah rubbed her hands together in a fruitless effort to warm herself. "Whatever you say."

"No spunk tonight?"

"Your people just destroyed my gardens."

"My people?" Noah arched his thick eyebrows. "I wouldn't call them destroyed. You want us to find who did this to Ezra, right?"

"Of course."

"We didn't have a choice. Come on now. You get it. No stone left unturned and all that happy horse manure."

Hannah wasn't in the mood to be cajoled. "What do you want, Noah? I've told you everything I know already."

Noah sat back in his chair and crossed his arms. "There's definitely blood on that stone, as well as bits of flesh and what appear to be hairs."

As much as the thought sickened her, Hannah was relieved to hear that there could be evidence on the rock. "Ezra's hair?"

"Some are gray and white, like Ezra's. Some are brown. Only tests will tell for sure."

"Could they belong to Moose?"

Noah tapped a hand on the glass-topped table. "Hard to say without analysis. We should have that soon. In the meantime, I've asked for a search warrant for the inn. We'll have to go through everyone's rooms. Take some samples—"

Hannah had been expecting this. Dreading it—but expecting it. It didn't soften the blow. "When?"

"As soon as the warrant comes through."

"When will that be?"

Noah glanced at his watch. "Anytime now. We're supposed to serve a warrant before ten, but given the circumstances, I'm sure an exception will be granted. Whoever did this could try to destroy evidence. We need to make sure that doesn't happen."

"Are you searching my apartment too?" Noah didn't respond, but he didn't need to. "What do you want me to do with Moose?"

"Can you send him to stay with Reggie for tonight?"

"I guess I have no choice."

"I'm sorry, Hannah. I know you didn't ask for any of this."

Hannah's eyebrows shot up. "Then you've come to your senses and realized it wasn't me who killed Ezra?"

"No one has been ruled out yet, but I never accused you of killing Ezra."

"You said I had motive."

"And you do."

"I also have motive for wanting to see his killer behind bars, so search away. Just try not to destroy the place."

Noah started to rise, and Hannah motioned for him to wait a moment. "I know you can't say for sure whether that's the murder weapon, but assuming it is, why would someone go to the trouble of throwing the rock into the woods all the way over here?"

"You mean why not just toss it into the pond?" Noah asked.

"Exactly—where the blood would have been washed off and no one would be the wiser."

Noah said, "Maybe because they forgot to dispose of it in the heat of anger or panic."

Hannah took a deep breath. "Or they wanted to implicate someone else."

Noah bent his head, rubbed the back of his neck. He looked at her through tired eyes. "That's a possibility."

Noah didn't have to say it. They were both thinking it. Someone might have been trying to frame *her*.

* * *

It was after one in the morning when the police finally left the inn. Hannah had been provided a copy of the warrant as well as an inventory of the items removed, which included a hairbrush or comb from each living quarters and Hannah's computer. They'd left a copy of the warrant for Waylen, who still hadn't come back.

"I'll make sure you have your stuff returned quickly," Noah said before leaving.

"I kind of need my computer to run the inn."

"Understood." Noah squeezed Hannah's arm. "Look on the bright side. The rock may very well be a breakthrough in the case. Hopefully we're that much closer to finding who did this."

Hannah watched everyone pull out of the driveway. When they'd gone, she turned around to find Maura standing behind her. She was dressed in silk pajamas and was holding Turnip against her chest.

"Mind if he sleeps with me tonight?" she asked.

Hannah was about to say no, to claim him as her own, especially because Moose was with Reggie, when she saw the worry lines etched around Maura's mouth. Whatever she felt about the other woman, she had just lost her uncle, and now she was in a strange place and a different state and found herself a suspect in his murder investigation.

"Sure, take him. He doesn't like to be held for long, though."

Maura nodded. She turned toward her room, but stopped midway. "I'm sorry my family has caused you so much trouble," she said finally. "I saw your beautiful gardens. And now the inn." She glanced over her shoulder. "We didn't do this to Ezra. You must believe that."

Hannah watched Maura retreat to her suite, Turnip still in her arms. Maura seemed like a complex woman. High-strung, demanding—but not a murderer. They were all difficult—vultures, Ezra had called them—but none seemed capable of something as heinous as murder.

But if it wasn't a family member, who had killed Ezra? It seemed even more horrible to believe the murderer was someone from Jasper. Hannah reminded herself that could very well be the case. How well did anyone ever really know their neighbors?

She locked up the inn, leaving a light on for Waylen, and returned to her apartment for a restless night's sleep.

* * *

Morning greeted Hannah with a loud clap of thunder and the pitter-patter of rain against the inn's metal roof. She rolled over, searching for Moose, and then remembered the events of the night before. Feeling like a zombie, she stumbled into the shower before dressing in jeans and a clean linen tank top. It was 8:38. She'd agreed to meet Teddy at Ezra's house at nine.

Hannah texted Reggie to let her know she'd swing by to get Moose around ten-thirty. Then she climbed into her car, feeling guilty for driving the short distance to Ezra's house. The rain was still falling in sheets, though, and she couldn't very well pick Moose up on a bike.

Teddy was already at the house when Hannah arrived. She climbed the rickety steps to the front entrance and let herself in. Teddy was in the kitchen. He had a clipboard in one hand and a pen in the other.

"Inventory," he said by way of an unrequested explanation. "I should have done this sooner."

"I guess," Hannah said, putting her backpack down in the kitchen. "Considering the vultures were trolling around here."

"*Vultures?*"

"Ezra's term of endearment for his nephews, niece, and pretty much anyone who wanted to buy his property."

Teddy laughed. "Vultures. I like it." He opened a cabinet door and knelt before it, grimacing at the smell. "Bad onions." He stood up. "This place is a mess. I've already gone through half of it and haven't found anything of particular value or interest, but you can take a walk around if you think it'll help." He gave her a knowing look. "And don't forget the dog's stuff. The reason you're here, right?"

Hannah nodded. "Sure."

She left Teddy to his work in the kitchen and went upstairs to Ezra's study. On the way, she passed his bedroom. It was simply decorated, almost monk-like, with a full-size mattress, a single dresser, and a ladderback chair. The floor was well-swept pine, and there was no rug by the bed or extra pillows on the mattress. A small closet held a half-dozen flannel shirts, an old, dusty suit jacket, and one white dress shirt. His dresser contained two pairs of jeans, two pairs of stained Carhartt's, and socks, underwear, and white T-shirts. His scent—woods and tobacco—wafted from within, stinging her eyes with sorrow and regret.

A single prescription-pill bottle sat on his dresser next to a framed photo of Molly. Hannah picked up the pill bottle. Ademetionine. Hannah had no idea what it did, but it sounded like serious stuff.

She went from Ezra's bedroom to the third room. It looked more like the cluttery mess downstairs, with boxes of women's clothes, fabric, a sewing machine, books, and myriad other items scattered around the space. Water stained the ceiling, and dead moths littered the light fixture. Hannah wondered why he kept his own room so clean and tidy yet allowed the other rooms to fester.

She'd never be able to ask him.

The study was coated with dust. While Ezra's desk was stacked with books and notebooks and his bookshelves were lined with books, magazines, and three-ring binders, the insides of his desk drawers were filled with junk, as though someone—the police?—had simply dumped everything back inside. A quick perusal of the bookshelves told her what she should have realized had she been paying attention—that Ezra had been a botanist. College treatises, periodicals, professional journals all sat on musty shelves next to books about ecology, Vermont wildlife, indigenous cultures, and sustainability. A box filled with old newspapers and local magazines sat askew in one corner under a map of Vermont. The small closet was jam-packed with Molly's clothes and shoes, the closet doors barely able to be shut.

Hannah leaned against the wall. It would take her days to go through all of this, not an hour.

"Hannah?"

She peeked her head outside and saw Teddy coming up the stairs.

He smiled. "I see you found the study. Fun, huh? I still have to inventory it, which will take all day."

"I could help you."

Teddy's smile faded. Hannah could see his desire for expediency battling with his fiduciary responsibilities as executor. The former won out. "Friday? We meet here in the morning at, say, ten?"

"Sure," Hannah said. As she was leaving the study, she noticed a clear spot on the floor where something rectangular had sat. "That spot is dust-free. Someone took something, Teddy."

Teddy studied the room for a second. "The police *were* here. It was probably removed as part of the investigation."

"Didn't they have to give you a list of everything they confiscated?"

Teddy's eyes narrowed as he thought about the question. "Yeah, yeah. I can check my notes when I get back to my office. I'm sure they did."

"I also don't see his financial stuff here—his checkbooks and bank statements."

"I'm sure they're with the police too."

Teddy kept looking at the door, and Hannah could tell he was ready to go. This was the Teddy Smith she remembered. Impatient and decisive. "It's important, Teddy. What if his family members took something while they were here? Or Brian stole something important?"

"What would they want with this old stuff?"

Hannah followed him down the steps, wondering the very same thing.

Chapter
Twenty-Two

B y the time Hannah got back to the inn with Moose, the rain had subsided, and the sun was punching its way through the cloud cover. Hannah found Rebecca outside, cleaning up the flowerbeds from the prior night's search. She wore shorts, a sleeveless hoody, sunglasses, a pink bandana, and a pair of headphones. Her face was sun reddened, her upper arms sunburned.

When she saw Hannah walking toward her, her mouth turned down in disapproval. "Who did this?" She nodded toward the trampled beds. "They're a mess."

"The police were here last night, after you left. They found something in the woods that led them to search the property."

"They could have been a little more careful. It took us two years to create this habitat, and like that—" She shook a fist at the woods. "It was like they just didn't care."

Hannah said, "They had bigger things on their minds."

"I still think there was room for respect." Hannah started to walk away, and Rebecca said sullenly, "You have new guests."

"Fantastic. Who?"

"A young couple. I put them upstairs, in the vacant room." She took her sunglasses off and wiped them on her hoody. Her eyes looked bruised and red, as though she hadn't slept all night. "When can we rent the other rooms?"

"The other rooms are taken by Ezra's family."

"Really?" Rebecca looked surprised. "The woman moved downstairs, and the two adjoining rooms upstairs are empty. I think your guest is gone."

"Waylen left?"

Rebecca shrugged. "I didn't check him out, but it sure looks like he's gone."

Hannah sprinted inside, grabbed the room key, and jogged up the stairs. She didn't need the key—the set of adjoining rooms Waylen had claimed were unlocked and empty. Hannah went through the closets, the dressers, and even the bathroom drawers. Nothing. If it hadn't been for the unmade bed, it looked as though no one had stayed there at all.

She spun around and jumped. Rebecca was standing behind her, holding a shovel.

"See," Rebecca said. "Gone."

"It sure looks like he checked out. Did you see him at all?"

Rebecca shook her head. "I've been here since nine and, other than the young couple, no one has shown up."

Hannah hadn't heard him come back to the inn the night before, after the police left. Maybe after his falling out with Teddy, he'd skipped town, figuring there was no point in staying if he didn't stand to gain anything. Only Waylen didn't *seem* like someone who would give up without a fight. Another possibility occurred to her: maybe he'd gotten wind of the police activity, and he'd fled back to New York.

"Where are you going?" Rebecca asked as Hannah pushed past her.

"To call the police."

"Why? Do you think he stiffed you?"

Hannah hadn't even thought of the money, but of course he'd stiffed her. The cost of two rooms for over a week—gone. She exhaled and made herself focus. She'd get hold of Waylen eventually. Right now, there were more important issues at hand.

She reached Noah on the first try. "Waylen is gone."

"Gone as in—"

"Left the inn."

"Maybe he's just staying somewhere else."

"Where else would he stay? Unless he wants to go into Brandon or Killington."

"When did he come back to get his belongings? We left him a notice about the search."

"This morning. I never saw him, and neither did Rebecca, so he must have done it *very* early."

Noah was silent for a while. Hannah could hear traffic noises in the background, so she knew he wasn't in Jasper.

"Penny for your thoughts," she said finally.

"I think it's awfully coincidental that he left the morning after we searched his room."

"Me too. He would have seen the notice that you'd been through his belongings. Maybe it freaked him out. He seems temperamental."

Noah murmured something under his breath. To Hannah, he said, "Did you go into his rooms?"

"I did. There's nothing there—completely empty. Why?"

"I can't say much, Hannah, but if he calls or shows up, please give me a call."

"That's not very reassuring."

Noah was silent for a moment. "It's not meant to be."

* * *

"Waylen has motive, means, and he had opportunity," Reggie said later that afternoon. She had been helping Hannah clean the rooms Waylen vacated, and they were finishing the beds. "Isn't that how they do it in the detective shows? Sounds like a suspect to me."

"He certainly thought he was inheriting Ezra's estate," Hannah said. She plumped up a pillow and placed it inside a fresh, cream-colored cotton case. "You should have seen his reaction when Teddy told him he wasn't getting anything."

"Did Teddy tell him about you?"

"No, but Waylen figured it out himself. It doesn't seem like he told Rob or Maura—at least not yet."

Reggie stayed quiet while straightening the handmade quilt. Little bumblebees buzzed around embroidered daisies on a background of chambray patches. Hannah loved this room—its warmth and its simplicity. Each guest room featured a different pollinator, and this was the Bumblebee Room. She hated that it had been wasted on Waylen.

"I think that's it," Reggie said. She finished with a handwritten note and two Lake Champlain vegan chocolates.

"Now onto the other room," Hannah said.

"Why did Waylen need two rooms?" Reggie asked.

"No idea. He only used one. I suspect he wanted a buffer zone between him and his cousins, so they couldn't hear his calls and stuff."

"Pretty expensive buffer zone."

Hannah grimaced. "Not when you don't pay your bills."

Reggie sat on the desk chair and crossed her legs. She was wearing a pair of gray cargo trousers and a plum short-sleeved Henley. Her hair was back in her signature ponytail, and her nails, currently drumming the desktop, were trimmed and buffed but unpainted. She wore the serious look that in high school had meant a lecture about not angering their parents or using condoms or obeying the traffic laws. Hannah braced herself for whatever was coming.

"Speaking of bills, you need to let all this go, Hannah. It may be years before Ezra's estate is released from probate given the murder investigation. In the meantime, I looked at the inn's financials. There's not much left."

Hannah busied herself folding and unfolding a towel. She was all too aware of the inn's financial state. She didn't need a reminder from her sister.

"You may think you don't need to hear this from me, but you do. I know you're out there playing sleuth, and I was okay with it at first when we thought you were a suspect. But with this guy Waylen gone, it's looking more and more like the police should be focusing on him. Besides being dangerous, you have work—real work—to do around here." She looked up at Hannah, her brown eyes full of worry. "Please let the police handle things."

"I hear what you're saying," Hannah said.

"Is that your way of saying thanks, but no thanks?"

"I heard what you're saying, and I will take it under advisement."

Reggie shook her head. "At least I know where Peach gets her stubborn streak from."

* * *

Reggie's plea left Hannah with a dilemma. She'd been counting on her sister's connections to help her figure out what had happened to Ezra, but without Reggie's support, she needed to find another way to get to her mother's old friends—in particular, Tilda Howard. She didn't have contact information for Tilda. She thought about sneaking a look into Reggie's address book, but the new couple at the inn gave her a better idea.

They were young and excited about seeing Vermont's Green Mountains, so Hannah had given them a half-dozen nearby hiking options. They'd chosen the Devil's Mountain trails, and when they returned to the inn late that afternoon, they were enthusiastic about the views from the top—and about an encounter they'd had with a porcupine.

"We thought it was hurt," the woman said. She was digging into the cucumber gazpacho Hannah had made for the afternoon snack. "We followed it for almost a quarter of a mile, and then the little thing just took off."

"Seriously," the man said. "We thought we were going to need to track down a wildlife rehabber. We even found a few on social media. That little stinker was just playing us."

"It was so cute," the woman said.

Wildlife rehabber.

Hannah had left the cold soup and some sourdough bread out for the couple to enjoy on their own and headed back to her apartment. She didn't have Tilda's home number, true, but Tilda was a state-certified wildlife rehabber. That would mean that somewhere on the Web she would have an address or a phone number.

It took her only five minutes on her phone to find the contact information for A Place of Refuge, the organization Tilda ran out of her home. She called the number listed, and a woman answered immediately.

"Aunt Tilda?" Hannah said.

"Hannah," a warm voice answered. "I wondered when you would come calling."

Chapter
Twenty-Three

Tilda lived in an old, white farmhouse about forty minutes away from Jasper. Her property was close to a main road, although in that remote part of Vermont, a main road meant that a car passed by two or three times an hour. A hedge of daylilies acted as a border between the house and the street, and their bright-orange blossoms matched the faded pumpkin-orange of Tilda's front door. Acres of meadow stretched behind the house, and a small barn, also painted a subdued orange and surrounded with chicken wire, shared space with a yurt.

The woman who answered the door wore jeans and a pink long-sleeved linen shirt and carried a pair of gloves in one hand. Her graying black hair was pulled back from her face, and her dark skin stretched clear and taut over impossibly high cheekbones. As a child, Hannah had thought Tilda was the most stunning woman on earth. She caught her breath now. The years had only softened Tilda's beauty, not erased it.

"Come on in, Hannah. I'm finishing up with a new intake—sweetest little bunny you've ever seen. Give me five minutes and I'll join you in the kitchen."

"Can I see it?"

"Sorry, sweetheart. Not something my license allows. But you can pour yourself some iced tea from the fridge, and there are homemade cookies on the counter." She smiled, crinkling amber-colored eyes. "Just don't eat the square ones. They're for the squirrels. Might break your teeth."

Hannah wandered through the living room and into the kitchen. She'd never been at Tilda's house before, but the home seemed to suit her. The living room was a cozy retreat full of rich, colorful fabrics and vibrant prints. The kitchen cabinets, while old, had been painted white, and the space was filled with local pottery and bright linens. A metal container of oatmeal-raisin cookies sat on the counter next to a plate of what looked like hard, square, seedy granola bars. Hannah took a cookie, poured herself a glass of iced tea, and sat down at the round table in the corner of the room, admiring the view from the window. She hoped Tilda would be as welcoming once she knew why she was there.

True to her word, Tilda was back in a few minutes. She pulled off her latex gloves, disinfected them, and then washed her hands before pouring herself some tea and bringing her glass and the container of cookies to the table.

"It's been a long time, Hannah Telulah Solace, but I understand from Regina that you are back in Vermont and have been for a while."

"We were hoping you would come to the inn for book club. Reggie and I took over the Jasper Inn, and it was hosted there. I think you'd like what we've done with the place."

"I'd like anything better than what Chad did with it." Tilda scowled. "That man's bad taste in decor is rivaled only by his bad taste in paramours."

"I can drink to that." Hannah held up her glass, and the two women toasted. "Reggie is doing okay on her own, though."

"More than okay. Reggie is the toughest person in Jasper," Tilda said. "She just doesn't realize it."

Hannah broke a cookie apart and stared at the pieces. She didn't like lying to her sister, even lies of omission. But Reggie had a way of backing her into a corner. "Speaking of my sister, it would be great if we could not tell her about my visit today."

"Oh?" Tilda's eyebrows shot up. "Why is that?"

"Because she told me to stay out of the murder investigation."

"Do you always listen to your sister?"

"I almost never listen to my sister."

Tilda laughed. "That's the Hannah I remember. Look, I don't have any information that would help with a murder investigation, so I think we can call your visit a social one—one I will keep to myself."

"You told me you were expecting me."

"I was."

"Why?"

"I'd heard from Regina that you and Ezra Grayson had become friends. You'd naturally want to know more about why someone killed him."

"True."

"It doesn't take a psychologist to see that Ezra had filled a certain empty place in your life, perhaps becoming a father figure." Tilda's smile was tinged with sadness. "It's hard to lose a parent, no matter how they go."

Hannah could feel defensiveness rise in her belly. "Is that what Reggie told you? That he was a father figure to me?"

"No, Reggie just said you had an odd friendship. The rest was conjecture on my part."

"Ezra was my friend. If anyone parented anyone, it was me who was parenting him."

Tilda rubbed her forehead with long, slender fingers. Calmly, she said, "You know your relationship best, but there is no shame in looking up to someone, nor is there shame in wishing we had a different relationship with our own parents. Your father isn't an easy man to love."

"Neither was Ezra."

"Exactly."

Hannah finished off her cookie and took another. Was Tilda right? Had she been searching for some kind of father figure in Ezra? Had she been the daughter he'd never had, as Teddy had said? Hannah thought back to all the conversations she and Ezra had had about gardening, about companion planting and pollinators. and even the simple fixes he'd shared with her for things around the inn. Despite his curmudgeonly nature, Ezra had been patient and kind in ways her father never could be.

Tilda said, "Why'd you come, Hannah?"

Tilda's words were not unkind, but there was an edge to them Hannah also remembered from childhood. It took a certain kind of person to take in injured and orphaned wild animals, nurse them back to health, only to release them back into the wild and whatever vagaries of humanity they might encounter there. Tenderness balanced with resiliency. That combination of caring and toughness was Tilda's hallmark, and it was on full display now.

"I want to know what happened between my father and Ezra all those years ago."

"What do you mean, 'what happened'?"

"When my dad bought Ezra's property. When my father became rich, and Ezra didn't."

Tilda held up open hands. "Nothing happened. Your dad and Ezra made a deal. The deal paid off handsomely."

"This deal led to decades of animosity between Ezra and my dad, so clearly it wasn't as straightforward as everyone would like me to believe."

"Did you try asking your father?"

Hannah nodded. "He told me he paid Ezra fair and square, and that Ezra was upset because he thought the Jasper property was being bought for my family's personal use. He felt he had been misled."

"There's your answer."

"Is it?" Hannah drained the last of her tea and pushed the glass aside. "That hardly seems like a reason to hate each other for twenty years."

"Maybe if someone made enough profit off it it would. Imagine selling your homestead and finding out the buyer had bought it under false pretenses and then spun the sale into millions." Tilda broke off a piece of cookie and popped it into her mouth. After swallowing, she said, "I don't think it was just the Jasper property. As I recall, your mother told me Ezra sold your dad several pieces of land, including one in New York State. That could be a lot of profit to ignore."

"I suppose."

"You sound skeptical. Why is that?"

Hannah said, "Ezra was at my father's house the day he died, and my father had visited Ezra a few weeks before then. I can't help wondering if those visits were related to Ezra's murder."

"Related in what way?"

When Hannah didn't answer right away, Tilda put a hand over her mouth. "Oh, Hannah. Your dad isn't the easiest man alive, but he's not a killer."

"Think about what he did to Ezra. Isn't it a slippery slope to go from fraud to more serious crimes?"

"Fraud? Who said what happened constituted fraud?" Tilda's eyes narrowed. "I never much liked John, but I loved your mother, and Beverly Solace wouldn't have married someone capable of outright fraud, *or* murder."

Hannah sat back in her chair, thinking. She wanted to believe her mother had been a good judge of character—she had certainly surrounded herself with loyal friends—but she'd married a man who'd bullied her and cheated on her, so Hannah had to wonder. His indiscretions were no secret in Jasper, and surely Tilda knew about her father's affairs just as everyone else did.

A cell phone rang loudly, and Tilda jumped up. "That's the Bat Mobile ring. Give me a few minutes." She picked up the call, provided directions about the care of what sounded like an opossum, and clicked off. "I have about twenty minutes before an injured opossum arrives, so I need to wrap this up." She smiled warmly, although her eyes held a glint of sadness. "Let's get together for real sometime. Maybe dinner here? Or I could come to the inn."

Hannah stood up, placed her glass in the sink, and started toward the front door, Tilda following behind her.

"You know," Tilda said. "I knew Molly for a long time. She was a sweet woman. Caring, generous, and she loved Ezra fiercely."

"I remember her as someone kind and loving, but somewhere along the line she changed. At least that's what I keep hearing."

Tilda nodded. "We always attributed it to illness, but you'd think someone would share their medical troubles with their close friends."

"That does seem strange."

Tilda looked out the window, watching for her new charge. "Ezra was a botanist. He worked for the Fuller Foundation once upon a time. Loved his job. Did you know that?"

"Someone told me he'd been a botanist. I didn't know about his work for a foundation."

Tilda nodded. "It was a reputable nonprofit, and Ezra was trying to do good in the world, before . . . well, sometimes good intentions aren't enough."

"What do you mean?"

"That's in the past and doesn't matter now," Tilda said, nudging Hannah gently with her elbow. "Anyway, I think maybe you're asking the wrong question. Perhaps rather than asking whether your father defrauded Ezra, you should be asking why Ezra sold him his properties in the first place."

Hannah stepped outside into air, which felt oppressively humid. The clouds again had formed a bruised and threatening canopy in the sky.

Tilda's gaze traveled to the road in front of her house. A car was approaching, and Hannah could make out a Vermont license plate on a silver Tundra.

"Will she make it?" Hannah asked. "The opossum, I mean."

Tilda flashed Hannah that sad smile again. "With a little medicine, a lot of care, and a healthy dose of faith, I think maybe she will."

* * *

Why *had* Ezra sold his property to her father? The question plagued Hannah through dinner that night and well into the evening. By nine o'clock, neither Maura nor Waylen had returned to the inn, but the lights on the Airstream were on, telling Hannah that at least one of Ezra's family members was there. Rob didn't come inside, though, and at ten, Hannah turned off the common-area lights. Maura had the access code for the inn should she come back later. Hannah wondered where she was, and whether anyone had heard from Waylen.

Back in her apartment, Hannah spent the next two hours searching for anything helpful she could find about Ezra, his property transactions, and the Fuller Foundation. With Moose curled up on the floor beside her, she typed away on her phone, determined to figure out how Ezra's past had influenced his death. Ezra had no social media or internet presence, and she couldn't find public information about twenty-year-old land sales, but she did find material about the Fuller Foundation. Now defunct, it had been a nonprofit dedicated to forest stewardship and the ecological integrity of New England's woodlands, riverbeds, and watersheds. It looked like it had been in business until about seventeen years ago.

A search using Ezra's name and the foundation gave her no immediate hits, but when she dug back far enough, she found a short article that mentioned that the foundation had been the brainchild of two botanists, T. Moyer and E. F. Grayson.

E. F. Grayson. Ezra Frances Grayson.

Excited, Hannah thought about her next move. If anyone might know something about Ezra's days at Fuller, it would be his brother-in-law, Louis. On impulse, she shot Louis a text, offering to take him to breakfast at Benny's Diner before she had to help Teddy sort through Ezra's study the next day. Louis texted her back almost immediately: *Yes to breakfast, no to Benny's. I don't want a side of heartburn with my eggs. How about Breaking Bread? Eight? And next time, call. I don't accept dates via text. —LD*

Laughing, Hannah bent down to pet Moose's head. Her breakfast with Louis a date? Come to think of it, she supposed it was the closest thing to a date she'd had since breaking up with Chris three years ago.

Hannah had one more person to contact. She sent Tilda a text about T. Moyer and asked her for help in finding the man. Tilda didn't respond right away, but that was okay. Now Hannah knew where to find her.

Chapter
Twenty-Four

Nadia Taylor was dishing out coffee and biscuits when Hannah arrived at Breaking Bread the next morning. The bakery half of the shop consisted of a coffee bar with stools and a half-dozen bistro tables set on a polished concrete floor. The bike shop, though separate, was connected by a sliding barn door that Nadia and her partner left open during the hours they shared. Right now, the bike shop was closed and its interior dark.

"Coffee and the vegan carrot-cake muffin," Hannah said. She saw no sign of Louis yet, but it was only 7:53. She handed Nadia her credit card. "When an older man shows up shortly—you can't miss him, believe me—put his order on my tab as well."

Nadia had dark hair and even darker eyes, and those eyes studied Hannah with intense interest. "I'm sorry about Ezra. I should have said that the other day. I know you two were close."

"Thank you."

"They'll catch the bastard soon."

"I sure hope so."

Hannah escaped Nadia's stare and took the bistro table by the window. Only one other table was occupied, and Pastor Kendra gave her a little wave from her seat. She was typing away at a laptop, two large coffees and an untouched croissant on the table by one of the empty chairs.

Hannah was about to go and visit with Kendra when Louis arrived. He was wearing a pair of khaki quick-dry trousers and a light-blue button-down shirt. Over the shirt was a rust-colored fishing vest adorned with hooks and lures. Hannah hoped he wouldn't accidentally drop any hooks into his breakfast. That date would not end well.

"Kind of you to purchase my breakfast," Louis said when he finally sat down. He carried a plate bearing a wrap sandwich, two slices of avocado, and a cup of coffee. "The egg-and-cheese wrap is wonderful here. You must try it."

"I'll keep that in mind, Louis. Thank you for joining me." Hannah gestured toward his outfit. "Quite the fishing vest you've got there."

Louis beamed. "It's a vintage Heavy 3 AM fishing vest." He leaned in conspiratorially. "These sell for over a thousand dollars. I had it in the shop for over a year, and one day someone offered me a hundred for it. Can you imagine? Rather than basically giving it away, I kept it for myself. What a find, right? I'm a walking advertisement for the shop."

Hannah nodded. It *did* make a statement. "I didn't know you fish."

"I don't really, but I rather enjoy the look. I will make a few casts and then spend the rest of the time reading a book and watching for loons. It's a pleasant way to spend a morning."

"You know another pleasant way to spend the morning? Telling me about Ezra's affiliation with the Fuller Foundation."

At the mention of the foundation, Louis's contented smile vanished. "You do know how to kill a date. It's no wonder you're single. Why do you want to know about that place?"

"I thought it might help me understand Ezra's past."

"For your Nancy Drewing?"

"Now she's a verb?" Hannah smiled. "Sure, for that."

Louis stared at his uneaten egg-and-cheese wrap. He picked up his coffee cup, took a small sip, and placed it carefully back on the table, arranging it so it was at exactly two o'clock in relation to his plate.

"You don't really want to go there," he said.

"Why not?"

"Because it will dredge up some ugly stuff, stuff that is unlikely to lead to Ezra's killer."

"Like what?"

Louis carefully cut a slice of his wrap and popped it in his mouth, chewing slowly and avoiding eye contact.

"*Louis?*"

Another pause. "This goes back more than twenty years, Hannah. I like solving mysteries as much as anyone, but not at the expense of someone's reputation."

"Reputation?"

"As in Ezra's," Louis said finally. "It's not a story with a happy ending."

He took his time eating the rest of the wrap. When finished, he placed his napkin over his plate and sat back. Hannah watched as Jay Birk entered the shop and joined his wife at her table. She smiled as he sat down and handed him a coffee.

Louis glanced in their direction before saying, "Maybe we should finish up here and go for a walk."

Outside, he ambled toward the small park, chatting as he went. "The Fuller Foundation was Ezra's baby. He and a man named Thomas Moyer were botanists for a chemical company in New York a lifetime ago. Weed killer or some such thing. Ezra hated the job, hated everything about it. The two of them decided their time would be better spent back in Vermont, protecting plants rather than killing them."

"Which aligns with the foundation's mission statement," Hannah said.

"You did your homework. Good." Louis stumbled on a loose stone and grabbed her arm for balance. "Young mind, old feet."

Hannah patted his hand. "Ezra helped to start the foundation?"

"The *idea* of it, at least. The foundation was financed by a wealthy benefactor, the family member of someone who'd started a successful chemical company. I shan't name names, but how's that for symmetry?" Louis stopped fifty yards from the park and turned to look at Hannah. "Her name doesn't really matter. She wasn't involved in the day-to-day operations. That was Ezra and Thomas. Ezra was so proud of that foundation—or so we all thought."

Hannah looked at him quizzically. "He wasn't actually proud of it?"

"He left abruptly. He didn't tell me why, but Anita told me he was asked to go." He tilted his head downward at looked at her knowingly over the bridge of his nose. "Embezzlement. Or so she heard. Of course, my dearly departed wasn't fond of Ezra, so it didn't take much to convince her he'd done something wrong. I believe if he had done something so egregious, he had a very good reason."

This time, Hannah had to grab Louis's arm for support. *Ezra, embezzling?* "No way."

Louis shrugged. "Follow the money, my dear. Ezra left, and the foundation eventually folded. No charges were ever pressed, but with foundations like that, the seed money is typically invested and there are enough earnings to cover expenses. They rarely fail because of financial ruin. They spend only what they have."

"Who handled the foundation's investments?"

This time it was Louis who patted her hand. "Ezra."

*　*　*

Hannah felt a burning need to tell Reggie what she'd learned. What if the money in Ezra's accounts, the money she was due to inherit, was the fruit of illegal activity? The possibility of Ezra embezzling was too much to bear alone. Only Reggie had asked her to stop poking around the murder investigation, and Hannah decided that poking that bear wasn't worth the momentary release. Instead, she called Tilda from the safety of her car.

"That didn't take long," Tilda said.

"Did you get my text?"

"I did, but I chose to ignore it. Let the police do their thing, Hannah."

Hannah slammed her head against the headrest. "Reggie got to you."

"Reggie did no such thing. I remember how headstrong you can be, and as soon as I mentioned that foundation yesterday, I thought, 'You fool, Tilda.' I saw it in your eyes. You're like a beaver with a log, Hannah. You can't let go."

Hannah refused to bite. She knew her own reputation, but she also knew that that reputation was fifteen years old. "Please tell me how I can find Thomas Moyer."

"By heading to the Mount Pleasant Cemetery. Thomas passed away many years ago."

"Then give me another name. Someone who might have known what really happened."

Hannah heard Tilda sigh into the phone. "I didn't know Thomas well, but his wife Marjorie is still alive. She lives in Chittenden, near the reservoir. I know because she works at one of the restaurants near Rochester. Darien's Brewpub. She's the hostess."

"Thank you!"

"Slow down. What are you going to do with this information?"

"Talk with her."

There was a long pause before Tilda spoke again. "Has it occurred to you that she might not want to talk to you?"

"I can't force her to."

"No, you can't." She drew out the syllables. "Has it also occurred to you that there is a murderer on the loose, and if you keep asking questions, you may trip right into their crosshairs?"

"The thought has occurred to me, yes."

"And you're out there anyway, consequences be damned?" When Hannah didn't respond, Tilda said, "Maybe you're more like your father than you think."

"Ouch."

"Food for thought."

"Don't be angry, Tilda." She meant it. She realized it mattered to her whether or not Tilda was angry.

"Just be careful."

"Is she okay?" Hannah asked. "The opossum, I mean."

"As a matter of fact, she's doing surprisingly well." The warm smile had returned to Tilda's voice. "It'll be a long, winding road to recovery, but that little girl is strapped in and ready to rumble."

* * *

"I wasn't sure you were going to show." Teddy glanced at his watch. "You're late."

Hannah threw her backpack on the kitchen table. "Sorry. I got hung up."

"At breakfast?" Teddy smiled. "I saw you with that older man on Main Street. New boyfriend?"

"Don't be crude."

Teddy smirked. "Shall we head up into the study? I'd like to play a round before the storms set in tonight, so I thought we could divide and conquer."

Hannah wasn't so sure he was supposed to let her do that, but she wasn't about to point it out. "No problem."

Teddy gave her the boxes on the floor to go through while he took the desk. He handed her a clipboard and a pen. "I've gone through the desk and the shelves already. Just make a list of what's in the boxes. No need to sort them or throw anything out, or even be too specific in your notes. We just need to catalogue what's here, especially anything of value."

Hannah cleared a space between the boxes and the desk and sat cross-legged on the floor. The first box was easy to record—old Vermont newspapers and magazines. Hannah made a few notes and moved on to the second box—old credit-card bills. *Ezra's hoarding tendencies continue*, she thought. The third box was smaller and contained photographs, mostly of Molly.

"Are you almost done?"

Hannah looked up to see Teddy staring down at her from his perch on the office chair. The clipboard sat on his lap, and he'd finished with whatever he'd been cataloguing.

"What are those? Pictures?"

Hannah nodded.

Teddy glanced again at his watch. He chewed on his lip, looking around the room. With a resigned sigh, he said, "Why don't you finish up without me? Just make sure you don't throw anything away or take anything from the house."

"Okay."

"I don't see anything of importance here. You?"

"Not at first glance."

Teddy nodded. "A lot of it is garbage. I'd just throw it all out, but because of the ongoing investigation, I need to leave his house intact."

"Did you ever find out whether the police removed anything from the room?" When Teddy looked confused, she added, "You were going to check on that because it looked like a box was missing. And maybe his banking information."

"Yeah, yeah, that. No, I owe Booker a call. Thanks for the reminder."

But Hannah knew that Teddy wouldn't call Noah. His dismissive tone told her that. The new, improved Teddy was all about golf and as little stress as he could manage. She watched the lawyer leave, and as he exited he made her promise again not to take away or destroy anything in the room.

When he'd gone, Hannah returned to the photos. She knew her job wasn't to sort, but she couldn't resist the urge to go through them one by one, not because she was looking for clues, but because she couldn't look away from the journey into Jasper's past the photos presented. There were photos of Main Street when it had been just a dusty road lined with Benny's Diner, a stripped-down version of the general store, the church, and Ezra's house, looking pin-straight and freshly painted. There were photos of the horse farm, photos of Devil's Mountain in its prime, and photos of people—some of whom she recognized.

Familiar faces in one yellowing photo caught her attention, and she picked up the picture, holding it carefully so as to not smudge the surface. It was a photo of her mother, Tilda, and Molly standing together in front of Ezra's Victorian house during what looked like a picnic. Molly's smile was wide and welcoming. Her graying hair was pulled into a bun, and she wore slim-fit pants and a cardigan set. Older than the other two women by twenty years, she was standing as one would expect a hostess to stand, her posture proud and open and welcoming.

Tilda looked as beautiful as ever, her sculpted cheekbones and slim neck lending her a movie star's profile as she gazed at someone off camera, dark eyes in a mid-laugh squint.

But it was Hannah's mother who truly captured the camera's eye. She stood slightly apart from the other two women as though distancing herself just a little bit from their gaiety. Her golden-streaked hair was long and loose, cascading around her shoulders in waves. Her hands rested on her swollen belly, which protruded from a plain, knee-length, faded cotton dress—a contrast to the more fashionable clothes Tilda and Molly were wearing. Her lovely face looked lined and worried, the shadows under her eyes captured by the angle of the sun and the photographer's lens. It was a face with character, and the camera loved it.

That was me in there, Hannah thought. Her mother would have been close to forty. In the photo's background, Hannah could make out a gangly eleven-year-old Reggie standing with Phyllis, who's stern countenance was visible even from a distance. John Solace, if present, wasn't in the picture.

Hannah held onto that photo for a long time. She remembered her mother as kind-hearted but weak, unable or unwilling to stand up to her father when he'd singlehandedly uprooted their life or berated her daughters. But this picture portrayed a different side of her mother—someone tired and worn and worried. Maybe they had been poorer than Hannah remembered. Maybe struggling financially had taken a toll on Bev and she'd been happy with the change. *Maybe my memories were clouded by the angst and self-centeredness of a child.*

Hannah put the photo aside and was reaching for the next when her cell phone rang. It was Noah.

"I need to talk with you. Are you at the inn? I'll come to you."

"No, but I can be there in fifteen."

Hannah hung up and took a deep breath. Noah had refused to say more over the phone, but clearly something had happened. She put the pictures back and was about to pick up the box and take it with her when she remembered her previous conversation with Teddy.

I promised not to take anything with me, she thought, *but I didn't promise not to come back.*

Hannah ran down to the basement. She'd only been in its dank recesses a few times, but she knew there was a window there with a broken latch. Ezra had stored little down there because the basement was prone to flooding, but she found what she needed—his old utility ladder resting against the wall of the crumbling foundation. She propped the ladder in front of the broken window and headed back upstairs, happy to be above ground again.

She wondered for the millionth time why Ezra had let his house fall into disrepair when he had so much money at his disposal. And she wondered what, if anything, that had to do with his murder.

Chapter
Twenty-Five

N oah handed Hannah her computer and other items he had confiscated during the search.

"Thank you," Hannah said, placing the materials on the table in her private apartment. "Did you come here just for this?"

"I came here to tell you that you that I'm worried."

Noah hadn't wasted any time getting down to business. He'd been at the inn when she arrived and had insisted that they speak in her apartment with the windows closed. Now he was looking at her with a mixture of brotherly concern and professional gravity that made her throat go dry.

"What are you talking about?"

Noah took a seat in her apartment's small living room. He pushed his disheveled hair back from his face, and Hannah noticed the haggard lines around his eyes, the untrimmed beard. He was clearly under stress and probably not sleeping.

"We got DNA tests back on the rock your niece found. The blood is Ezra's."

"Then the rock *was* the murder weapon."

"We're waiting for a full report, but it looks that way."

"How does that put *me* in danger?"

Noah was looking at Moose, who was sitting in the doorway, his attention on Hannah. "Can you sit down? That dog won't settle until you do."

"He's fine."

"He's guarding you."

Hannah sat on the room's only armchair. "Better?" When Noah nodded, she said, "What else did the DNA report reveal that has you concerned?"

"There were several fibers and three hairs on the rock. The fibers matched Ezra's flannel shirt. One of the hairs was Ezra's and another was consistent with the fur of a short-haired dog."

"Moose."

"Correct."

"And the third?" Hannah was preparing for him to say it was hers. After all, she'd been at Ezra's house the day he had died and most days before that. It wouldn't be so improbable to think that some of her long, curly hair could have gotten on her friend's clothing.

"It matched the sample we took from Waylen Grayson's room here at the inn."

"So he . . .?"

"Is officially a suspect." Noah rubbed the back of his neck while he spoke. "Look, you said yourself that it would have made more sense for the killer to have thrown the weapon into the pond. The water would have washed away the blood on the rock—it would have been just another rock on the bottom of a lake. Maybe the killer panicked—that's a possibility."

"Or maybe the killer purposely placed the rock there to throw attention elsewhere, as we said the other day." Noah nodded his agreement, and Hannah continued, "The hairs were visible. Even

I saw a few on the rock. Why go to the trouble of framing someone else and then leaving evidence behind?"

"Good point, and we asked the same thing ourselves." Noah rose, looked at Moose, who'd lifted his head to watch him, and sat back down. "Are you sure that dog is friendly?"

"He loves Peach, and not all animals love Peach. Just ask the cat."

Noah smiled. "I'll take your word for it. Anyway, you're right, but the third hair was in a small crevice on the rock's underbelly. It's unlikely they even knew it was there."

Hannah let that sink in. She didn't particularly like Waylen, but he seemed too precious to be a killer, especially one who would traipse out into a marsh to take another's life. If Waylen was going to kill someone, he'd hire a hitman or plant a bomb. Ezra's death was too messy for him.

Although that day at the inn, he *had* come back with mud on his legs, Hannah reminded herself. Maybe he wasn't as averse to getting dirty as she thought. The mud sparked another thought.

"The day of Ezra's death," Hannah said, "Ezra called me to say he was coming over. That was around four in the afternoon, a few hours after I'd left his house. I went kayaking around seven thirty and found Ezra's body shortly thereafter. Moose was with him."

"Moose got loose. We established how he broke through the screen door."

Hannah held up a hand. "Right. He was left behind, must have heard Ezra, and went running to the pond. You said Moose might have been the only witness. I don't think that's right, Noah. Whoever did this must have been gone a while before Moose arrived."

Noah narrowed his eyes. "I don't understand what you're getting at."

"Moose is a sweet dog, but he can be protective. You can see that yourself today. Let's say he heard Ezra struggling and broke down a door to get to him. Had the killer still been anywhere near the body when Moose arrived, Moose would have attacked. When I saw Waylen the next day, he had mud on his legs, but I didn't see any wounds."

"Maybe he just had time to get back to the inn before the dog arrived."

"Think about it, Noah. There is no direct route from the side of the pond where Ezra died to the inn other than *through* the pond. The banks are muddy and nearly impassable by foot. That means whoever killed Ezra was either quite efficient and got back to Main Street, drove to the inn, and placed the rock in the woods all before seven, when I left for the pond, or—"

"Or they borrowed a boat, tossed the rock into the woods, and disappeared before you came outside."

"Exactly. Moose's presence narrows the window a little bit."

Noah closed his eyes and sat silently for a moment. When he opened them again, he fixed his stare on Moose. "Did you or Reggie see anyone come or go from the property between five thirty and seven thirty?"

"Just Rebecca, but then, we weren't looking for anyone either."

"Had any of the inn's kayaks gone missing?"

"Not that I noticed, but guests use them frequently, so I don't usually check."

"Were any wet when you headed out on yours that night?"

Hannah thought back to the night in question. She pictured the six kayaks they kept by the path to the pond: two blue, two yellow, and two green. She'd grabbed one of the blue ones. "By seven thirty, they were all accounted for, but I wasn't paying attention enough to notice whether any were wet."

"Right. Plus, taking a boat would have required premeditation. The killer would have had to kayak to the other side, lure Ezra out to the pond, kill him, and then kayak back."

Hannah nodded. "It seems unlikely."

They sat quietly for a few moments. The afternoon sunlight was streaming through the windows and fell in slashes across Moose, who was snoring softly, basking in the warmth. The mantel clock was ticking, and Hannah glanced up to see Turnip walking along the top of a chair, her small feet balanced precariously on its edge.

"There is another possibility," Hannah said. "There's a walking path that leads from Devil's Mountain to the pond. It's occasionally used by mountain bikers, but it's not well marked, and it's a hike for someone carrying a boat. This means I rarely see ski-resort guests at the pond. It's possible that the killer hiked up the trail to the resort parking lot and then planted the rock at the inn at a later date."

Noah's brow furrowed. "It would be another way to distance him- or herself from the murder scene."

"Right, and without incurring the wrath of Moose. Waylen wasn't seen most of the day Ezra was killed. Maura told me that."

"And the rock's presence would throw suspicion off him."

"And onto me."

Noah chewed his lower lip in a way Hannah found endearing. He folded his trim body in on itself, leaning toward her in the process. "If someone planted that rock later, that could mean it was anyone, not just someone staying or living at the inn."

Hannah thought about that. "But you'd think we'd notice a stranger on the property."

"Not if they weren't a stranger."

Hannah cocked her head. "If you're talking about Reggie, don't be absurd."

"I'm talking about a laundry list of possibilities, people who might come and go without you having a second thought. Chad, for example. Think, Hannah. Who has been here?"

"Ash and his crew. Rebecca. Reggie and Peach. Reggie's book club on the night the rock was found."

One of Noah's thick eyebrows shot up, and Hannah rolled her own eyes. "Please. They were accounted for, and besides, their average age is north of sixty. I don't think any of them was carting around a three-pound rock in their Kate Spade bags, looking for the perfect chance to plant the murder weapon in the garden by the forest." Hannah smiled. "Although it would make for an interesting mystery novel."

Ignoring her attempt at humor, Noah asked, "Who else has been here?"

With another glance at Moose, who was twitching wildly in the throes of a doggy dream, Hannah said, "I don't think I can give you a satisfactory answer. If someone came here to dispose of the rock, then they would have done so on the sly. They could have entered the property on foot in the dead of night for all I know."

"Your security footage should show that."

"If we *had* security footage."

"My god, Hannah." Noah shook his head. He rose and walked to the window. "I think it's far more likely that whoever did this did it in plain sight, which means that Waylen is our number-one suspect. Not only was his DNA on the murder weapon, but he had a strong motive, and now it appears he's fled." He swung around to face Hannah, his face grave. "That's why I wanted to see you in person. We haven't been able to find even a trace of Waylen. There's no credit-card trail, no car sightings—and a red Porsche is hard to miss. That could mean he's lying low."

"Or it could mean he's working with someone else, and they're protecting him right now."

"Exactly," Noah said. "Until we know more, please pay attention to safety. Lock your doors, look under your car, keep Moose nearby. Waylen knows you inherited Ezra's estate, so others may know too." His eyes darkened. "You could be a target, Hannah."

Hannah walked Noah to the door and locked it behind him. She felt queasy at the knowledge that Waylen's DNA was on that rock. She thought about Moose's reaction to Waylen the other evening at Ezra's house. Hannah had thought Brian Lewis was the dog's target, but maybe it had been Waylen.

Or maybe the dog had been reacting to both of them. After all, if Waylen had an accomplice, who could it be? Brian would make sense. He'd been salivating over Ezra's land for years, desperate to get rid of the eyesore next door. Together, he and Waylen would both benefit from Ezra's death.

Hannah watched Noah pull out of the inn's parking area. He'd been kind to come here, but it had been a wasted trip. She'd already known she was in danger. She'd known since Teddy first told her about the will.

Chapter Twenty-Six

The next day, Hannah went through the motions of an innkeeper, but her heart wasn't in it. She served the new couple an afternoon snack of fresh fruit, eggless crepes, and homemade lemonade. Rob hadn't emerged from the Airstream all day, and Maura's car wasn't in the lot. The new couple seemed appreciative enough, but they declined the invitation to go for a hike or use the kayaks.

That suited Hannah just fine. She wandered outside into the gardens and helped Rebecca with the new plantings. Pink bee balm and echinacea, purple coneflowers, New England asters, and deep-red cardinal flowers were replacing the trampled plants that couldn't be saved. Rebecca had worked quickly and efficiently, and only a few flowers were left to plant.

"You finish these, and I'll work on the garlic bed," Rebecca said gruffly. Rebecca pulled off her gloves, revealing hands twisted and swollen from work, age, and arthritis. "The bulbs can't go in yet, but at least we'll be ready to plant in the fall."

Hannah agreed. There was nothing quite like fresh garlic, and the scapes and the heads would nourish her guests next year. "Before you head over there, I need to ask you a question."

Rebecca waited, hand on her slim hip.

"Do you recall seeing anyone unusual at the inn over the last week or so?"

"What do you mean by 'unusual'?"

"Anyone who's not typically here. I know about Ash and his crew, and of course the guests, but I'm wondering if anyone else has been at the inn when I wasn't around."

Rebecca pushed a steely strand of hair away from her face. "Not really." She turned to leave, walked five paces, and turned back around. "Yarrow was here the other day. He's not really an unusual guest, but—"

"*Henry* Yarrow?"

"One and the same."

"What was Henry doing here?"

Rebecca shrugged. "Don't know. He didn't tell me, just picked up that dark-haired guest and left."

Dark-haired guest? "Man or woman?"

"The woman. Maura."

Henry Yarrow at the inn to pick up Maura was an interesting development, Hannah thought. Henry had been divorced for years, and while not exactly voted Jasper's most eligible bachelor—that designation went to Ash—he had money and a touch of saccharine charm. Plus, Maura hadn't been staying at the inn regularly. Could she have been shacking up with Henry?

"Was he here for long?"

"I'm not paid to chaperone the guests."

"When was this?" Hannah asked, ignoring Rebecca's sarcastic tone. "Do you at least remember the day?"

"It was before the police ruined my flower gardens. I remember everything as Before and After," she practically growled. "Definitely before."

Hannah stared at the spot where Peach had made her discovery. Henry had been at the inn before the rock was found—that was something at least. He was another person with motive, and while his motive wasn't as strong as the family members', he nonetheless had a reason to profit from Ezra's death. Hannah could envision a scenario in which Henry and Ezra had argued over the sale of Ezra's property, the situation became heated, and Henry killed Ezra in a fit of anger. Panic-stricken, he could have decided to shift suspicion onto the relatives, or even Hannah, by tossing the rock near the inn.

But would Henry do that? She didn't know him well. A relative newcomer to the state—he'd been there only fifteen years—he did seem desperate to expand the resort. And if he was hooking up with Maura, maybe she'd convinced him to do something he wouldn't have otherwise done. Hannah sat back on her heels, remembering what Ash had told her—that Ezra's family and Brian Lewis had been walking around Ezra's property like they owned the place. Maybe Ezra's murder had been a group effort, and they all wanted a piece of the estate.

Hannah shook her head. *You sound nuts*, she told herself. *This is all useless conjecture, and what you need are facts.* She would plant the last of the coneflowers, call Noah to tell him about Henry, and then try to track down more information on Ezra and the Fuller Foundation. She couldn't stake out the cousins, but she could do some digging on her own. And if that meant a night out at a pub, so be it.

* * *

That night at Darien's Brewpub was hopping. Hannah found a parking spot next to a Hummer with New York plates and made her way past a small crowd outside, waiting for a table. It was a beautiful late summer evening. Temperatures had cooled to the low sixties, the sky was clear, and a hint of autumn could be felt in the crisp, dry air. Soon the leaves would start to turn, and the leaf peepers would come to New England by the busload, but right now the atmosphere was low-key and pleasant, and the pub patrons milling about on the deck just seemed happy to be there.

And why wouldn't they? Hannah thought as she wove her way through the crowd. Vermont was beautiful in late summer. Hell, Vermont was beautiful all year—except maybe in mud season, when the top layer of every dirt road was topped with a foot of mud and the black flies swarmed so thickly you couldn't take a breath without inhaling some. Hannah smiled to herself. Since returning to her home state, she'd learned to take each season in stride and enjoy what it had to offer. And right now, it offered hard cider and good beer.

Inside the pub, the air was smoke-tinged from the wood-fired pizza oven. Eight people stood in line, waiting to be seated, and the bar was two people deep. She looked around for the host, but the first host she saw was a man—clearly not Tom Moyer's wife. By the time she was third in line, an older woman had joined him. She had short white hair, a pouchy jawline, and the nervous tics of a caffeine addict. She smiled as she greeted guests, but wariness clouded her eyes when Hannah asked for her by name.

"Who wants to know?" the hostess asked.

"My name is Hannah Solace. I was a good friend of Ezra Grayson's."

The wariness turned icy. The woman had already started to turn her back when Hannah reached out and touched her shoulder.

Hannah said, "Ezra's dead. He was murdered earlier this month."

"I know. It was in the papers." The woman turned to face her. "What do you want from me?"

"Just a few questions about what happened at the foundation."

"Oh, is that all?" The woman snorted. "I'm sorry. Even if I wanted to talk to you, you can see we're swamped."

"What time do you get off?"

"Not for three hours. I'll be tired—"

"I'll buy you a drink. And some dinner, if you'd like."

The woman's expression softened, but only slightly. "I'll take the drink. But I'm not waiting around. If you're not here when I finish, I'm going home."

"Deal," Hannah said. She eyed the bar. If it would be a while, she'd get a drink as well.

* * *

Hannah was on her second beer when she received a text on her phone. It was from Reggie, and she wanted to come to the inn for a movie night.

Yikes, Hannah thought. *Sorry, out with a friend,* she texted back.

Since when do you have friends? Her sister retorted.

Funny lady. Call me tomorrow. With Reggie, less was more. Anything she said could and would be used against her.

Hannah was about to put her phone away when it buzzed again. This time the text was from Ash. *Come here often, beautiful?*

Hannah looked in the mirror over the bar and saw Ash's chiseled face staring back at her. He was sitting at a high top across from a petite brunette. The woman was scrolling on her phone, and Ash looked mildly bored. He gave Hannah a two-finger wave.

Paid someone to go out with you tonight? Hannah wrote back.

If I had, he responded, *this would be way more fun.*

Hannah laughed. There wasn't much of a nightlife in Jasper, unless you considered bonfires and drinking in the woods a nightlife, so she wasn't surprised to see Ash here. Nevertheless, she felt something odd inside herself that she recognized as a niggle of jealousy. Who was that woman? And why the hell did she care?

Hannah opened her cell phone and started making notes about Ezra's death. She jotted down what she knew about the foundation, the information she'd gleaned from Noah about the DNA, and the facts surrounding the will. With disgust, she realized that what she had amounted to mostly nothing.

Her phone buzzed again. *Can I buy you a beer?*

Hannah looked in the mirror and saw that now Ash was sitting alone. He shot her that mischievous, maddening grin. Hannah texted him: *What happened to your date?*

She absconded with the bartender.

Good choice on her part.

Join me and I'll buy all your drinks.

I'm not that easy.

She saw Ash smile. *How about if I finish planting the conservation meadow over the weekend?*

Now you're talking.

With that, Hannah happily left her uncomfortable bar seat and joined him at his high top. *At least now I'm not lying to Reggie,* she thought. *I am out with a friend.*

* * *

"I don't think I've ever seen you outside of Jasper," Ash said. He'd ordered them each a beer and was sipping his while they talked. "Imagine my surprise when I looked up and saw you trolling for men at Darien's Brewpub, of all places."

Hannah laughed. It felt good to laugh. "I'm not trolling for men."

"Then what *are* you doing here?"

"I'm waiting to talk to the hostess."

Ash gave her a quizzical look. "Why? Looking for a job?"

"Hardly. The hostess knew Ezra. I thought it would be worthwhile to talk with her."

"I guess I'm missing the connection." Ash regarded her through dark, heavy-lidded eyes. "Are you sure this doesn't have anything to do with his murder?"

"What would give you that idea?"

"I may play the part of the not-so-smart but mysterious and sexy outdoorsman, but I'm actually not that obtuse. I've seen you around town here and there, asking questions."

"Ezra was my friend. I want to see justice done." Hannah swirled the foam on her beer with one finger. "What do you know about Henry?"

"Henry Yarrow?"

Hannah nodded. "Rebecca says he was at the inn the other day with Ezra's niece, Maura. Doesn't that sound like an odd coupling?"

"I guess, but I'm not sure I'd believe what Rebecca says."

"Why not?"

"She's a little strange herself."

A waiter stopped by the table, and Ash ordered Hannah another beer and a Coke for himself. "Don't look at me like that. I'm working for a difficult client tomorrow," he said when the waiter was gone. "I need to be up early."

Hannah laughed. "Rebecca. Spill."

"There's nothing to spill. She and her husband Mark used to own the general store. They sold it to my cousin Annette a few years ago for a very large sum. Rebecca doesn't need the money, but she acts like that job at your inn is her life. Whenever I'm there, she just gives me the stink eye." He shrugged. "Not my favorite person."

"You're just not used to being around women who don't fawn over you."

"Funny." The pub crowd was thinning out, and the waiter returned with the beer and the Coke. Ash settled the bill. "In all seriousness, Hannah, I've watched her with your guests. She's a fantastic gardener, but she's not great with customer service."

Hannah downed half a beer in one gulp. Ash's opinions weren't a surprise to her. Rebecca *was* a strange bird. Ezra hadn't cared for her either, and she didn't seem to have many friends in town. Still, she was a great gardener, and she seemed to value her job.

"That doesn't mean she was lying about Henry."

"No," Ash said, "But she may have mistaken someone else for Henry, or she may have thought they were together when they weren't. In any case, why worry about it?"

Hannah debated how much to tell him. She settled on, "Because a man was murdered, and now his niece appears to be in a relationship with a person in town who wanted the dead man's property, so it seems logical to question—" Hannah turned her head in time to see Marjorie Moyer glance her way. She had her purse over her shoulder and keys in her hand. She made fleeting eye contact before racing out the front door.

Hannah stood up, nearly knocking over her beer. "Wait!"

She started to go after the woman, but Ash grabbed her wrist. "Hannah, stop," he hissed. "What are you going to do? Tackle her to the ground? She clearly doesn't want to talk."

Hannah felt herself go limp. He was right of course. She couldn't force Marjorie to talk to her. She nodded. Ash let go, and

Hannah ran outside in time just to see the other woman getting into a silver Honda Civic.

Hannah stood there and watched her drive away. Marjorie had been her chance to learn about the Fuller Foundation and whether what Louis had said was true. Short of stalking the woman, she didn't know how else to reach her.

Ash joined Hannah outside. "Come on. I'll drive you home."

"I can drive." But as the words left her mouth, she knew she shouldn't. When it came to drinking, she was a lightweight, and drinking and driving wasn't a line she'd ever cross again. She followed Ash to his truck.

The air inside the Toyota smelled of wood smoke and aftershave—Ash scents. Hannah buckled in and nestled back against the seat. As Ash left the lot and began the drive back to the inn, she found herself wondering how she was going to get her car the next day. She couldn't very well ask Reggie for a ride.

"I'll take you back tomorrow," Ash said, as though reading her mind. "I plan to get to the inn early."

"Thank you."

Ash slowed the vehicle and pulled to the side of the road. He turned to face Hannah. "Are you okay? You don't quite seem yourself these days. I can tell you're distracted. Is this about that woman?"

"I don't quite *feel* myself." Hannah glanced out the window, into the night and away from Ash's prying stare. "It's Ezra. Because he died on the inn's property, and because of our friendship, they considered me a suspect."

Ash was quite for a moment. She heard the rhythmic sound of his breathing, and for some reason found it comforting.

"You asked me about Rebecca earlier. I know the inn was searched earlier this week. I know because she told people the police searched your property. I wouldn't trust her, Hannah, and I wouldn't trust Mark. I'm not sure she's the friend you think she is."

Hannah looked down at her hands, clasped in her lap, and then up at Ash. "Rebecca's okay. She's just different."

"You asked me what I thought, and I told you. Take it for what it's worth."

"Thank you."

Ash smiled. "That's two thank-you's in one day. What's the world coming to?"

They drove the rest of the way to the inn in silence. When Hannah climbed out of the car, Ash got out as well.

"No need to walk me inside."

Ash pushed her hair back, away from her face. Even in the chill of the late August air, Hannah could feel his heat, smell that mix of musk and smoke. His touch against her bare skin was a thousand little jolts.

"Be careful," Ash said softly. "I know you're upset about what happened to Ezra, but it's not worth getting yourself mixed up in something dangerous."

"What if I'm already mixed up in something dangerous?"

Ash leaned down so their faces were just inches apart. The night was absolute, and a blanket of stars shown brightly overhead. Hannah, feeling the last tendrils of intoxication entwine with the beauty of the night and Ash's nearness, stood on tiptoe and kissed him.

Ash's eyes widened in surprise. He leaned into the kiss, clasping Hannah's hand in his own. Hannah stayed there for a moment, eyes closed, before she drew back.

"I'll be careful," she said and disappeared inside.

Chapter Twenty-Seven

Hannah woke up with a rock-splitting headache and the overcoat of dread that comes with knowing you've done something stupid. She rolled out of bed and stumbled to the shower. Even ten minutes of hot water couldn't clear her head. She needed coffee. Lots of coffee.

She dressed quickly and went into the inn's kitchen to make fresh coffee and put the apple-crumb cake she'd been storing in the freezer into the oven. As she was placing fresh berries on the counter next to small plates and pitchers of water and orange juice, Maura opened the door to her room and entered the common space.

"Can I get some fresh towels?" she asked, eyeing the brewing coffee.

"Sure. Do you need a room refresh too?"

"No, I'm okay." Maura stretched her arms over her head. Her normally straightened hair stuck out in frizzy waves, and mascara smudges ringed her eyes. "Just need coffee."

Maura looked worse than Hannah felt, so she poured her an extra-large mug of coffee as soon as the pot was ready. Maura took it with a drawn out "thank you."

"Give me a second, and I'll grab the towels," Hannah said.

She ran into the locked laundry room, and when she came back with a stack of fresh towels, Maura was sitting on the couch, looking out into the yard, her eyes red and wet.

"Are you okay, Maura?"

Maura swived around to look at Hannah. "We can't locate Waylen."

"I'm sorry to hear that."

Maura maintained eye contact for a few uncomfortable seconds before tearing her gaze away. She glanced around the room, finally settling on Turnip, who was sitting on the floor by the French doors, cleaning herself.

"Waylen was supposed to handle the will on our behalf." Maura sniffled, then blew her nose into a crumpled paper towel. "Yesterday, I went to see Uncle Ezra's attorney, a man named Theodore Smith. He says Waylen had already been to see him, and he had explained to him that we weren't inheriting anything." She blew her nose again. "Can you imagine that? Not one red cent for any of us."

"I'm sorry," Hannah said, her pulse quickening. She waited for the accusations and watched as Maura poked around in her sweatpants pocket for another tissue.

"I just don't get it," she said as she blew her nose. "When Uncle Ezra inherited all my grandfather's properties and money, I figured, *well, so what—he has no children. Eventually the family land will make it to us.* I know we weren't terribly close, but holy hell, to leave everything to a nonprofit? I mean, did he hate us so much that he left them everything?"

"A nonprofit? Is that what his attorney told you?"

"Smith? He was as worthless as deep conditioner for a bald man. Smith only told me that we weren't named in the will. He refused to say who was." Maura rubbed her knees with her hands, over and over. "If not us, then who? It has to be a nonprofit. Uncle Ezra was always going on about the environment or this issue or that issue." She sobbed again. "He must have really hated us."

Hannah left Maura in the living room with the clean towels, a box of Kleenex, a preoccupied Turnip, and a fresh cup of coffee. If Maura didn't know she was the heir, then that meant Waylen hadn't told her. Was that because he'd simply failed to mention it, or because he disappeared before he had a chance to spill the coffee beans?

Two Excedrin had helped Hannah's head return to normal, but she was still feeling a little hazy. The fresh towels reminded her that she hadn't cleaned or refreshed the Airstream since shortly after Rob's arrival—cleaning services were once a week for weekly Airstream guests—so she gathered her cleaning supplies and headed there now. Rob didn't open until the third knock, and when he did open the door, the force of his action nearly knocked Maura over.

"I haven't seen Waylen either, if that's what you're here to ask, and I'm not covering the bill for his damn room."

Rob looked better than Maura, but only by a fraction. His blond hair was unkempt, his face sported three days'-worth of stubble, and he'd either been smoking pot or had been sprayed by a skunk recently. Hannah took a step backward.

"That bad?" Rob asked.

"It looks like you could use some coffee."

"Maybe if it were hooked up to an IV." His face twisted into something like a smile. "I'd ask you in, but I need to straighten up a bit first."

Hannah held up the cleaning caddy. "I came to give a refresher clean and bring you some new towels. Do you want me to come back later?"

"Another time." He hesitated in the doorway, and behind him Hannah could see discarded clothing and crushed beer cans. "Simone and I are having some issues, and then Maura called me with the news about Ezra's will. It hasn't exactly been a banner day, and it's only, what—?"

"Nine-thirty."

"Right." He sighed. "Tell you what. I'll take those towels. Let me take a quick shower, and then I'll come up to the inn for some coffee."

"It'll be waiting."

On the way back to the inn, Hannah caught Rebecca watching her from her perch near the vegetable garden. She wasn't even scheduled to be there today. Hannah was about to walk over to her when Rebecca's cell phone rang. The other woman turned around to speak in private.

I'll catch her on the way out, Hannah thought, remembering that she still needed to get her car. That thought led to memories about last night and the kiss with Ash. She shook her head. *Me and alcohol don't mix*. She went to make more coffee for Ezra's family—and to down another cup herself.

*   *   *

"I can run you to Darien's now, if you're ready," Ash said later, through the kitchen window.

It was after eleven, and Hannah had been attending to inn tasks the since her conversation with Rob. She put away the last of the continental breakfast now that her guests were gone and planned to go find Rebecca.

"Sure," she said. She tried to detect whether Ash was having any reaction to the night before, but he just looked like normal Ash to her—slightly amused and very confident. She was certain random kissing was something that happened frequently in his world. At least more frequently than it did in hers. "Give me five minutes, and I'll meet you at your truck."

Five minutes turned into ten, and when she got out to Ash's truck, she found him talking with Noah. Noah looked from Ash to Hannah and back again.

"Your date was with Ash Kade?" Noah asked. He rocked back on his heels. "Huh. I hadn't thought of you as one of Ash's groupies."

Seriously, Reggie, Hannah thought. Her sister was a Swiss vault any other time. "No, *this* wasn't my date. I guess you were talking to my sister?"

"Ran into her at Benny's Diner. I told her I had some updates I wanted to share, and she suggested I wait until later today because you'd had a date last night."

"I told Reggie I was out with a friend. She made up the rest." Hannah slid into Ash's truck. "Ash is taking me to get my car. Can I call you later today?"

Noah looked torn, but he nodded. "Just don't forget."

On the way to the pub, Ash didn't mention the kiss. She figured he'd make some snide comment or use the chance to gloat—after all, *she* had kissed *him*—but instead they talked about the rain garden, the Yankees, and whether extra dark maple syrup was better than amber. When they reached her car, he waited until she was behind the wheel.

"Thanks for the ride," Hannah said.

"Thanks for the kiss," Ash said, and drove away.

Amused, Hannah slipped the car into drive. The lunch shift for Darien's was just arriving, and Hannah drove past two waitresses chatting in a shady corner of the parking lot. Behind them was a car she recognized from the night before—Marjorie's silver

Civic. A few seconds later, the hostess got out of the car and started to walk toward the entrance.

Hannah backed into a spot, parked, and ran after her.

"Are you kidding me?" Marjorie asked over her shoulder. She sped up, but Hannah got in front of her. "Now you're stalking me."

"This is a coincidence, I swear. I came back to get my car and happened to see you."

"Uh-huh. If you expect me to believe that, you're as clueless as Ezra." Marjorie reached out to push past Hannah, but Hannah stepped aside before she made contact.

"Please," Hannah said softly. "Just five minutes of your time. After that, I'll go away. I promise."

Hannah watched as annoyance gave way to resignation. "Fine, five minutes. I'm going to hold you to it. Follow me."

Marjorie led her to a picnic table behind the pub. She threw her bag down on the table and sat down, hard. "I can't imagine what you want to know. It's been years since Ezra and my husband parted ways."

Hannah took the seat opposite her, debating how to approach the topic. "I understand Ezra and your husband were the brains behind the Fuller Foundation."

Marjorie had foxlike features that she pinched into a scowl. "Is that what you heard? I suppose at the beginning that was true. Ezra and Tom came up with the idea together."

"While at the chemical company."

"Yes. They were both botanists. As Tom told it, they realized they'd gone to school to learn how to study and help nature, and instead they were spending their time killing it. Tom was originally from Burlington and Ezra from Jasper, and we all wanted to go back to Vermont." She leaned on the table, scraping the wood with her arm. "The foundation allowed us to go home."

"But things didn't end well?"

"If by 'didn't end well' you mean Ezra embezzling tens of thousands of dollars and leaving my husband holding the bag, correct, it didn't end well."

"Yet charges were never brought."

Marjorie's jaw clenched. "There was never any question regarding whether Ezra did what he did. He didn't even try to hide it. He claimed he was going to pay it back, but that's not how a trust works. You don't get to just *borrow* money whenever you'd like."

"Why didn't the foundation go to the police?"

"The foundation was just Ezra and Tom, plus a few support staff. Ezra's actions put Tom in an awful position—he could either call the police and turn his friend in, thereby risking the reputation of the foundation, or he could turn the other cheek. Tom did neither."

Marjorie's hand had begun to shake. Clearly Hannah had evoked bad memories, and she felt sorry about that, but she pressed on. "What did he do?"

"He told Ezra that if he didn't pay the trust back in full, he would call the police. He gave him a week."

Hannah's pulse quickened. The properties he sold—could they have been to cover the funds he'd stolen? "And did he?"

"Eventually, yes, but it took much longer than a week and caused a lot of problems, problems the foundation couldn't recover from." Marjorie glanced at her watch and stood up. Her uniform was too small, and the buttons stretched tautly across her chest, exposing a violet-colored bra. She covered her chest with her purse. "Your time is up."

"If it's any consolation, I think Ezra regretted what happened."

"Oh, I know he regretted it. He came to see me a few weeks before he died."

Stunned, Hannah said, "You talked with him?"

Marjorie snorted. "No effing way, and don't look at me like I'm some kind of witch. After what happened, my husband lost both his confidence and his career. To add insult to injury, their benefactor eventually pulled her funds. The foundation closed shortly after that." She stopped and stared squarely into Hannah's eyes. "But that wasn't the worst part. My husband took his own life because of what Ezra did. He lost everything, and he never got over feeling cheated by someone he'd trusted."

Hannah watched Marjorie walk away, feeling guilty. But beneath the guilt was another feeling—fear. Not the kind of icy, soul-gripping fear that comes with immediate danger, but a low-lying, lingering fear that she, too, had been played by Ezra Grayson. She had never thought her friend capable of embezzling funds or betraying a business partner. Apparently, Ezra had not been the man she'd thought he was.

Chapter
Twenty-Eight

Reggie called while Hannah was driving home from the brew pub.

"How was your date with Ash?"

Hannah made a left turn onto Route 100 and debated whether to be amused or annoyed. "I guess you spoke to Noah. Do the two of you communicate by police dispatch these days or is this just the Babysit Hannah Club?"

"Neither. He wants to talk to you, and I wanted to make sure you're okay."

"I'm fine."

"You're being kind of curt this afternoon."

"Am I?"

"Is it because I told you to stay out of the investigation? You know I meant well. I worry about you. It wasn't that long ago that you were in a relationship—"

"Are we going to rehash that again, Reggie? I was in a toxic relationship. I get that now, and I regret having stayed with Chris as long as I did. I'm also very grateful to you for helping me see the light. But that was three years ago. Can we please, please move past it?"

"It's not that easy, Hannah. I worry about you. Other than Peach, you're all I have."

"Yeah, well, you need to ease up. I can take care of myself."

"This is different. I just don't think you understand the dangers."

Hannah glanced in her rearview window. Something caught her eye—a flash of red six cars back. She rounded a curve and accelerated up a hill. She looked back again, hoping to see the profile of the vehicle as it rounded the same bend. There it was—a red Porsche Cayenne.

"Hannah?"

Two cars turned off the road, and now there were only three cars between Hannah and the Porsche. She strained to see the driver, but at that distance, they were only a dot behind the wheel. On impulse, she slowed, hoping the car behind her would pass and she could get a better look. *You're being paranoid, kiddo*, she thought to herself. Even if it was Waylen, what could he do out here?

"Hannah, are you okay?"

"I need to go, Reggie. I'll call you when I get to the inn."

"Hannah, something's wrong. I hear it in your voice. What's happening?"

"Later, Reggie. I'm fine." Hannah clicked off her phone.

The car behind her passed her in the next passing zone, but the driver behind them wasn't so patient and passed Hannah on a blind curve. *Jackass*, she whispered to herself. Now there was only one car between her and the Cayenne. Hannah tightened her hands on the wheel and willed herself to focus. She tried to see the Porsche's driver, but they were maintaining their distance, and she still couldn't make out a face.

At the next crossroads, the car behind her turned, leaving just her and the Porsche on the road. Hannah accelerated, debating whether to turn off onto a side road. In this area, most of the roads were gravel backroads, and she didn't want to be trapped on some country dead-end street with someone who meant her harm. Instead, she pushed down on the gas pedal. If it wasn't Waylen, she reasoned, the driver would maintain their distance. If it was Waylen—well, she'd figure out what to do.

She had her answer quickly. The Porsche was closing in fast. Hannah was nearing seventy miles per hour now in a fifty-five zone, and she could feel her chest constrict as she tried to breath. She had a sudden flashback of the drive with Chris, the crash that had marked the end of their relationship. Hannah's mouth went dry, her pulse pounded in her temples, but she accelerated further. The Porsche matched the increase.

Hannah wanted to call Noah but was afraid to take her hands off the wheel. She was coming up to a straight section followed by another curve. After that, there was just wilderness and limited phone reception for miles. Her Prius couldn't outrun a Porsche. She hit the power button on her car and jammed her foot on the gas, hard. The small car gunned forward, and Hannah aimed for the curve, hoping to get round it before the Cayenne caught up. Hannah knew this road like she knew the lines on her sister's face. Before the lonely stretch of road on the other side of the bend was a hiking trail and a small turnoff. If she could get to that, she could run up the trail. Waylen had a fast car, but he would never be able to catch her on foot in the wilderness. She was in shape; he was a desk jockey.

Only the Porsche was bearing down on her.

The SUV came at her like a high-speed train. They reached the curve at the same time, and the Porsche came up beside her, forcing her over. Hannah slammed on her brakes and slid into the small ditch at the side of the road. Her body was shaking; her eyes had narrowed to slits. The Porsche zoomed off into the distance. She locked the car doors and hit the speed dial for Noah.

"You wanted to see me?" She asked between panicky gulps of air. "Now would be a good time."

"Slow down. I can barely understand you. Are you okay?"

"I've been better. Waylen just ran me off the road, and I could use some help."

Chapter Twenty-Nine

Noah oversaw the tow truck that pulled Hannah's car out of the ditch, then followed her home. She'd had time to digest what had happened, and though still shaken, was calm by the time they reached her apartment.

Noah said, "Let's go for a walk."

"Now?"

"I still want to talk to you. After what you went through, I think you can understand the importance."

Hannah pulled on a pair of hiking boots and followed Noah outside. They walked down the path toward Devil's Pond. About halfway down the trail, Hannah put her hand on Noah's arm.

"I haven't been back here since I found Ezra."

"Don't you think it's time?"

Hannah shook her head. "I'm not so sure I'm ready. Especially after today."

"What if I needed you to? What if I said it's important to the case?"

Hannah clenched her hands together. Overhead, the trees formed a comforting tunnel of dark-green leaves, and the ground underneath them was a nurturing mixture of humus, pine needles, and wet leaves. Up ahead, though, she could see the glitter of sun on water. The pond, once a respite, now felt unwelcoming and even malign. And soon it would be the golden hour, just as it had been the day Ezra died.

"Noah—"

"Come on." He grabbed her hand. "Just come with me. I'll help you."

Hannah took a deep breath. Together they walked to the end of the path and out into the light. Noah chose to sit on a large boulder by the water's edge, near the boat launch, and he patted the spot next to him. Hannah refused to join him, preferring a smaller rock nearby. She pulled her knees up to her chin and wrapped her arms around her legs. The lake was beautiful this time of day. The water was still, and the trees reflected off the glass-like surface, mirroring the breathtaking view.

An eagle flew overhead, swooped down, and landed on the top branches of a maple tree, watching them. Noah followed its progress with his eyes. He said, "Did you know Ezra's niece Maura is having an affair with Henry?"

"Rebecca mentioned that she'd seen them together, and I'd noticed that Maura doesn't always sleep at the hotel."

"Why didn't you tell me?"

Hannah turned to look at him. "Because I just found out. I meant to tell you, but with everything that was going on, it slipped my mind."

Noah picked up a stone and tossed it into the water. "Did you know that Maura has a record? She was charged with forging checks about ten years ago, and a few years after that, she was arrested for identity theft."

"I had no idea." *But it explained why she didn't want me to call the police when someone tried to break into her room*, Hannah thought.

233

"I figured as much." He paused, studying the tiny ripples running on the mirror-surface of the lake. "We're watching her, Hannah. I thought you should know."

Hannah considered what he was telling her—the substance as well as the very fact of it. "Does that mean you think Henry could be part of this too?"

"Maura has an alibi for the evening Ezra died, and it's Henry, who conveniently forgot much about that day. We questioned them both, and they denied any wrongdoing. You and I both know that may or may not mean they're innocent." He shrugged. "All of them have an alibi except Waylen, who claims he was out driving that night—to clear his head."

The eagle flew from its branch, circling overhead. It swooped near the water's surface out by the marsh but soared upward without prey. Hannah thought back to the day she had found Ezra's body by the lake. Moose, sitting vigil by his human companion, waiting—for what? For Ezra to wake up? For a chance to sink his teeth into the person who'd killed him? She thought of Ezra's niece and nephews circling the property like birds of prey, watching and waiting for their turn to gain a profit from Ezra's death.

Had Maura, Waylen, and Rob known how wealthy Ezra was? Had she been the last to find out? And what about Henry Yarrow? He was in a race to get that property before Brian Lewis or even Chad. Had he been part of a conspiracy to finally force the sale of Ezra's piece of Jasper? It seemed unthinkable. For that matter, Maura seemed to be the least likely relative to be in on any plot, but here was Noah, someone she trusted, saying that she might have had a role in Ezra's murder.

Hannah said calmly, "A week ago, you thought *I* was involved."

"I never *thought* you were involved. We had to explore all possibilities. You had the most to gain. That's just a fact."

"I had the most to gain, but I didn't know it at the time Ezra died. What if someone else *thought* they had the most to gain and acted on that belief?"

Noah nodded. "Which is why the family members are still the most likely suspects."

Hannah stood up. The boat launch was just a small, rocky beach that sloped gently into the water until the bottom dropped to fifteen feet about ten feet from shore. Hannah slipped off her hiking boots and waded out, feeling the pinprick of tiny rocks on the tender soles of her feet.

"What about Waylen?" she asked over her shoulder. "The DNA linking him to the rock sounds like a real lead, not just conjecture. He ran me right off that road just now." Hannah took a deep breath, remembering the feeling of helplessness that had coursed through her as his vehicle sideswiped hers. "He could have killed me, but he didn't. It was a warning."

"Did you get a good look at him?"

"How could I? I was too busy trying not to crash."

"I know that must have been terrifying."

Hannah turned around. "It doesn't sound like you really *know* anything."

Noah didn't respond, and Hannah instantly regretted her harsh words.

"Why are you telling me any of this, Noah? Why drag me out here? How have I gone from person of interest to confidante in days?"

Noah climbed off the rock and stood on the shore, at the edge of the water. In the afternoon light, his face was all planes and shadows. "Waylen knows you've been chosen to inherit Ezra's estate, right?"

Hannah nodded.

"Assuming it *was* Waylen, his actions today were most likely a warning, like you said. He wants you to stay out of the investigation, and he also wants you to know they're coming for you. Intimidation tactics. If he and Maura are working together, then she knows too."

Hannah looked downward at the water. "She hasn't given me any indication she knows, if that's what you mean."

"Remember what I said at the outset. She's a con artist. Just because she hasn't said anything doesn't mean she doesn't know."

The wind had started to pick up, and gentle waves splashed against Hannah's legs. She bent down and dipped her hands in the cold, clear water. "You want me to keep an eye on Maura."

"I want you to close the inn, but I know that's not going to happen. So yes, I want you to watch for suspicious behavior, odd visitors, that sort of thing. But that's it, nothing more." He moved toward Hannah. "Whoever did that today means business. You need to be careful. This isn't a game."

"Why don't you just arrest Waylen?"

"We would if we could, but we don't have enough to make anything stick."

Hannah raked her fingers through the water as she'd done a thousand times before. Before, though, the lake had always felt like a sanctuary. Now, the cold felt jarring and unwelcome. She looked up at the surrounding woods. and instead of their beckoning to her, she saw danger lurking in their shadows. Someone could be hiding in there, waiting.

Whoever had killed Ezra was responsible for this. They had stolen Ezra's life, and they had stolen her peace.

Nurturing that bloom of anger had been Noah's plan. It's why he wanted her to come out to Devil's Pond with him. He wanted to remind her of what she'd lost.

She said, "I'll do whatever you want."

"I want you to be extra vigilant. I'll have a car drive by the inn a few times every evening, but I need to know you'll call me if anything—I mean *anything*—happens."

Hannah's smile was sad. Yet she was happy to have reconnected with Noah, even under these circumstances. Suddenly he was more than the annoying crush she remembered from high school.

She said, "I don't see what coming after me would do for them now. If I were to die, Ezra's property would pass to my heir, who is Reggie. They'll never see his money."

"Someone wants that land. Whether it's for a commercial deal or another fancy Airbnb property, I can't say, but if they can't get it legally, they'll try to intimidate you into selling it."

"And if Maura, Waylen, and Henry aren't working together?"

Noah frowned. "Maura knows she's not an heir, but she claims she doesn't know who is. She and Rob will stick around to contest the will. It's best if they don't find out Ezra chose you."

"Why wouldn't Waylen have simply told them?"

"Maybe he did, and they're pretending not to know. Or maybe he really is doing this on his own and wants to hold all the cards himself."

Hannah grappled with what he was saying, trying to make sense of the possibilities. "You're telling me to be discreet."

"I'm *asking* you to be discreet."

As they walked back along the path, toward the inn, Hannah pictured Ezra's killer tossing the bloody rock in the woods by the trail to Devil's Pond. Rob, Waylen, and Maura were obvious suspects, but Rebecca, Ash, and Henry had been on the property before the day the rock was found. Any one of them could have done it as well. She just couldn't see it, though; she'd known the three of them for years.

And then there was the will. The damn will.

Even with the newest information about the DNA and Maura's liaison with Henry, Hannah couldn't shake the feeling that Ezra's past was somehow significant. There was the very fact of all his money, but there was also his strange behavior leading up to the time of his death. He'd sought forgiveness from Louis and Tom Moyer's wife Marjorie. He'd talked to her father about the zoning restrictions. Were these simply the actions of a dying man, or had Ezra had some other goal in mind?"

"Pinecone for your thoughts," Noah said, tossing a pinecone at her.

They'd arrived back at the clearing to the inn's property. Ash was gone, and the newly minted meadow looked fresh. From this vantage point, the inn was a charming homage to yesteryear, with its yellow wooden siding and purple shutters, broad wraparound porch, and screened-in sunroom. The flowers waving from their beds added gaiety and life, inviting the insects that were buzzing about, oblivious to a murder investigation happening in their midst. Viewed from here, Hummingbird Hollow was a place to be celebrated, a retreat from the real world. If Noah was right, it could also be harboring murderers—a thought that continued to unsettle her.

"I'm thinking something doesn't add up," Hannah said. "Three cousins came to Jasper to convince their uncle to move into a retirement home and to sell his property. When the uncle is murdered, they stick around. Even a con artist would know enough to leave town as soon as possible. Why stay?"

"Why, indeed?" Noah gestured toward the inn. "Yet two are still here, and one is pretending to be missing."

* * *

Reggie called at ten that night. Hannah had the inn locked up for the evening and was sitting on the couch, reading a book about homesteading, Moose at her feet. Turnip had decided that Moose was an acceptable houseguest, and was curled up against the dog's warm body, purring softly.

My little family, Hannah thought.

"Noah told me what happened today," Reggie said. "Are you okay?"

"I'm fine, but can we talk about this tomorrow?"

"I'll do you one better. Chad has Peach this weekend. Why don't we meet at Ezra's house and you can explain to me everything you've been doing related to his murder."

Hannah opened her mouth to argue and closed it quickly. Her sister's usual judgmental tone was gone, replaced by something eerily similar to actual interest. Surely this was a trap.

"I don't know what you're talking about."

"I'm talking about breakfast with Louis Driver, drinks with Ash, and a playdate at Ezra's with Teddy Smith. Unless you've ordered the Vermont Men of All Ages Sampler Platter, you're up to something. And the common link is Ezra."

"We discussed this earlier. I'm an adult, Reggie—"

Reggie sighed. "I know, and I'm sorry for giving you a hard time before. It's just that after Mom, and now with Dad . . . well, I can't lose you too. I need you, and Peach needs you." She paused. "When Noah told me what had happened, I realized I was wrong. I love you, Hannah. I don't say it enough, but it's true."

Hannah had left her cozy cocoon and was standing by the back window, staring out into the dark yard. "I love you, too, but that doesn't explain the change of heart."

"If you're going to keep slinking around town, then at least let me help you."

239

"What makes you think I can even get into Ezra's house?"

"Really, Hannah? I've been watching you sneak in and out of places since you were twelve. It's a cliché because it's true—there's safety in numbers. Let me sneak with you."

Hannah wasn't so sure about safety or her sister's ability to sneak, but she agreed to meet Reggie at Ezra's at seven the next morning anyway.

Chapter Thirty

Hannah showed up at Ezra's house at 7:03 the next morning. In an effort not to advertise her arrival, she parked down the road, near the church, and she and Moose walked to the house. The early-morning air was still heavy with the scent of evening primrose. Ezra's flower gardens, long gone wild, now tumbled into the yard like a child's unruly curls. Morning glory had taken over one corner of the house, and its vines had strangled the peonies and lilies that once thrived by the back windows. Hannah made a mental note to clean up the garden. It was something she could do, at least.

Moose seemed happy to be home, and he tugged her along the path that led to the side of the house closest to the forest. Rain-clouds hung low in the sky, and a thick mist, not yet burned off by the sun, had settled over Jasper. Hannah looked behind her, toward the outbuildings, feeling a heavy sense of unease. What if someone was watching her? Her run-in with the red Cayenne had her on edge, and she saw shadows everywhere.

Moose tensed, head cocked, and Hannah felt her own muscles tightening. "What's there, boy?"

Just then, Reggie popped out from behind a tree.

Hannah jumped, a scream gurgling in her throat, but her sister's grin was contagious, so she laughed despite her annoyance. "You're nuts."

"Broke the tension, didn't I?" She reached down and scratched Moose behind the ears.

"At the expense of my mental health."

Reggie glanced at the house and down at the dog. "I tried all the doors, and they're locked. Tell me, Houdini, how are we getting inside?"

Hannah handed the leash to her sister. "Go to the back door with Moose and wait."

Hannah found the broken window in the basement and shimmied her way through it. Her feet found the ladder she'd placed underneath, and despite the darkness in there, she was able to make her way down the ladder and onto solid ground. She put her cell-phone light on to find her way to the stairs and let herself up and into the house.

The first thing she noticed was the smell: the sharpness of creosote mingled with the damp, musty scent of mildew. Dust and soot had settled on the furniture, and the white fabric in the background of Ezra's Queen Anne chair was tinged gray. A listlessness could be felt in the house, and the sound of Hannah's shoes on wooden floors echoed in a way she did not recall. The house, barely habitable when Ezra was alive, was in the throes of giving up entirely.

Hannah opened the back door and ushered Reggie and Moose inside. The dog ran through the house, tail wagging, nose to the ground. *He's looking for Ezra*, Hannah thought. Tears stung her eyes, and she looked up to see her sister holding out a hand.

"Moose will be okay," Reggie said. "He needs this closure too." She grabbed Hannah's hand and together they walked through the downstairs. "Does anything look out of place?"

"It's hard to tell because the police and Ezra's vultures were here. What I really need to focus on is upstairs, in Ezra's study."

Hannah led Reggie to the top of the creaking stairs and into the study. The room looked as it had the last time she was here—with an extra coat of dust. The box of newspapers and magazines was still on the floor where she'd left it, as were the photographs.

"What are we looking for?" Reggie asked, pulling on a pair of latex gloves. When she saw the exasperated look Hannah was giving her, she said, "*What*? Who knows how long these boxes have been sitting here? They could be full of silverfish and who knows what else."

Hannah shook her head. Leave it to Reggie to think of silverfish at a time like this. She pulled the curtains tightly closed and sat down in front of the photographs, sifting through them one by one, while Reggie went through the media box. Moose had finished roaming the house, and after walking in a tight circle several times, finally settled down in the open doorway with a huff.

The sisters worked in silence punctuated only by Moose's gentle snores and the occasional sounds of a car heading down Main Street. Hannah listened closely for any cars stopping at Ezra's house. It was a toasty eighty-four outside, and with the windows closed, the upstairs of Ezra's house lacked ventilation. Sweat beaded on her forehead and trickled between her breasts. The room was dusty and stuffy and hot, but she didn't dare open a window for fear of alerting someone to their presence. Better uncomfortable than noticed.

Most of the photos in the box were of Molly. It was like looking at a time capsule—the woman had barely changed through the years. Hannah could tell the decade during which each picture was taken only by the clothing and the background. She even saw the Buick that Ezra kept abandoned in the barn, shiny and new. With each photo, Hannah felt a sense of melancholy settle around her like that morning's fog. Separated from the rest of his stuff, many of their edges worn from constant handling, these photos had clearly been important to him. Even more than that, they reminded her of her own family and her family's deep connection to this changing town.

It all goes by so very quickly, Hannah thought. One day it might be Peach looking back at pictures of us. What would her legacy be?

"These are just local articles," Reggie said, interrupting Hannah's thoughts. "Tell me why we're going through them? The man was a hoarder."

Hannah hadn't told Reggie about the Fuller Foundation and Ezra's role in its demise. Part of her was afraid to tell her even now, for fear she'd hold it against Ezra, so she answered, "Look for patterns or maybe the names of local companies or organizations that repeat. He may have been a hoarder, but there must have been a reason why those papers were kept separately. Everything else he has aside from his financial records and these photos is scattered around the house."

Reggie kept shuffling through the papers. "I guess." She sounded unconvinced.

Hannah got to the bottom of the box of photos and pulled out the last twenty or so. Most were of another neighborhood picnic. These pictures had clearly been taken by someone other than Ezra because he was in some of them.

At first glance, they were run-of-the-mill photographs, the kind you'd see taken during neighborhood cookouts across the country: groups of adults milling about, eating hot dogs and corn on the cob; plastic lawn chairs placed in circles, with people chatting and some playing volleyball or congregating around the food table nearby. Nothing extraordinary. Hannah recognized a handful of people—her mother and Tilda, Phyllis, Kendra and Jay Birk, and Ash's father. In two of the photos Ezra, looking younger, leaner, less hunched over, stood near the grill holding a spatula. He seemed alone, his focus somewhere other than on the camera.

There were only two pictures of the normally social Molly. In both, she was sitting in a lawn chair with a blanket over her lap, looking glum. One shot caught her alone, her gaze moist and faraway. In the second picture, she was with a man who was standing over her at an angle so that his mouth was pressed to her ear. He held her hand in his, and Molly's eyes were closed. She looked on the edge of tears.

The photo telegraphed deep sadness and total compassion. It was evident that the man holding Molly's hand was trying to comfort her, and she was letting him. It was an intimate shot, and anyone looking at the picture would have said the two were friends. Close friends. Confidants.

Hannah recognized the man's neatly clipped beard and bespoken style.

Louis Driver.

*   *   *

It was after ten that morning when Hannah and Reggie finished going through Ezra's study. Hannah had pulled several photos from the pile, and she placed them on the floor in front of her sister. There were four in total, one from each decade up through 2002.

"Before and after," Hannah said.

Reggie pursed her lips. "Before and after what?"

"That's the question."

"You're talking in riddles again, Hannah." Reggie bent lower and shined her cell phone light on the photos. "These are all of Molly Grayson. What does Molly have to do with Ezra's death?"

"That's just it, I don't know." Hannah slid onto her stomach, propping her head on her palms, and looked again at the photos. She pointed to the first one, a very old black-and-white picture. "Molly in her twenties, full of smiles." She flicked the second photo toward Reggie. "Molly in her thirties, acting like the hostess with the mostess at some neighborhood event." She tapped the third picture. "Molly presiding over a picnic like she was serving the president." Hannah looked up at her sister. "In every one of these, Molly looks happy and comfortable to be in the spotlight. Now look at this one."

The fourth picture was dated August 20, 2002. It was the photo from the picnic during which Louis was talking with a visibly upset Molly.

"What do you see?"

"Molly looks ready to cry, and some man is trying to comfort her. So what?"

"I couldn't find another happy picture of Molly after this shot. In fact, there are hardly any pictures of Molly or Ezra after this picnic."

"Still not following."

Hannah stretched her way into a sitting position. "I've visited Ezra nearly every day for more than two years. In all that time, he gave me no inkling that he had money or that he planned to leave me his estate. That's bothered me, Reggie. Why would he hide that from me? He obviously trusted me enough to be his heir."

Hannah ran a finger across the fourth photo and placed her nail on Louis's head. "Before Ezra died, he paid a visit to that man. He's the vintage-clothing-store owner I told you about—Ezra's brother-in-law, Louis Driver. Louis told me Ezra went there to make amends. He told me that his wife Anita had been worried about Molly because she had suddenly become very withdrawn, and she blamed Ezra for her sister's condition. Within a few years of that photo, Molly died."

Reggie let out a familiar sigh of exasperation. "Hannah, this sounds like your imagination running wild—"

Hannah gave a warning head shake. "Do you want to help me or not?"

Reggie nodded, and Hannah went on, "There's more." She told her about the Fuller Foundation and Ezra's trip to see Tom Moyer's widow, Marjorie. "It was as though he'd been going through the AA step of making amends, only with Dad he was confrontational."

"The Fuller Foundation. That's awful," Reggie said. "He committed fraud, and a man took his own life because of it."

"He sought forgiveness."

"People do that when they're facing their mortality. They try to make amends. It's not uncommon, but it doesn't excuse what happened."

"No, it doesn't. I just can't believe Ezra would do something like that." Hannah stared at the photo. "One of those people he met with was Dad."

"You told me that before." Reggie frowned. "You think he wronged Dad?"

"He sold that land to Dad, and afterward they stopped talking. Then suddenly he saw Dad twice in as many weeks? Dad said he wanted him to petition to pass a zoning law, but what if there was another connection between the two of them?" Hannah stood, extending her arms upward, and threw her head back. She felt a headache creeping around the edges of her skull. "Why would Ezra keep boxes of old news clippings? His house is full of random piles of newspapers and magazines, yet he kept them in a separate box. Nothing makes sense, and now he's dead, and I can't ask him a goddamn thing."

Reggie held up a hand. "What date did you say was on that last photo?

"August 20, 2002."

"Hannah, look at this." Reggie started pulling magazines and newspapers from the pile. "Every article, magazine, and newspaper in this box is dated between August 2002 and January 2007."

Hannah stared at the pile. "That's bizarre. Why would he keep only those?"

Reggie handed her a paper from Manchester, Vermont, and another from Brattleboro. "I have no idea, but he did. There are no notes or highlights, either."

"The dates coincide." Hannah crouched down, pulling the papers and magazines together and placing them back in their boxes.

"What are you doing?"

"Taking these with us. Before you say a word, Teddy's not going to care or notice. I can't find any of Ezra's financial documents, and Teddy still hasn't contacted the police to find out if they have them. I won't destroy anything."

"Suit yourself."

Hannah was expecting opposition. She felt oddly disappointed.

"Where to next?" Reggie asked.

"We drop Moose off at the inn, and then on to Louis Driver. It seems my new friend has lied to me."

Chapter
Thirty-One

A Vintage Look wasn't open. Hannah knocked on the door in case Louis was inside, but no one answered and the interior was dark. The shop had no listed hours; a sign on the door said simply, "CLOSED."

Hannah texted Louis, but she received no immediate response. A call also went unanswered.

"He's avoiding you," Reggie said.

"Why would he do that?"

"Maybe he has something to hide."

Hannah slid back into the driver's seat. "*Please.*" But even as she said the word, she considered what she knew about Louis—almost nothing. He *had* been one of the people Ezra visited before he died. Maybe Louis had been lying to her all along and had a reason to want Ezra dead.

Hannah looked at her sister. "You know, all this time, we've been thinking of the people who had something to gain from Ezra's murder: money; access to his property. What if Ezra was killed for another reason altogether—like to cover up a secret?"

Reggie leaned back against the seat. "What kind of secret?"

"A crime, perhaps? Think about what we *do* know. Around the summer of 2002, Molly changed. She may have been ill, but those close to her deny knowing anything about an illness."

"She could have been depressed or suffering from anxiety," Reggie said.

"Maybe," Hannah said. "And there was certainly more stigma about mental health issues back then, but what if the reason she changed was linked somehow to Ezra? We also know that during that time Ezra was accused of embezzling money. Then he sold his land to Dad. Clearly, he needed money."

"Gambling addiction?" Reggie asked, sitting up straighter in her seat.

"That's a possibility, and if Molly knew, maybe she withdrew from her circle of friends out of shame or embarrassment."

Hannah started the car. "I know someone who might be able to tell us." She pulled away from the curb, trying to remember her mother's friend's address. "Phyllis. She was also in those photos from the picnic in 2002. If Ezra had a gambling addiction or other problem, she might know about it."

*　*　*

Phyllis was just getting into her car when Hannah and Reggie pulled up next to her. They climbed out of the Prius and walked to her parking spot.

"Twice in one month! People will begin to think we've reconciled." Phyllis grinned. She opened her arms wide and gave them each a hug.

"Can you spare ten minutes before you go wherever you're going?" Hannah asked.

Phyllis glanced at her watch. "I have a doctor's appointment, so make it quick."

Hannah opened her bag and pulled out the photo from 2002, the one of Molly and Louis, and showed it to Phyllis. "It looks like the summer of 2002 was about the time Molly started to withdraw. You were at this picnic. Do you remember anything she might have said or done that day?"

Phyllis squinted at the photo. Then she reached into her large leather bag, pulled out a pair of reading glasses, and gave the photo another long look. Finally, she shook her head and handed the photo back to Hannah. "I'm afraid I don't remember much of anything about that day." She made a drinking gesture with one hand. "We enjoyed a few beers when we got together. I was probably two sheets to the wind, as they say."

"How about Ezra?" Reggie asked. She told Phyllis about the Fuller Foundation. "Is it possible he had a gambling or other problem back then?"

Phyllis looked from Reggie to Hannah and back again. "You've been doing your research." She sighed and leaned back against her Subaru. "Everyone knew something was going on with those two, but no one knew exactly what. I didn't know why he'd left the Fuller Foundation, but that makes sense given the aura of secrecy at the time. So unfortunate. Molly withdrew, as you know, but Ezra was acting strange as well. Maybe that was it, or maybe there was something else going on in their lives."

"It seems like everyone who would know is either gone or not talking." Hannah studied her mother's best friend, looking for some suggestion that she wasn't being completely truthful. She saw only concern and curiosity.

Reggie said, "It's too bad Molly's sister isn't still alive."

"Anita?" The concern and curiosity morphed into confusion. "Why would you want to talk with Anita? She wouldn't have been able to help you."

"Why not?" Hannah asked, thinking about the letters Ezra had written to Anita before Molly died. "They'd been close."

"I don't know who told you that, but it's not true. Anita wasn't a very nice person. We all put up with her because she was Molly's sister, but the two of them rarely spoke. I think Anita blamed Ezra for the rift, but it wasn't his fault." She shook her head in emphasis. "Louis was the one Molly was close to. They were like brother and sister, those two. If you have a question, ask him."

Hannah and Reggie exchanged a look. Phyllis glanced at her watch.

"The ophthalmologist awaits," she said. "Next time we get together, no more murder talk, please. I retired from law for a reason."

Hannah was about to suggest a dinner date when her cell phone rang—Rebecca's ringtone. She pulled it out of her bag and answered. Rebecca rarely contacted her unless it was urgent.

"Everything okay?"

"The police are here. Someone broke into the Airstream, and your guest is pretty upset."

"Be there in twenty minutes." Hannah hung up and told the two women what had happened.

"Related to the case?" Phyllis asked.

"Who knows," Hannah said. "At this point, nothing would surprise me."

*   *   *

Two police cars and Noah's truck were at the inn when Hannah and Reggie arrived. Noah and the uniformed officers were talking to Rob, who was standing near the inn's entrance looking shaken. Rebecca was in the vegetable garden, weeding between the tomatoes as if nothing had happened. She glanced at Hannah and shrugged her shoulders.

"What's happened?" Hannah asked as she approached the group.

"Someone broke into the Airstream," Rob said. "So much for small-town safety."

"Did they take anything?" Reggie asked.

"It doesn't look like it," Rob said. "They made a mess of the place, but my money and other stuff is still in there."

Noah glanced toward the Airstream and frowned. "Whoever did it used force to break the lock. We dusted for prints but didn't pull up anything on the door—it was wiped clean. Inside, we only found Rob's prints, so we're assuming whoever did this wore gloves."

"We all know who it was," Rob said. He had his hands on his hips. His reddened face and clenched jaw contrasted with his forcedly calm tone of voice. "Isn't it obvious? He's been missing for days."

"We don't know for sure that it was Waylen," Noah said.

Rob made what sounded like a low growl and walked away, into the inn.

"He's pretty upset," Hannah said. "I can understand why."

"He seems convinced this was Waylen and that it's related to Ezra's death, but he can't—or won't—tell me how. For right now, we have no reason to believe this was anything other than a break-in."

"They didn't take any money," Reggie said. "If it had been kids or a thief, they'd have stolen *something*."

"Not necessarily," Noah said. "According to Rob, there was no cash lying around. Thieves like easy targets and no fuss. They could have been spooked by Moose's barking or the sound of a car and left before they had the chance to find something of value."

Hannah looked at the Airstream that she, Reggie, and Ash had so carefully restored. Its door was gaping open. "This is the second break-in attempt at the inn, once with Maura and now with Rob. Maybe Rob's right and this *is* Waylen's work." Hannah looked at Rebecca, who was squatting in the garden, her back to them. "Have you talked to Rebecca?"

"She says she arrived after the break-in, which happened around eight this morning."

"She was supposed to be here by eight."

Noah shrugged. "HR problems are not in my purview." He cracked his knuckles and directed one of the uniformed officers to have another look around. "Then we'll be out of your way, Hannah."

"No Maura?" Hannah asked, noting the woman's absence from the yard and her car's absence from the lot. If she were here, Maura would be part of the action.

"No Maura," Noah said. "I can only assume she's with Henry."

*   *   *

Hannah went inside to find Rob pacing the common area, his hands clasped behind his back, his breathing labored. When he saw Hannah and Reggie, he looked up and shook his head.

"What a mess! First my uncle is killed, and now my cousin is missing. I tried telling the cops that Waylen broke into the Airstream, but they wouldn't listen. He's looking for something, I know it. Maura said someone tried to get into her room too. Unless you're breaking into your own guests' rooms, it must be Waylen."

Hannah put her bag down on the counter. "What would he be looking for?"

Rob continued pacing. Hannah thought he was ignoring her question, but then he added, "He's paranoid, always has been. I'm sure he thinks we're holding out on him. That one of us struck some sort of side deal with Ezra before he died."

"Did you?" Reggie asked.

"Of course not," Rob scoffed. "Ezra had zero interest in selling that property, and now that he's gone, it's probably going to go to some third party with no tie to the land or the house."

"The house has been in your family for a long time," Hannah said.

"My mom and her siblings, including Ezra, grew up there. At one time, my grandfather owned half of Devil's Mountain. Who do you think sold it to the ski resort?"

"And yet he gave what was left to Ezra?" Hannah asked.

Rob walked to the island in the kitchen and poured himself a cup of stale coffee. "Ezra was the eldest male. Maura's mom was the oldest child, then Ezra, then Waylen's dad, then my mother. My grandfather was a misogynist. He believed only men could manage things other than a household."

"That must have angered his daughters," Hannah said.

"Of course—as well as Waylen's dad. We—the cousins—figured that we'd see the family property when Ezra passed, but it sounds like we'll have to fight for it." He looked at Hannah over the rim of his mug. "Maura talked to Ezra's lawyer. The whole estate goes to some unknown third party, even the damn dog."

Hannah studied Rob for some indication that he knew she was that someone, but if Waylen had told him, he didn't let on. "I'm sorry. About your uncle, about his estate, about the break-in. This can't be easy for you."

Hannah's words seemed to act like a valve releasing the steam fueling his agitation. Rob sank down onto a stool and stared into his coffee cup. "I think my wife is leaving me," he said quietly. "I came up here hoping Ezra could offer us a fresh start in a new place."

Reggie said, "You wanted to move here?"

Rob looked up at Reggie, then Hannah. "Before Ezra died, I stopped by his house alone. We talked about the old days, about the woods and his love of nature. He seemed oddly melancholy. I thought I'd convinced him to move to a smaller place. I offered to take over the house and fix it up so he could move back in later, with us, if he wanted." Rob shook his head. "I had visions of becoming part of this community—with Simone."

"Simone seems like more of a city girl," Hannah said. "Was that what she wanted?"

Rob gave her a hard smile. "She doesn't know what she wants. She'd learn to love it here."

Hannah wasn't so sure, and from the skeptical look on Reggie's face, neither was she. "Did you know your uncle was ill?"

Rob looked at her sharply. "Ill as in . . .?"

"Terminal liver disease."

"Waylen hinted at it, and the police asked me about Ezra's health, but I didn't know for certain until after he died." Rob stood up, began pacing again. "That makes sense. He didn't quite seem himself, and when I suggested renovating the house so he could move in with us, he laughed at me. I thought . . . well, I thought he was laughing at the idea of living with Simone and me."

"But he may have been laughing at the idea of *living*," Reggie said quietly. She was sitting on the couch with Turnip on her lap, and she stroked the cat's fur without looking up. "If none of you knew for sure Ezra was sick, why this trip? Why now?"

"The fire," Rob said. "We knew he needed to move out of that house."

"Ezra said you were pushing him to sell the property," Hannah said.

"Maybe *they* were, but not me. I love Vermont. I wanted to live here."

"What was in it for them if Ezra sold now?" Reggie asked.

Rob shrugged. "Lock in a high price? Make sure our uncle could fund his own retirement? They thought his insistence on staying was ridiculous, especially Waylen. Waylen wanted him to sell everything to the highest bidder, move somewhere that could take care of him, and have funds to ensure that care would be paid for without dipping into the proceeds from the property. He was worried Uncle Ezra would become a burden on us if someone didn't help him manage his money." Rob's handsome face darkened with anger. "Waylen was sneaking around, trying to shore up some deals, pit one bidder against the other. If he knew Ezra was sick, he likely had an angle—maybe he was even trying to get a piece for himself."

Hannah thought about the three cousins, about Ezra's description of them as vultures. "You, Waylen, and Maura were seen walking around the property a few days ago with Henry Yarrow and Brian Lewis. Was that about pitting one bidder against another?"

Rob gave a halfhearted laugh. "Pretty much. Waylen's idea—back when we all thought we were inheriting."

"What are you going to do now?" Hannah asked.

Rob rubbed his eyes with big, callused hands. "Until we know more about Ezra's heir, I refuse to believe it's not us. I'll wait a few more days until the police dig their heads out of their asses, and then I'll head back to New York. For now," he shrugged again, "I'll put my belongings back together again and wait. We're going to contest the will. We just need to identify our opponent."

Rob looked so forlorn that Hannah couldn't help but feel a tug of empathy. "Do you want a new room? It might be strange staying in the Airstream. I can put you in the rooms Waylen had."

"No, that's okay. A fresh lock would be nice, though. And some new sheets and towels. No rush on the sheets and towels." Hannah agreed to get a locksmith out right away. "In the meantime, you can put your stuff in the spare room. I'll show you to it."

"Thanks, Hannah."

You won't be thanking me soon, Hannah thought, dreading the day Rob and Maura learned that *she* was their opponent.

Chapter
Thirty-Two

Reggie needed to spend time at the office on Monday, so Hannah headed to Louis's house on her own. The man still hadn't responded to her text messages or her call, so she was left with one choice—to wait for him at his home. As she pulled into his driveway behind his car, she realized there would be no waiting. She found Louis outside, building what looked like a small fairy village in his flower garden. When he saw Hannah, he stopped what he was doing and stood up. He wore spotless work pants, a button-down chambray shirt, suspenders, and a large khaki breezer hat.

"What brings you here, Ms. Drew?"

"Your refusal to answer my calls or texts."

Louis smiled. "I've been out here working. Do you like my village? I bought these miniatures at an auction. They look rather darling in the garden."

They did look cute, but Hannah was too annoyed to tell him so. "I need to talk to you, Louis."

"Clearly, or you wouldn't be here."

Hannah took a deep breath. *Stay calm.* "You lied to me."

"I did no such thing."

"You said you didn't know why Molly withdrew. But you do know."

Louis took his time tidying his garden tools. When he was finished, he said, "Come in for some tea. Let's make this a civilized conversation."

"Civilized? A man is dead—*murdered*—and you want to have tea?" *Great, so much for staying calm, Hannah.* "I don't want tea. I want answers."

Louis looked ready to argue, but instead he said softly, "Let's at least sit in the shade. My old ticker can't take much of this heat."

Hannah joined him in a set of red Adirondack chairs toward the back of his property. They were situated under a large maple tree that bordered the forest, and the maple provided a wide canopy of shade and dappled the harsh sunlight filtering through its leaves. It was a nice spot to relax, and if it weren't for the task at hand, Hannah would have enjoyed sipping tea under the tree's generous branches.

Instead, she pulled the photo of Louis and Molly from her purse and handed it to Louis. "Take a look."

"What exactly did you glean from this?" Louis asked.

"That's the body language of two people who care very much for each other."

"Molly was my sister-in-law."

"I was Chad's sister-in-law, but he never comforted me like that."

Louis handed the photo back to her with a flourish of his hand. "You're reading far too much into one picture."

Hannah's chin jutted forward. "Others have told me that Anita and her sister were never close. You were close to Molly, not Anita. Why did you lie?"

"I never lied to you. Anita *was* worried about her sister. She *did* blame Ezra for what happened. I spoke carefully and truthfully."

"You obfuscated the truth."

"Hannah, you came here out of the blue asking me for information about my family members. I shared exactly what a man in my position would with a practical stranger." He let out a long, slow breath. "I shared the letters from Ezra. I told you about the Fuller Foundation when you asked."

"You left out things that mattered. Like why Ezra needed money."

Louis's mouth tightened into a tiny knot. "You haven't figured that out as well? I had hoped you would have sleuthed your way through all the town's nasty secrets by now."

Hannah readjusted herself in her seat so she was leaning forward, meeting Louis's gaze. "Shortly after August 2002, when that photo was taken, Ezra was caught embezzling funds at his workplace, a foundation he had loved and helped to start. You told me that, and I met with Marjorie Moyer, Ezra's partner's wife. I know that Ezra intended to return the money. Around that same time he sold his property to my father. Clearly, something had happened that caused Molly to withdraw and Ezra to need money."

Louis's eyes widened. "Well done."

"Why did he need money, Louis?"

"Why do people generally need money, Hannah?"

"Illness, an unexpected expense, a new home, divorce— but those are things people share with others. Yet no one seems to know what was happening with them back then." Hannah tilted her head back and let out a heavy sigh. "Enough with the theatrics. Tell me, because all I can think of are blackmail or extortion, but why the hell would someone blackmail Ezra?"

Louis's expression became suddenly grave, the amused look gone from his eyes. He gazed out at his backyard and pointed to a set of sliding-glass doors and, under them, a rectangular, wooden, unadorned patio that protruded from the house and into the yard.

"It happened there," he said. "It all seemed innocuous enough at the time. Molly and Ezra had had an argument, so she came here looking for solace. Anita was away, playing bridge, and Molly and I did as we so often did—we sat on the patio drinking wine and nursing our hurts and talking about our dreams. I can't even remember what started her fight with Ezra. It doesn't matter now. She hadn't had more than two or three glasses of wine, and it was cheap stuff." Louis eyes had a faraway glaze. "She left late. It was dark and rainy. I told her to spend the night, but she insisted on getting home. She didn't want Ezra to worry. She felt bad about the fight." Louis paused, swallowed. "She never even saw him."

The hairs on Hannah's arms stood at attention. "*Him*?"

"The man she hit. Donald Devereaux McDonald. A hard name to forget."

"My god." Hannah tried to process what she was hearing. There had never been any local talk of Molly hitting someone in her car, so that meant—

"She hit him and raced away from the scene. Illegal, immoral, awful, whichever way you turn it, it was wrong."

"I can't believe it."

"I couldn't either. And nor could Ezra."

"How was the man?"

"Dead on the scene."

Hannah shook her head in disbelief. "And no one ever knew." Her eyes widened. "*You* knew. *You* blackmailed them. That's why you never told Anita."

Louis slapped his pant leg and gave out a chuckle. "I'd be mortally offended if the prospect weren't so amusing. Did you hear me tell you Molly and I were close? I don't know what 'close' looks like for your generation, but for mine it meant not blackmailing your friends." He sneezed and wiped his nose with a pressed, white handkerchief. "I knew because Molly told me, but I certainly never blackmailed her. In fact, I swore to keep her secret. And I have. Not even my dear beloved knew. I told no one. Until now."

"But she *was* blackmailed, so *someone* knew."

Louis nodded. "Someone who saw the incident demanded a lot of money or they would go to the police. Molly was bereft. She wanted to turn herself in, but Ezra would hear none of it. He tried to borrow funds from the foundation, and when that didn't work, he raised the money by selling his family's land. By then, he'd dug himself quite a hole."

Hannah didn't know what to say. She'd known on some instinctual level that something was amiss, but she'd never imagined this. "What does this have to do with Ezra's murder?"

"Possibly nothing," Louis said. "Which is why I haven't come forward to the police."

"You were playing with me."

"I was impressed by your gumption. It's not every day that someone comes along and decides to do something gutsy. Most people sleepwalk their way through life." Louis touched Hannah's hand, and she pulled it back. "You have an old hippy's soul, Hannah Solace, and I wanted to trust you with this secret. It's been burning a hole in my own soul for more than twenty years. I'm glad you got as far as you did."

They sat in silence for a few minutes. Hannah listened to the breeze blowing through the maple trees and thought about what life must have been like for Louis to keep that dark secret for so many years, even from his wife. And if it had been hard for Louis, it must have been devastating for Molly and Ezra. It felt like everything that befell them thereafter had its roots in that one reckless act.

"Will you tell the police now?"

Louis took off his hat and rubbed the back of his neck. His face was red, his brow sweaty, even in the shade.

"Do you think I should? Molly is dead, Donald Devereaux McDonald is dead, and now Ezra is dead as well." Louis slumped back in his chair. "I'm not sure what good rehashing all this would do. Some secrets should stay buried."

Hannah wasn't so sure. Head still spinning with these revelations, she asked, "Who blackmailed Ezra?"

"I have no idea, and that's the truth. I was hoping perhaps you would figure out that part."

Hannah rose to leave, and Louis joined her. They walked to her car without talking. The August air was humid and warm, but patches of gold and orange in the trees announced autumn's lurking presence. It wouldn't be long before the ground was frozen and the maple trees had shed their glorious leaves.

"Can you forgive me, Hannah? I'd like us to be friends."

Hannah got into her car and studied Louis, with his old-fashioned sensibilities and his odd sense of loyalty. "I can try." Before pulling out of the driveway, she asked, "Ezra didn't come here just to apologize, did he?"

"No, he didn't."

"What else did he want?"

Louis bent toward the open window, hat tipped so that Hannah was only looking into one eye. "He was angry that I wouldn't give him the money back then. He believed if I'd just lent them the funds, none of this—the Fuller Foundation, the loss of his land, Molly's depression—would have happened. He wanted to talk about that."

"What did you tell him?"

"Foremost, I told him the truth—we didn't have the money. I would have had to take some drastic action, like remortgaging the house, and I couldn't have done that without alerting Anita. Then I told him that paying the miscreant had been the wrong thing to do. It was. Molly should have gone to the police. And finally, I quoted Sophocles. 'Thou thyself art thine own bane.'"

"From *Oedipus.*"

"*Oedipus the King,* to be exact." Louis's smile was colored by sadness. "He didn't appreciate my response, but he did like the quotation, That was Ezra. He always loved a good twist."

Chapter
Thirty-Three

M onday afternoon brought thunderstorms, the kind that start as fat, lazy drops of rain and change into something angry and vindictive. Hannah drove from Louis's house to the office of Solace & Little Realty Management & Sales with a heavy heart. Blackmail. Hit-and-run. A dead pedestrian. Donald Devereaux McDonald; it *was* an easy name to remember, and when she got home, she would look him up. At least now she understood why Ezra had sold his properties. The question was: What properties had he sold?

There were two vehicles in the office's parking area, and Hannah braced herself for another world war between Chad and Reggie, but she was pleasantly surprised to find them sitting at the conference table looking at something with Peach. No one was shouting.

They all looked up when Hannah came in. Peach grinned. Chad practically snarled.

"Hey there," Reggie said. "I'm glad you came by. Peach and I were going to stop over tonight, but with the storm coming, we thought we'd head home instead."

"No problem. Am I interrupting something?"

"Peach was just reading us the book she wrote while she was with Chad and Karen for the weekend." Reggie's wide eyes and arched eyebrows told her to go along with whatever was happening. "Would you like to sit with us while she reads the last page?"

"Sure." Hannah took a seat opposite Chad and listened as Peach read from her book, which consisted of several pieces of copy paper stapled together. Inside were crayon drawings of a curly-haired girl wearing a cape and a billowy dress.

"And then the warrior princess put all the frog killers in prison, where they will rot for forevermore. The end." Peach closed the book and flipped it over to the cover. "That's me," she said proudly, pointing to the cape-wearing dress-clad girl. "Did you like it, Aunt Hannah? It's about a superhero who protects frogs."

"I loved it," Hannah said, meaning it.

"The bad guy hurt the frogs, so the princess threw him in jail."

"She wanted to do what was right," Hannah said.

Peach patted Hannah's hand. "I like frogs."

"Me, too, kiddo."

"Let's talk outside," Chad said sternly to Reggie, still glaring at Hannah.

Reggie's rounded eyes turned to eyerolls. "Back in a moment," she said to Hannah.

While Reggie was outside with Chad, Hannah asked Peach how her weekend was.

"Daddy took me to a petting farm. I played with piglets. He called them all Bacon. I didn't think that was funny, and he told me to stop being like you, Aunt Hannah. Then we had ice cream and watched baseball on TV. He lets me eat whatever I want." She yawned. "I don't like my bed at his house. It's scratchy."

Hannah nodded. "Good sheets are important."

"How about you. What fun did you have?"

The question was asked with such sincere interest that Hannah wasn't sure whether to laugh or cry. Her niece, with her crazy curls and her mixed-up colorful outfits and her fierce stubborn streak, was a breath of cool autumn air in a heated world. What fun *had* she had? She supposed the faux date with Ash had been a highlight. She settled on "I got to stay up late on Saturday."

Peach clapped her hands. "That's *so* fun!"

Indeed. Before Hannah could say anything else, Reggie stormed back inside. She kissed Peach on the head and sent her into the bathroom to wash up. When Peach was out of earshot, she said, "He wasn't a fan of Peach's book. Called it 'violent' and blamed you."

"*Me*? I'm trying to save things, not kill them."

"Apparently that kind of 'zealotry' incites violence." Reggie shrugged. "You know how he gets. Anyway, Peach's book is great. I love her sense of justice. I'm just wondering if she's heard a little too much talk about Ezra."

Hannah figured Chad's anger had more to do with Hannah's refusal to do his bidding than Peach's book. "Maybe."

Reggie glanced at the bathroom door. "Tell me about Louis before Peach gets back."

Hannah gave her the two-minute version. "How's that for a new twist?"

"You were right. There *was* something more going on."

"Yeah, but what the hell does it have to do with Ezra's murder?"

Thunder rumbled, and Peach came flying out of the bathroom. "It's coming! Count, Mommy! Count!"

"We count after we see lightning."

"Oh yeah." Peach looked deflated. "Can we leave soon? I'm bored."

"Give me fifteen minutes, Peach. I'm going to walk Aunt Hannah outside."

"How many Dora shows is that?"

"Half a Dora show."

Peach looked satisfied with that answer, and Hannah hugged her good-bye. Back in the small parking area, Hannah and Reggie huddled under the building's oversized awning.

"I think you need to tell Noah what you found out," Reggie said. "He deserves to know."

"I've thought about it, but to what end? There's no direct link to what's happening now."

"Isn't that for him to decide?"

"I guess. I'll call him tonight." Hannah remembered why she'd come in the first place. "Can you do me a favor?"

"Whatever you need."

"Use your databases to find the list of properties Ezra sold to Dad?"

"Don't we know what Dad bought?"

"The property in Jasper wasn't the only one. Several people, including Aunt Tilda, mentioned multiple properties. I'm just curious what else Dad has going on."

The rain increased its tempo, and Reggie gave Hannah a quick hug. "Sure, I'll look now before I go and text you the results later."

"Better not go beyond half a Dora show."

Reggie laughed. "I wouldn't think of it. Now scoot. Before the storms pick up."

*   *   *

Hannah returned to an empty inn. The Airstream lock had been fixed, but the trailer was dark. There was no sign of Maura's car, and the young couple staying on the second floor had checked out that morning. Even Rebecca was gone. Moose greeted Hannah with the pent-up love and relief only dogs and wound-up toddlers can show, and she hugged the big canine tightly, happy for his company.

She'd carried in the box of news articles Ezra had saved and placed it on the table in her apartment. Given the emptiness of the inn, she opted not to put out an afternoon spread and settled on a bowl of fresh fruit and some nuts. Moose continued to prance around her. She looked outside and promised him a walk once there was a gap in the storms.

Back in her apartment, she began sorting through the newspapers and magazines, trying to figure out why Ezra had saved them. She made neat piles, sorting by date and then further sorting by type of media. Given the dates—the earliest was from the summer of 2002—she assumed they had something to do with the accident. Her first thought was that Ezra had been looking for information about the hit-and-run, tracking whatever news might have covered it. Only there were no police reports or obituaries in the piles.

As thunder boomed outside, Hannah scanned each piece, looking for some clue into Ezra's mind. Feeling frustrated, she moved to her computer to look up the hit-and-run victim, Donald Devereaux McDonald. Because the accident had happened so long ago, there wasn't much about the man himself. A date-specific search turned up a few short pieces about the accident, but all that was mentioned was a hit-and-run, the date, and the location. Another dead end.

At 5:12, her phone beeped. It was her sister texting her the results of the property search. Hannah read them over, mystified. She'd had no idea her father had bought—and subsequently sold—two pieces of property that later became industrial spaces.

There had been an abandoned paper mill in New Hampshire that was started up again, and a large piece of property by a river in upstate New York that was sold to a plastics company, Grand Pero Corporation.

Hannah looked back through the newspapers and magazines to see whether there was any reference to the mill or Grand Pero, but she couldn't find anything. She did a search for each and found dozens of hits for Grand Pero. As a company, it had been investigated and fined for contaminating local rivers and drinking water with PFAS, a toxic chemical known to cause diseases in humans and animals. The New York factory had been shut down in 2017. Dozens of residents near the plant had come forward with tales of cancer and other illnesses.

Stunned, Hannah considered this new piece of information. On its face, it was an environmental tragedy, but for Ezra, it must have been even more. He'd sold his family's land to her father, who in turn had profited from the property by selling it to Grand Pero. People got sick, the river was polluted. Ezra the botanist who wanted to protect New England must have been outraged.

Hannah returned to the box of news articles. She put herself in Ezra's place back in 2002. He'd paid a blackmailer to save his wife from prison. In order to do that, he had sacrificed his integrity at the Fuller Foundation, taking money from the nonprofit in the short term and eventually paying it back by selling his family's land. His sale of the family land had resulted in a rich development—something Ezra would have detested—and environmental crimes—something he would have hated even more.

The accident was bad enough; the blackmail tipped the scales. How to discover the identity of the blackmailer? *Look for people suddenly spending money they'd never had before*, she thought. She reviewed the news pieces again through that lens and found articles about new businesses, property sales, announced ventures. Had Ezra found his blackmailer in this pile? Is that why he stopped looking five years later? If so, she was holding their identity in this pile too.

Moose whined, causing Hannah to look up from her work. The rain had stopped, and a sliver of sun was peeking through the clouds. "Want to go for a walk, old boy?" Hannah asked the dog. He responded with a giant yawn and a big, loud fart.

* * *

The earthy smells of rain and dirt mingled with the cinnamon-scented goodness coming from Breaking Bread. Main Street was hopping for a Monday evening. The bakery stayed open late one Monday a month and hosted games—Bingo, Quizzo, pinochle, trivia—and from the crowd congregating inside and on the sidewalk, Hannah knew tonight was trivia night. She was tempted to stop by for a cup of tea, a vegan scone, and a glimpse of Cheating Chad making a fool of himself, but she had Moose with her, so she kept walking. She was about to cross the street in front of the church when she heard Kendra Birk call to her from the bakery. Hannah stopped and waited for the older woman.

"Nadia's got the whole town in there tonight," Hannah said.

"And then some." Kendra reached out to touch Hannah's arm lightly. "I've been meaning to catch up with you. To see how you're faring."

Kendra was wearing faded jeans and an orange performance T-shirt. Her thick hair was tied back, away from her face, which was makeup-free and suntanned. She looked more like a Long Trail hiker than the local pastor, which is something Hannah had always appreciated about her.

"I'm okay," Hannah said.

"Really?"

"Still reeling, I guess." Hannah wiggled Moose's leash. "Thankfully, I've got this guy to keep me company."

Kendra bent down so she was eye-to-eye with the dog. Moose wagged his tail furiously and licked her face. Kendra smiled, but when she stood back up, her expression had darkened.

"Are the police any closer to finding who did this?"

"They have some leads, but nothing definitive."

"And you—no one has learned about the will?"

Hannah glanced around. Satisfied that no one else was outside, she said, "Just Ezra's nephew Waylen. He figured it out, but if he's shared it, no one has told me."

"Yeah, I heard he disappeared." Kendra looked at Ezra's house, which seemed to tilt farther than the day before, if that were possible. "The police have been by the property a few times. I heard they took Ezra's bike." She placed her hands on her hips. "Someone had placed a device on his bike to track his movements. At least that's what Lakshmi told me.

Hannah took a step back. Noah hadn't mentioned that. "Someone was tracking his movements?"

Kendra nodded. "It doesn't sound like it gave them any real leads. Lakshmi is a friend of mine. She came by to ask a few questions, but I'm afraid I wasn't much help."

Hannah had met Lakshmi Gupta on a few occasions. The state trooper had been on the scene when Ezra's body was first discovered. "If they figure out who put that device on his bike, they might find the killer."

Kendra shrugged. "Maybe. Or maybe someone did it to track when he was in and out of the house. Based on what you told me, he had money. Someone else may have known that too. That would be a pretty smart way to know when someone was away from home."

* * *

Hannah left Pastor Birk at the church and meandered onto Ezra's property. She watered his container flowers, checked to make sure the bears hadn't knocked down his birdhouses and walked Moose around the property. As they reached the rear of the property, the place where meadow gave way to forest, Moose pulled her in the direction of the barn.

"Whoa!" Hannah called. "Stop pulling."

But the hundred-pound dog had no intention of stopping. He dragged Hannah to the barn and whined and barked at the door. The entrance was padlocked.

"Sorry, Moose," Hannah said. "Whatever creature you smell will have to live another day. You're not getting in there."

But as Hannah left Ezra's property, she wondered if Moose hadn't sensed something she didn't. She called Noah's work number, then his personal cell. He didn't answer, so she left him a message. "I've learned some stuff you might find interesting," she said. "Call me. And you might want to send someone over to check out Ezra's barn. Moose was agitated. He seemed to pick up a scent."

Despite Moose's comforting presence, Hannah felt that deep sense of unease as she walked home. By the time she reached Dirt Road, dusk was upon her, and thunder was rumbling in the distance once again.

Chapter
Thirty-Four

Hannah put Moose in her apartment and headed out to the Airstream to bring Rob some fresh towels and sheets before the storms started again in earnest. She knew it would be empty because Rob's car was gone, but she knocked twice anyway before letting herself in. The Airstream smelled of stale beer, and Hannah regretted not having brought her cleaning supplies while the place was mostly empty. She quickly changed the sheets and remade the bed. She'd head back inside the inn, grab his belongings, and put them in the Airstream, saving him a rainy trip later.

Rob's things had been put in one of the unused guest rooms. Hannah let herself in, picked up the two suitcases, and brought them outside. She unlocked the Airstream and placed the bags in the kitchen area. The rain and wind were picking up, and she stood on the porch for a moment, watching the trees sway. From the look of the sky, it would be one of those stormy nights when she'd lie in bed listening for the snap of branches or the slow creak and sudden bang that meant a tree had fallen. She hoped there'd be no flooding. The last major flood had set Jasper back years.

Inside, she hurried upstairs and surveyed the rest of Rob's belongings. She debated whether to leave everything until morning, when hopefully the rain would have stopped, but she'd be running the risk that he'd come home late and want his things then, disturbing her sleep. Better to place his computer bag and other materials inside a fresh garbage bag, keeping them dry for the trek to the Airstream.

The rest of the house was still—too still. Only the howl of the wind and the tapping of rain against the metal roof could be heard from inside. Hannah found Turnip in the inn's sunporch, and she put the cat in her apartment so they could all be together when Hannah turned in for the night. She pulled two garbage bags from under her sink and ran upstairs in the main part of the inn to fetch the rest of Rob's belongings.

She was in the midst of putting his computer bag inside the garbage bag when the clasp came undone and everything fell to the ground. The computer, an older Dell model, seemed unharmed, and she put it carefully back in the leather bag. She was collecting the papers that had fallen from a folder when one document caught her eye. It was a trust agreement. Hannah put down the leather bag and skimmed through the document. From what she could tell, it put Ezra's property on Main Street into a land trust, and it was dated three days before he died. Frantically, heart thumping, Hannah sorted through the other documents in the folder. She found Ezra's bank and investment statements, his checkbook, and paperwork for creating a 501(c)(3).

Confused, Hannah stared at the documents, wondering what they meant. *Ezra intended for his property to be put in conservation— not bequeathed to me*, Hannah realized.

Why does Rob have these documents?

Hannah had trouble swallowing. These papers meant one thing—Rob had taken them from Ezra's house. He'd come to Jasper expecting to inherit Ezra's property. He might have known

Ezra was ill, but maybe he didn't. Either way, he thought he could have a fresh start here in the Green Mountain State. That much of Rob's story she believed. He must have been snooping around Ezra's house and found these documents. He would have realized what they meant: the house and money were going to nonprofits, not to him and his cousins. Whether he took them before or after Ezra's death, she didn't know. Clearly, Teddy hadn't seen them. Rob clearly hoped that by hiding them, he could contest the will and still get a piece of Ezra's estate.

As Hannah read through the documents, a more sinister thought occurred to her. What if Rob had found the documents before Ezra died. What if he'd lured his uncle out by the lake to convince him he could take care of the property—no land trust needed. But when Ezra refused to entertain the possibility, he'd killed him, thinking *he* was set to inherit.

Only killers couldn't inherit. That meant he would have had to frame someone else.

Like an innocent innkeeper. Or his obnoxious cousin.

Oh god.

Maybe he was acting alone. Maybe he had help—like his cousin Maura. And Henry Yarrow.

Hannah's cell phone rang. Noah. She answered, nearly dropping the phone with her shaking hands, and said, "Noah, Waylen isn't the killer."

"Hannah, where are you?" The force of Noah's voice scared her.

"At the inn."

"Get Moose and lock the doors. I'm sending a patrol car over there. Do not open the door for anyone. Do you understand? Not for anyone."

"Noah, Waylen's not the killer—"

"I know. Waylen Grayson is dead. We just found the remains of his body in the chipper in Ezra's barn." He paused. "Lock your doors, Hannah. Please."

Hannah stared at the phone in her hand, thinking. *Waylen, dead?* That meant two murders. If Waylen was dead, who had chased her down in the Porsche? Her mind flitted to Rob. He'd woken up that day looking awful, had downed a pot of coffee, and then she'd lost track of him. He could have followed her. He could have tracked her for all she knew.

He wasn't here now—at least his car wasn't. With sudden panic, Hannah realized the inn was open to anyone with the code. That included Rob.

She dropped the documents on the floor and started to run back downstairs when she heard the unmistakable sound of high heels on hardwood. Maura—not Rob. As she rounded corridor on the ground floor, she came face to face with a woman, but it wasn't Maura.

It was Simone Long, and she was holding a gun.

Chapter
Thirty-Five

"Put the gun down, Simone," Hannah said. "You don't want to do this."

"Oh, but I do. I've wanted to do this for a very long time."

Simone was looking over Hannah's shoulder, and Hannah turned to see Rob standing behind her, holding the broken handle of a rake. "Listen to the lady. Put the gun down, Simone."

Simone let out a high-pitched wail. She'd traded her dragon-lady heels and head-to-toe black for jeans and a sweatshirt, and Hannah saw just how tiny she was without her Manolo Blahniks.

"It was bad enough you messed up the plan, but why did you have to kill *him*, Robby?"

"That's what got you here finally?" Rob asked. "Waylen?"

"When I hadn't heard from him . . ." She waved the gun. "Where is he?"

"Ground up like hamburger," Hannah said, looking over her shoulder at Rob. She wanted to add to the tension between them. While they were focused on each other, they weren't focused on her.

Rob lifted the handle over his head. His five o'clock shadow was now nine o'clock shadow, and the stench of booze emanated from him along with the sour smell of dried vomit. His short blond hair was slicked back with sweat. He rubbed one hand on his stained NYU T-shirt and let out a low moan.

"You should get out of here," he said to Simone.

"Not without some answers. Waylen said the money isn't ours."

"It's hers." Rob pointed the handle at Hannah. "He told me before he . . . well, before."

Simone said, "Before you killed him."

Rob's hand was shaking. Hannah weighed the chance of a successful tackle. He seemed unsteady and mentally unstable, but that could cut both ways. Simone was a complete wild card. Was that gun for Rob—or for her? She didn't relish the idea of testing either hypothesis.

"I found the trust documents," Hannah said, hating the weakness in her voice. She forced her chest out, her head up, her voice louder. "Ezra was going to leave his land and money to environmental causes."

"Not *his* land or money. *Our* land and money. The *family's* land and money. It was bad enough that he sold my grandfather's property and that he ran that house literally into the ground, but then to give it all to charity?" He poked Hannah with the dull end of the broken handle. "Or to you? Such bullshit." Rob shook his head. "Put the gun down, Simone. I can forgive you. Let's just get out of here."

Simone released the safety on the gun and aimed it over Hannah's shoulder, at her husband. "Admit what you did."

"I didn't mean to kill Ezra. We went for a walk and argued about the trust. He made me angry. It was an accident."

"I'm not talking about Ezra. I mean Waylen. Admit you killed him. You found out about us, and you killed him."

Rob's face turned brick-red. The hands holding the rake handle were a bloodless white. "I found out that he knew what I did, and I killed him. The fact that he was sleeping with you only made the act that much sweeter."

Simone fired. Hannah dove to the ground, and the bullet missed both Rob and Hannah, instead shattering the front-door sidelights.

"You've got to be effing kidding me!" Rob lunged for his wife. She backed up, tripped, and fell on her butt, dropping the gun. Rob grabbed it.

While Rob was wrestling with his wife, Hannah took advantage of the situation and ran out the front door, into the night and the rain.

*   *   *

The rain fell in sheets, clouding her vision and blocking any glow from the moon or stars. She'd left her shoes inside, and the mud and wet grass were slippery against her bare feet. Only the light spilling from the inn lit her path. She zigzagged through the yard, and when she reached the darkened rear of the property, she had to navigate from memory: through the new conservation meadow, past the kayaks, then into the woods on the path that led to the pond. She could have chosen the road, but there was nowhere on Dirt Road to hide. If either Rob or Simone came after her, she'd be an easy target. At least in the woods, she had cover.

Hannah stopped by the kayaks to grab a paddle and a life vest. She tucked both under her arm and continued half-running, half-walking down the wooded trail, pausing every few minutes to quiet her jagged breathing and listen.

It was during one of these quick breaks that she heard the unmistakable sound of a gun going off. It came from the yard, not the house. She had no idea who had shot whom, but she wasn't going to wait to find out.

Another hundred yards and she could feel dirt and packed pine needles give way to rocks. She heard the sound of rain pelting water. She was within twenty feet of the pond now. She stepped carefully through the slippery clearing and felt along the ground for a rock. When she found one the right size, she tied the life vest's belt around it, then waded a few feet into the water, carefully testing the depth of each step, and dropped the rock, letting the life vest float. It wasn't much, but if one of them came along the path, the reflective tape on the vest would distract them. Even a few moments could help.

Then Hannah made her way back to the entrance to the trail, the kayak paddle over one shoulder, and waited.

Chapter Thirty-Six

The rain had slowed just enough for her to hear footsteps on the path. Hannah had been standing there for what felt like hours but was probably minutes, her arms and legs cramping, her feet stinging from rocks and tree needles. She tensed, readying the paddle. He came through the opening to the lake without glancing her way and ran toward the water and the floating life jacket. It was still dark, but Hannah's eyes had adjusted to the blackness, and she could tell he was lurching to one side as he moved. Simone had wounded him. She wondered what he'd done to her.

Rob stood there, staring out into the water, looking for her. He picked up a rock and threw it into the pond, muttering "Come on" under his breath. When that did nothing, he aimed his gun at the water and pulled the trigger. The sound reverberated, hurting Hannah's ears. She gripped the paddle hard, as much to calm her quaking nerves as to ready herself for a battle. She wasn't a fighter, and she didn't know whether to run down to the water now and head him off, banking on the element of surprise, or wait until he was closer, when landing a shot would be a surer thing.

The gun convinced her to go with the surer thing. If she ran at him and he heard her, he'd have time to aim and shoot.

She watched as Rob scanned the horizon, wiping the rain from his eyes—a fruitless task. She watched as he threw more rocks into the water and then finally waded out into the pond, picking up the weighted life vest and uttering "Shit" at top volume.

It was obvious he didn't care if he was heard. He wasn't trying to hide. He was the hunter, and she was the prey.

The thought enraged her, and she raised the paddle over her head. As Rob Long came back up the trail, muttering a string of expletives that would have made a soldier wince, Hannah swung her kayak paddle with every ounce of strength she had left, hitting him square on the head and knocking him to the ground. The gun flew from his hand and off into the forest.

Rob's hands flailed about, searching for his gun. Instead, he found Hannah's ankle, grabbed it, and flipped her over. She was still holding the paddle, and she unclasped the clip that held it together, pulling the two ends apart and exposing the sharp metal pin inside. She stabbed a disoriented Rob, hard, then started to spring up so she could escape. He howled in pain and surprise, but his firm hands gripped her shoulders, digging in and pulling her back toward him. With an unexpected surge of energy, Hannah pinned him to the ground with half the paddle, sitting on his chest and using her knees to press down on the paddle ends. Rob bucked and clawed, but she found strength she hadn't known she had. For that moment, she was Peach's warrior princess, and Rob Long had killed all the frogs.

"This is for Ezra," she whispered in Rob's ear.

It wasn't until Noah Booker and Officer Gupta pulled her off him that Hannah finally let go of her paddle. Even then, her cold, cramped hands remained curled into claws.

Chapter
Thirty-Seven

The ambulance driver wanted to take Hannah to the hospital for a complete physical, but she refused. Other than a few pebbles embedded in her feet, a dozen scratches, and one particularly nasty mosquito bite, she was fine. She needed a hot shower, a cool bed, and Moose.

None of that was meant to be.

The inn had become a makeshift hospital and police department. Simone had a gunshot wound to the leg and contusions to the head. She would spend the night at the hospital, where the police would try to figure out how she was involved with Ezra's death, if at all. Rob was badly injured, and he and his crushed larynx were also on the way to the hospital, where he'd be treated and questioned and carted off to jail.

When most of the officials had gone, Noah brought Hannah a cup of hot tea, which he handed to her along with a plate of apple cake. "Are you ready to talk?"

She thanked him, and sat down on the inn's couch, placing the tea and cake on the end table beside her. "I told you everything."

"Not everything."

Hannah stared at her hands, which finally had feeling again. "You want to know what I found." When Noah nodded, Hannah told him about her quest to dig up Ezra's past—from the hit-and-run accident to the sale of his properties, to the Fuller Foundation, to the revelation that Molly had been blackmailed.

"By whom?" Noah asked.

"Still a mystery."

"And your father? Still convinced he was part of this?"

Hannah shook her head. "As a matter of fact, I think he's the reason Ezra has so much money. My father has felt guilty all these years for profiting from a misunderstanding. Ezra never wanted him to develop that land. He didn't want a plastics factory in New York. He wanted to get some money and transfer title, but my father saw a way to make his fortune. Ezra never forgave him for that."

"He paid him off?"

"I think those bank statements will show that my father paid him part of what he made off the deals. Ezra saw it as blood money, and never touched it. Twenty years of investing turned the cash into another small fortune."

"Ezra felt guilty."

"*Thou thyself art thine own bane.*"

"What?"

Hannah smiled. "Something someone once said to Ezra. He wanted to blame everyone else for what happened, but I think in the last weeks of his life he started to look inward. He realized that from the moment he decided not to go to the police but to pay Molly's blackmailer, he triggered a domino effect that would alter the trajectory of their lives. And those effects went well beyond their family or even our little corner of the world."

Noah shook his head. "How did you fit in here?"

"That I can't answer. My best guess is he thought I was better than his vultures. He knew I would at least take care of Moose and make sure the land didn't end up in the wrong hands."

Noah smiled. "That so?"

"You're laughing at me," Hannah said. "Two dead, two injured, and you're laughing at me."

"I'm surprised by you. That's different."

Hannah turned away, startled by the intensity of his gaze. Moose was sprawled out on the floor by her feet, and she bent down to pet him, happy for the distraction. "What about Waylen and Maura?" Hannah asked.

"We found Waylen's head buried in the woods behind Ezra's house and his car abandoned near an old logging trail. As I told you, his body went through the chipper." Noah grimaced. "I'll never forget that scene as long as I live. Thanks for the tip, Moose."

"He's a good dog."

"A good dog with a trust fund."

Hannah smiled. "If that holds up. I spoke to Teddy briefly on the phone, and it sounds like the only one who can contest the will at this point is Maura, but Teddy doesn't think she has a shot. Ezra's intent to create a land trust presents a wrinkle, but since nothing official came of it, Teddy doesn't think the probate court would enforce it."

Noah watched her, his expression unreadable. "Is that why Ezra wanted to see you that night? To tell you about his plans for the trust?"

"I think so." Hannah stretched her legs in front of her and wiggled her sore toes. "He knew he was dying. With the so-called vultures circling, he wanted me to know he was ill and the reason for his intentions. I think he was headed here with those documents when Rob intercepted him."

"And Rob had no idea Ezra had already changed the will—to you."

Hannah nodded. "I'm going to go through with the trust, Noah. Teddy will have to figure out the specifics, if he can find time between golf games. But one way or another, the land will go into a trust and the money will be set aside for an environmental cause. It's what Ezra wanted."

Noah stood, stretched, and stuck his notebook in his pocket. "It's late, you must be exhausted, and I've had enough death talk for one night."

Hannah followed him to the door. Before he could leave, she hugged him.

"What's this for?" Noah asked, hugging her back. They stayed like that for a few seconds before Hannah pulled away.

"For peeling me off Rob before we had another death in Jasper."

Noah smiled. "I thought maybe it was for some other reason."

"Don't get all cocky on me, Booker," Hannah said. "If I wanted to ask you out on a date, I'd suggest something like the concert in the park Friday night."

"And I'd say something like 'Sure, how about seven o'clock?'— as long as you're not already dating Ash."

"I'd say I'm not, so great, see you then."

As Hannah was closing the door, she thought of one more thing. "Noah," she called after him. "That device you found on Ezra's bike—the one I'm presuming Rob put there to keep track of his uncle—where did Ezra go the day he died?"

Noah stood in a puddle of light, looking up at her from the driveway. "To your dad's, but you already knew that."

"Nowhere else?"

Noah thought. "The day before he visited someone else, someone not related to the case." He gave Hannah the name. "Why do you want to know?"

"No reason," Hannah said and wished him goodnight.

Chapter
Thirty-Eight

"What do you have there, Peach?" Hannah watched as her niece put a plate of thumbprint cookies down on the inn's kitchen island. "I hope those are for me."

"They're peanut-butter cookies. I made them with my own thumbs," Peach said, grinning. Her hair was pulled back into a ponytail, but thick escaped curls framed her round face, and the rest of them looked like they were planning their escape as well. "Mommy says I can only have one." Peach's face dissolved into laughter as though everyone knew she could never eat just one.

Hannah snuck a cookie, holding finger to mouth. "Don't tell." She handed her niece one too, eliciting giggles.

Reggie came in moments later with a large green salad. Hannah would add a plate of black-bean burgers and sweet-potato fries to the mix. The corn on the cob from the garden would be steamed at the last minute, right before they sat down to eat.

"Looks like a Labor Day feast," Reggie said.

"It does," Peach said with her mouth full. She slipped Moose a piece of cookie and giggled again.

"Your grandfather's coming for dinner," Reggie said. "Leave some cookies for him. Besides, no chocolate for dogs."

"Daddy says Grandpa won't eat black-bean burgers," Peach said. "Or any of our rabbit food."

Hannah and Reggie exchanged an amused look. "We'll see about that," Hannah said.

Peach ran out of the room, and Reggie gave Hannah a hug. "I'm so glad you're okay. I should have been here."

"Why? Then we both would have been in danger." Hannah smiled. "It all worked out. At least now we know it was all Rob—Rob who killed Ezra *and* Waylen, Rob who planted the murder weapon at the inn, Rob who cleaned out Waylen's rooms and forced me off the road using Waylen's car. He'd been hoping the police would blame Waylen for the murder he committed." Hannah shivered, thinking how close she'd been living to a killer. "I'm just grateful we got some justice for Ezra."

Reggie looked around. "His niece is gone?"

"Henry picked her up yesterday. Apparently, they've been seeing each other for a few months now. No one knew, because Henry didn't want even the suggestion of a conflict of interest when he bid for Ezra's property."

"Think the relationship will hold up now that Ezra's property is off the table?"

"Time will tell." Hannah glanced at the oven clock. "Think inviting Dad was a bad idea?"

"Probably," Reggie said. "Time will tell that too."

Hannah looked out the window and saw Rebecca pulling into the inn's parking area. She wasn't supposed to work today, but her presence here was no surprise. She seemed to come whether scheduled or not.

"Back in a few," Hannah said to Peach and Reggie before disappearing outside.

Rebecca was just putting her water bottle in a shady spot when she saw Hannah coming toward her. She put her backpack on the patio and nodded curtly at her boss.

"I need to talk to you," Hannah said.

Rebecca stood still, her body suddenly tense. She followed Hannah to the set of swings by the lilac bushes and sat on one stiffly. The day was sunny and warm, the sky a clear lapis lazuli blue. The trampled flower gardens were perking up again, thanks to Rebecca, and the Three Sisters garden was still providing its generous bounty. Purple asters complemented the white-and-yellow pearly everlasting flowers and the white common yarrow that bloomed throughout the inn's borders. Butterflies and dragonflies flitted through the gardens, and a single hummingbird fed on purple asters near the patio.

Hannah couldn't have asked for a more beautiful Labor Day. She just wished she didn't have to have this conversation.

"What I can't understand is why you let him get away with it," Hannah said softly. "And why you continue to let him get away with it."

"I don't know what you're talking about."

Hannah leaned backward, feet straight out ahead, and pushed herself on the swing. "Don't play games, Rebecca. I know Ezra visited Mark the day before he died. Noah told me. Ezra was dying. He'd spent his last weeks on some sort of 'this is your life' journey, making apologies to some people and confronting others. He'd figured out that Mark was the one who blackmailed Molly. He went there to confront him."

Rebecca was silent. She didn't swing, didn't move. Her attention seemed fixated on a row of hydrangeas, their white flowers heavy with moisture.

Hannah said, "When I first learned Ezra had visited Mark, I brushed it aside as coincidence. But Ezra left newspapers behind, and once I began to see the world through his eyes, I saw patterns. He'd kept an article on the grand opening of a new and improved Jasper country store. Purchased in 2004, two years after the accident, and two years after Mark blackmailed Molly."

"I had nothing to do with it."

"Then why did you break into Maura and Rob's rooms?" When Rebecca's eyes widened in surprise, Hannah said, "Yeah, I figured that out too. You had access to room keys, but you made it look like an outside job. Why?" When Rebecca didn't answer, Hannah said, "Mark sent you in to see if they had anything on him, didn't he?"

"No."

"Then why did you do it?"

Rebecca started swinging. She clasped the sides of the swing and moved back and forth, her long, graying hair flying behind her. She went so high that Hannah was afraid she'd flip over the bar.

"Rebecca, talk to me."

Rebecca's face was tilted toward the sky. She said nothing.

"You need to go," Hannah said.

Rebecca slowed to a stop. "What do you mean?"

"I mean you're fired."

Rebecca stared straight ahead, her jaw clenched in defiance. Hannah felt awful—Rebecca loved the gardens even more than she did—but she couldn't work with someone she didn't trust, and she didn't trust someone who stood by while her spouse did something so vile. If only Rebecca would talk about it, maybe Hannah could understand. But Rebecca gave her nothing but that stony, determined stare.

Later, after a quiet but satisfying meal with her family, Hannah reflected on the way Rebecca had left that afternoon, her body upright and unbending, her conscience just as unyielding. Noah had called earlier that weekend to tell Hannah he'd looked into the death of Donald Devereaux McDonald. The sixty-year-old had been hit by a driver who didn't stop. The accident wasn't the cause of death, however. Donald died of a heart attack. Noah told her he'd already been dead when Molly hit him.

The news had made Hannah cry. If Molly had come forward, she would have learned that his death wasn't her fault. As a result, perhaps she wouldn't have sought solace in solitude or spent evenings needlessly worrying about the death penalty. Perhaps Ezra wouldn't have spent two decades in despair, his only friend a young innkeeper who barely knew what she was doing. As it was, Molly and Ezra's lives were ruined, and perhaps Rebecca's too.

The choices we make define us, Hannah thought as she snuggled on the couch next to Moose and Turnip. Peach and Reggie had left hours ago—John Solace too—and she was alone at the inn. But she had reservations for leaf-peeping season—the inn would be full, her work would continue. Sometime in the coming weeks, she'd hold a memorial for Ezra and make plans for the trust. In the meantime, she could hear the croak of bullfrogs outside, and the constant hum of crickets kept her company.

She'd take this life, she decided, and make it her own.

Recipe

Hummingbird Hollow's
Bean & Veggie Chili

This versatile chili recipe is a great base for your favorite seasonal vegetables. In summer, try adding a cup of diced zucchini or yellow squash and a handful of diced fresh red peppers, and in the winter try it with diced sweet potatoes or butternut squash. It's delicious on its own, but at the inn we often serve it over brown rice or baked sweet potato.

Ingredients

1 tbsp. olive oil
1 large red onion, finely chopped
2 large carrots, finely chopped
3–4 cloves of garlic, finely chopped
2 tsp. chili powder
1 tbsp. ground cumin
½ tsp. chipotle chili powder
½ tsp. Mexican oregano

Pinch of cinnamon

1 14.5-oz. can crushed fire-roasted tomatoes

1 14.5-oz. can finely diced fire-roasted tomatoes

½ tsp. unsweetened cocoa powder

½ tsp. turbinado or brown sugar

½ tsp. salt

1 14.5-oz. can of black beans, drained and rinsed

1 14.5-oz. can of pinto beans, drained and rinsed

1 14.5-oz. can of red kidney beans, drained and rinsed

1 14.5-oz. can of cannellini beans (or a second can of black, pinto, or kidney beans), drained and rinsed

2 cups water

1 cup fresh or frozen corn

1 tbsp. masa harina mixed with 5 tbsp. of water (optional—but adds a nice flavor)

¼ cup chopped cilantro (optional)

Directions

Sauté onions and carrots in olive oil over medium heat until the onions are translucent, about 7 minutes. Lower the heat, add chopped garlic, and sauté another 2 minutes. Add the chili powder, cumin, chipotle powder, oregano, and cinnamon, and stir, careful not to let the spices burn (add a few teaspoons of water, if needed). Add the crushed and diced tomatoes, the cocoa powder, salt, and sugar and bring to a boil. Add the beans and 2 cups of water. Return to a boil, lower the heat and simmer, partially covered, for 45–60 minutes, stirring occasionally and adding more water if the chili is too thick. Whisk the masa harina with the 5 tablespoons of water and add this and the fresh or frozen corn to the chili. Return to a boil, lower the temperature, and simmer for 15 minutes or until the corn and carrots are tender. Add salt and pepper to taste and sprinkle with chopped cilantro. Serve with diced avocado and drizzle with chipotle crema—or add your favorite toppings.

Chipotle crema: Whisk together ½ cup vegan mayonnaise, ¼ cup plant-based milk (we prefer oat), and ½–1 tsp. chipotle powder (to taste).

Acknowledgments

S pecial thanks to my tireless agent, Frances Black, for believing in this project from the first mention of Hummingbird Hollow Bee & Bee. A warm thank-you also to the team at Crooked Lane, including my editor Faith Black Ross, Rebecca Nelson, Dulce Botello, Mikaela Bender, Thaisheemarie Fantauzzi Pérez, and Stephanie Manova. It's always a thrill to see a vision come to life, and this book has been a passion project from the start.

I learned a great deal while doing research for this novel, but one of the most fascinating people with whom I spoke was Karen Rose, a Vermont-licensed wildlife rehabilitator in Vermont and the brains, brawn, and heart behind Monty's Wildlife Rehabilitation. Thank you, Karen, for your generous time and for all you do for the woodland inhabitants of our beautiful community.

And finally, thank you to my family and friends, especially Ben, Ian, Mandy, Matthew, and Jonathan Pickarski, Angela Tyson, Sue Norbury, Kim Morris, and Carol Lizell. Your support means everything to me.